W9-AQO-489

What You Call Winter

What You Call Winter

STORIES

Nalini Jones

Alfred A. Knopf • NEW YORK • 2007

This Is a Borzoi Book Published by Alfred A. Knopf
 Published in the United States by Alfred A. Knopf, a division of Random House, Inc., New York, and in Canada by Random House of Canada Limited, Toronto.

www.aaknopf.com

Some of the stories in this collection have been previously published in different form in the following: "What You Call Winter" in Glimmer Train Stories *(Spring 2004); "This is Your Home Also" in* Dogwood *(Spring 2003); "In the Garden" in* Ontario Review *(Spring 2002).*

Library of Congress Cataloging-in-Publication Data

Jones, Nalini, [date]
What you call winter : stories / by Nalini Jones.—1st ed.
p. cm.—(Borzoi book)
ISBN 978-1-4000-4276-0
1. India—Fiction. 2. Catholics—India—Fiction.
3. Intergenerational relations—Fiction. I. Title.
PS3610.O6275W47 2007
813'.6—dc22 2007001464

Manufactured in the United States of America

First Edition

For my father and mother

Contents

Now the whisper of trees is gravel under cars,
a polluting pearl lies over the city across the bay,
an innocence gone.

It may return, as we have returned. Here lies
a lesson we have lacked. Until the tide turns,
footprints leading outwards on the beach
point us the pathway back.

—from "A letter completed from another time,"
So Far

GERSON DA CUNHA

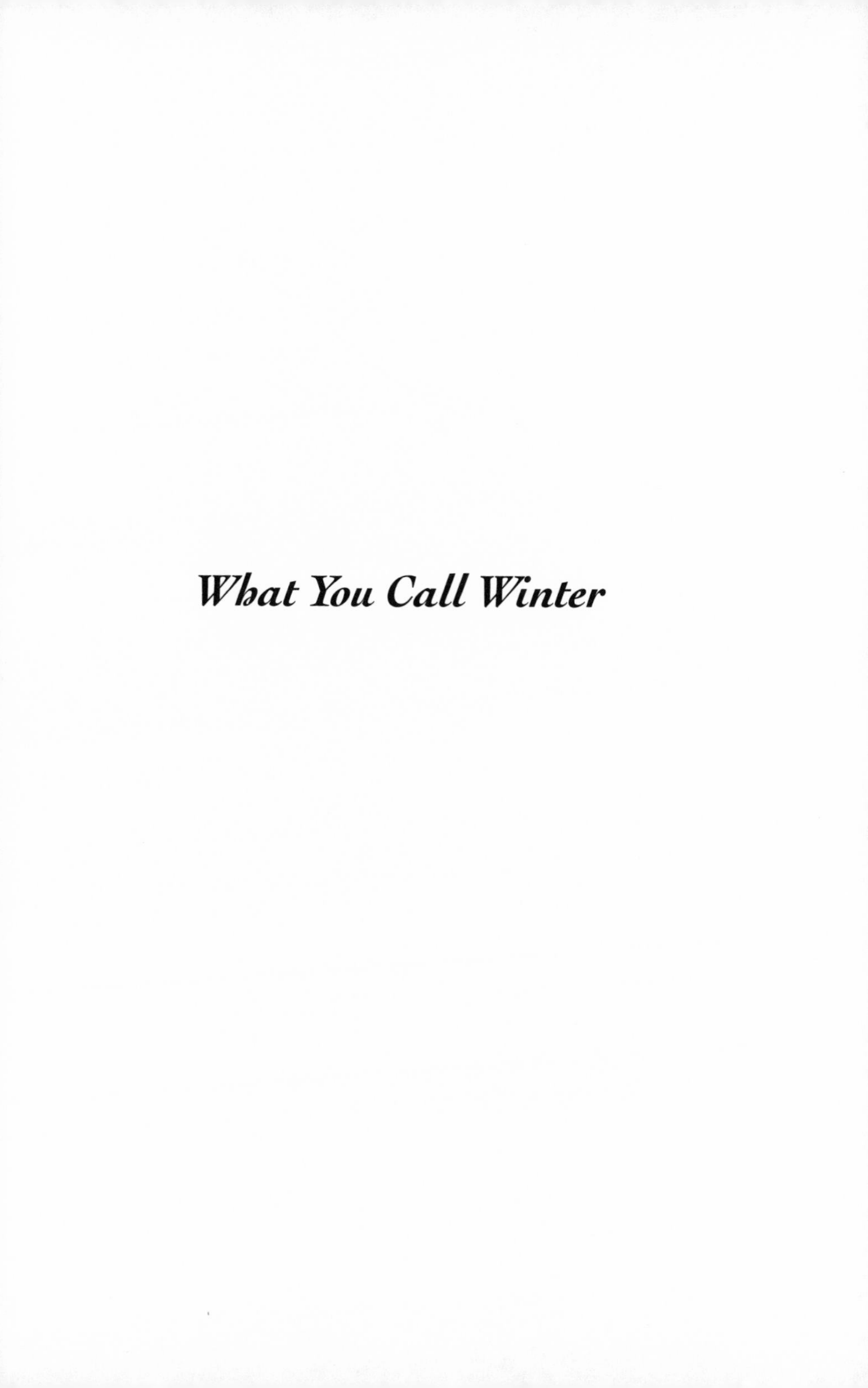

What You Call Winter

In the Garden

Three days before her tenth birthday, Marian Almeida came home unexpectedly early. Usually her afternoons were spent at Uncle Neddie's, who was no uncle of hers at all but the nearest neighbor with a piano for her practice. Of course, Uncle Neddie and his wife and his three unmusical children spent the drowsy stretch of hours before supper curled on narrow mattresses, napping through the merciless heat. The shops were closed, dogs panted under wiry trees, shadows darkly spotted the roads and yards. The servants sifted rice or ground spices; the dancing grains and elliptical rhythm of mortar and pestle lulled even the restless children to slumber. Marian, seated before the scarred wooden box of Uncle Neddie's piano, touched her fingers to the yellowed keys so lightly that she did not make a sound. She practiced her fingering in silence while the household slept. "It shouldn't make a difference, how hard you thump," her mother had decided when she arranged for Marian's practice sessions. "You can just learn the *shapes* of songs for now." On lesson days, when Marian perched on the glossy black bench of St. Jerome's piano, the noise of her own playing startled her.

But Uncle Neddie's wife, known to the neighborhood as Aunty Neddie although it was commonly believed that she must once have enjoyed a name of her own, met Marian at the door with the news that one of the children had fallen ill. "Go on, then." She shooed the girl away. "Tell Mummy not another week, at least. We can't have you carrying anything home."

Marian imagined carrying the germs of the sick Neddies in her belly. She thought of the careful way she would have to lower herself into chairs. Her own mother, she'd been told, was carrying twins.

The afternoon spun before her, golden and dusty, suddenly free. Marian walked home with a mounting sense of excitement. She had two hours, at least, before her mother finished tutoring, perhaps longer if she stopped off to market. (Marian's daily bouts at the piano lasted ninety minutes, with extra time, her mother reasoned, for imagining the sounds.) Usually, Marian had just enough time to change out of her school uniform skirt before her mother arrived and homework began. Sometimes, if she hurried to reach St. Hilary Road before six, she might run into her father, home from the university but on his way out again to meet his friends at the Santa Clara Gymkhana. Perhaps this was the day she could go with him, she thought. Some of his friends were Parsees, named for their jobs and not for saints like Marian and all the Indian Catholics. Her father's name was Francis, but the Parsees called him "Frinkie," which made him laugh in a way he never laughed at home.

For a moment Marian thought of her brother, Simon, two years younger and still trapped at his desk, and she felt a pang of sympathy that threatened to spoil her own enjoyment. Twice a week Simon took special classes after school to prepare him for seminary, which both of them agreed was rotten luck. But every second day he was allowed to bowl for the cricket team, she reminded herself. Nobody had ever suggested he take up piano, Marian further realized, and found she could once again rejoice in her good fortune. The road flew beneath her feet in jerks and rushes as she began to skip—past the tall gates of St. Jerome's Church, where families of beggars held out their hands to the Catholic ladies. One small girl, whose hair was thick and matted, the color of clay, looked sorrowfully as Marian sped by.

"Wait, madam!" the child called in English, and Marian, shocked, stopped and turned to face her. Marian and her family and most of the middle-class Catholic families spoke English in their homes, but to many others—insurance salesmen, shopkeepers, servants, taxi drivers—they spoke Hindi or Marathi or some swirl of all three. Beggars almost never spoke English.

The small girl glared at her, continuing in Hindi. "You could buy me an ice cream, at least."

"No, I can't."

The child scowled.

"I'm going now," Marian told her.

A boy came to stand beside the girl, jostling her shoulder. "Why do you bother with schoolgirls?" Marian heard him scolding.

Her father's house, squatting in the sun behind a black iron gate, seemed transformed with nobody filling its rooms. Marian couldn't remember the last time she'd been home alone. Only Togo, napping in a patch of shade at the foot of the porch steps, lifted his head for a moment and whined before dropping to sleep again on the cool tile. Marian had to use her key to open the door at the head of the stairs. Inside, silence settled, thick and swampy, on stacks of books, the radio, the teapot and stained spoons left out from lunch. The hands of the clock drifted slowly toward evening, as if through water. Marian moved quietly in the shadowy green light, checking bedrooms, the kitchen, the back balcony, where washing hung on slack lengths of line. She felt she'd entered a private world, interrupted only by the low whir of fans. Even Martha was gone.

Marian's mother gave all her servants the same Christian name. Several Marthas had come to Bombay from the villages near Mangalore to live with Marian's family. Easter Almeida, attentive to their equal need for literacy and the Lord, had launched the careers of every girl with the instructive tale of their common namesake, a friend of Jesus's "cumbered about much serving." Marian could remember listening to three such beginnings, leaning against the doorframe, twining a strand of hair around her finger. "What are you doing, hanging about?" her mother snapped at her the last time. "You gawk like a hawk." *Thou art troubled about many things,* Marian thought, staring at the stout braid of her mother's hair before she slipped away without a word. The shapes of retorts were enough for Marian. That was nearly two years ago, just after she won St. Jerome's Sunday school prize for reciting Bible verses.

Marian untied the red ribbons from the ends of her braids and peeled herself a sweet lime before she wandered through the living room. Threads of light needled through the woven shades and fell across the tile floor in a golden mesh. She stepped past the print of the Virgin, whose eyes followed her onto the front balcony: a bank of windows over a balustrade with wooden doors that could be closed in the monsoon season. Now they were latched open. Marian hoisted up the shade just enough to see a single bright stripe of lawn below, then higher and higher, revealing the guava tree, the gate, the street gutter, the road. An Ambassador taxi buzzed slowly past like a fat summer fly, and she could hear the lazy calls of crows. She tried to imagine what every member of her family might be doing at that precise instant. Her father, on a train; her mother, in a classroom; her brother, bent over the book on his desk. Martha, sent to market, with just enough coins in her drawstring sack. She glanced again at the road. A stream of bullocks trickled ahead of a boy with a stick. Marian listened to the thin ringing of their bells, broken into pieces by the rise and fall of each bony shoulder, and thought that even the shape of the cattle's song turned drowsy in the afternoon. Her stomach had begun to ache, and she thought she might curl up on her bunk and read.

But she didn't want to waste her free time sleeping. Instead, she began to rummage through the wardrobe her parents shared. She pushed past the skirts and blouses her mother used for everyday wear and began to run her fingers along the silken folds of her mother's saris. Most of the Catholic women of Santa Clara wore their good Indian outfits only for church or weddings or parties—and of course to go to the city, a forty-minute ride on the commuter train. The girls wore uniform jumpers to school and frilly dresses or kameez and churidar at parties. Only when Marian was fully grown would she have her own saris and blouses. But she was searching for an old cotton sari, which she had once been permitted to try on.

Her mother had had to help her tuck it, nearly doubled at the waist, and three paces across the room the fabric slipped from Marian's waist and shoulders. You're too small, her mother had protested, but she had been smiling. Finally Marian tensed the muscles of her arms and legs into marionette stiffness and made it across the length of the living room. Her mother clapped her hands and called her a little rani. Her father bowed and asked for a dance, and Simon clowned about like a footman behind her, lifting a trailing edge of cloth.

In three days, Marian would be ten years old. Old enough to help with the babies when they came, her mother told her. Old enough to play the piano in a recital, old enough to listen without talking back, old enough to write letters to Aunty Trudy in Bangalore, who answered them in envelopes addressed to Miss Marian Almeida. Old enough not to fuss when Simon called her Miss Marian, Marian, Quite Contrarian. (*Suffer it to be so now,* thought Marian, armed with her Bible verses, whenever he annoyed her.) Old enough, she was certain, to put the sari on herself. She would surprise the whole family when they came home. She would set them all laughing. Her mother might let her choose a bindi for her forehead. Simon would lose the pinched face he wore whenever he came home from school. Martha would look on from the kitchen and flash her broad grin, putting one finger over her mouth where a tooth had rotted away. Hushing the shape of her smile. Even Marian's father would stay home from the gym, and when he'd had his cup of tea, he would find the red cushion and stand on his head. He would stay upside down until all the old stories of when he was a boy came rushing back from wherever they'd been lost. They fell into his feet and couldn't find his mouth, he used to tell Marian, or they wiggled through his arms to the tips of his fingers, or they hid in his stomach with last night's fish. "They've gone down to my bottom this time," he exclaimed when her mother was out of the room, and he'd smack the back of his pants to get them moving again. Marian was old enough not to believe him, of course, but still she missed the game. Usually he came home just in time for supper, then spent the evening at his desk, rubbing the back of his neck. Marian used to cover her head with her pillow when her parents argued, but now they fought only in small bites and jabs. She fell asleep most nights, listening to ice cubes in her father's glass, her mother's pen scratching across the page. The shapes of shouting, she thought, even in the quiet. She wondered if the twins could hear what her mother was thinking.

Marian picked through toppled piles of shirts, sagging against one another on the crowded shelves. She flicked past her mother's kameez tops to reach the saris, her fingers lingering over the soft squares of cotton, and then she strained to reach farther back. Hangers poked into her shoulder and she could hardly see through the thicket of clothes to the fabric she was touching. She struggled to untangle herself, but two saris slithered to the ground from the hangers, one on top of the other, like twin snakes. Discouraged, Marian hopped backward, out of the cupboard. The ache in her stomach began throbbing again. She bent slowly to pick up the first sari, suddenly near tears though she knew she was old enough not to cry, and there, hanging behind her mother's good silks, Marian found the dress.

Before she'd even touched it, she knew it was meant for her. Before she'd held it carefully to her chest, mindful of the satin bow, before she loosened the top button, in the shape of a flower, to slide the hanger from its shoulders, she'd abandoned the idea of the sari. She laid the dress out on her mother's bed and the skirt stood up stiffly from the mattress. Her school pinafores were flat and limp as rags. Marian loved the way the dress held the shape of a ten-year-old girl, as if hoping for her to climb inside. She thought of her mother kissing both her cheeks, the grown-up way, for her birthday. She imagined Simon, too impressed to tease. Martha would gasp and forget to cover her mouth. Her father would teach her to dance properly: on the floor, not balanced on his feet.

Marian hurriedly replaced her mother's saris, listening for the sounds of evening. She had forty minutes at least, she gauged, before anyone else arrived home—time enough, surely, to try on the dress. She couldn't wait a whole three days and nights. "Come now, my girl, you've got to be patient," her mother told her when she wondered about the twins, boys or girls. Whole weeks passed before any of her piano pieces had any sound to them at all, and then never as she imagined. She'd grown tired of waiting; she wanted a taste of this dress. Just a peek at herself in the glass, looking different than she'd ever been, and then back into the closet without anyone knowing. She didn't want anything setting her mother off, or the evening could shatter like glass.

Fear, longing, excitement pierced her sharply, throbbing in her belly, the way she used to feel when her father told stories of tiger hunts. Only this time she felt as if she were the one walking into the jungle, with a pounding heart and slow, careful steps. *I mustn't dirty it,* she thought.

She scrubbed her hands and face, wishing she had time to run a bath. Instead, she splashed a bucket of water over her dusty feet and rubbed her arms and legs with a cold damp cloth. She shucked off her jumper and blouse and hung them quickly on a peg, making sure to leave the bathroom tidy. The dress, a delicate leafy green, waited on the bed. Marian's dreams had spread through the neighborhood. She would walk into church in a pale green cloud and float up the aisle. Who is that marvelous girl? people would wonder, and when she turned into the Almeida pew and everyone recognized her, her parents would beam. She would practice piano with the skirt billowing over her rickety stool, and even the little unmusical Neddies would rise from their sickbeds to hear the shapes of her songs. They would beg her to give concerts, as softly as she liked.

The day began to rouse itself, flushed and warm, from the afternoon sleep, and the noise from the street grew louder. Marian heard motorcars, the chatter of women, the wailing calls of merchants. She knew her father would soon be home.

She held her breath as she stepped into the dress. The fabric was smooth and cool as fresh sheets. Marian waited until she had zipped up the back, twisting one arm behind her waist and the other one over her shoulder. She fastened three regular white buttons and the top one with its silver petals before she slid her feet into her good white slippers and walked slowly to the mirror.

Marian was not especially tall for a ten-year-old. For most of her life she'd been much smaller than her classmates. She wouldn't get her height until she turned thirteen, according to her mother, which was when all the women of her family got their height. (It did not occur to Essie Almeida to consider when the women of her husband's family might begin to grow.) Marian's arms and legs were slender, and her feet were so narrow that the mochi (who made shoes) had to use a special pattern for her slippers. But in the past year she had shot up. She could stand back-to-back with her friends, and her right hand on the piano could stretch over six keys. Her chest had begun pressing against her thin school blouses, and she was glad her uniform jumper covered her fully.

But in the leafy green dress, Marian felt just the right size. The skirt brushed past her knees, the sleeves puffed lightly over her shoulders, and a panel of white lace veiled her chest. The single flower button gleamed like a jewel at the base of her throat. *Sing unto the Lord a new song,* thought Marian. She paced back and forth to hear the skirts rustle—the shape of grown-up whispers—and smiled shyly at her reflection. Suddenly she stopped, cocked her head, and undid her braids, combing her fingers through the long, dark waves until her hair rippled down and touched the hem of the dress. Marian gazed at herself as if at a stranger, wondering if she looked like her mother or her father. Wondering if the twins would be girls and whether they would look like her. She pinched color into her cheeks, then through the window she heard the shouts of schoolboys, out of their sports clubs. Her father would arrive any minute.

It was only her mother who would mind, she realized. Her father would like it, she was sure. She wanted someone to see her before this new Marian disappeared again and the old one returned, patient and ordinary, sitting down to her prep work. She watched the girl in the glass before her. One person, to see her just this way, with her hair down even though she knew that on her birthday her mother would insist on braids. You'll tangle in two minutes, she'd say. I'll need a pair of shears. Worse, she might laugh or call Marian vain. Her father would only be proud, Marian decided, slipping quietly down the outdoor stairs. She would hide in the garden and surprise him.

The grass tickled her ankles as she ran to crouch behind the banana tree. The branches spread into a thick green canopy, just over her head, and from time to time she leaned past the trunk to check the street. Nothing but black bars, where the gate threw its cage of shadows. Noises began and grew louder and faded away again, and she tried to pass the time by guessing the shapes of the sounds. A bullock cart, an autorick. Marian wished she had a watch. Her father had a pocket watch that he carried every day to the university where he was the registrar. He tucked it into his vest pocket, keeping it very snug so it couldn't fall out, and attached the free end of the chain to his belt loop so a small bit of it always hung in view. (In those days, despite the heat, he wore a vest to work each day. People must feel they could look up to him, he told Marian. It was fitting for a man of his position.) She shifted from one leg to the other. A woman calling her daughter. A chicken clucking. Some servants speaking Marathi. Her back felt tired from standing so stiffly, and the waiting seemed to grip the muscles of her stomach. She tried to think of the martyrs. A motorcycle hummed past in fits and starts. Finally, she heard the jangle of the latch and the gate creaking open. She smoothed her skirt and took care not to slouch.

"Togo!" her father called, just before he came into view. Marian heard the dog's chain rattling from the back garden, where he slept beneath the kitchen balcony, and then her father stepped past the trunk of the tree and froze. He'd been holding his pocket watch in one hand and dropped it at the sight of her. Even in the shade of the low-hanging branches, Marian felt her cheeks grow hot. She could see the light glinting off the glass face, hanging down from his belt by the golden chain.

"Marian. Sit down."

His voice was the shape of a knife blade. She felt a tight

coil of fear in the pit of her stomach, and her legs gave way before she thought of asking why. She dropped on all fours to the dusty ground, banging her knee against a root.

"Now, keep your head down," he said quietly. "Don't stand up. And come slowly this way."

Marian crawled toward the gate with her head so low that her hair trailed in the sparse grass. Her father waited until she'd reached him. She could see the hems of his pant legs, coming loose, as she knelt beside him. Then he put his hand on her head.

"Stay just where you are," he told her. "Don't turn around."

He moved past her slowly, taking sideways steps. Marian crouched on her knees. She might have stained the dress, or torn it—the idea struck her like the back of her mother's hand. She hadn't asked permission to wear it, it might be ruined forever, her mother would like the new daughters better—each new thought bent her double, like so many lashings. But she kept her back turned. From the corner of her eye, she saw her father take up the field-hockey stick she'd left propped on the porch. Togo came running around the house to greet him, stretching his lead to the limit, but her father snapped, "Sit down, sir!" and the dog flattened himself in the grass, whining.

Old enough not to cry, she began to anyway. She couldn't remember her Bible verses. She heard a great flurry behind her: branches snapping, leaves thrashing, Togo snarling and barking, straining at his lead. Then one final crack. *Please,* she thought. The shape of a prayer. At last her father's voice, panting. "You can get up now, Marian."

She stayed huddled to the ground, rocking on her heels. Twigs fallen like the remnants of a ravished nest. Leaves scattered as if a monsoon wind had brought them down. At first when she looked up she didn't see it. Her father stood beside the banana tree, the hockey stick still in his hands, and pointed to a bright green snake lying broken in the dust, its head crushed. Marian sprang from the grass.

"I got it," he told her, dropping the stick and walking slowly to Togo, who stood at attention, growling. He ruffled the fur of the dog's neck and head, murmuring softly to him. Marian stared at the snake. It lay perfectly still, as if waiting to strike.

"Don't go near it," her father warned, still facing Togo.

"Daddy?"

"It's dead, but I don't want you handling it. Hang on, let me just tie him up in back." He took Togo by the collar.

Marian couldn't imagine wanting to touch the terrible bright skin of the snake. She'd never seen a snake like this before, only thin brown garden snakes, wisping away beneath a leaf or rock. Occasionally, near the carnival rides on the beach at Juhu, she and Simon saw cobras dancing from charmers' baskets. Her mother always frowned and shook her head when Simon wanted to go closer.

This snake wasn't a cobra, wasn't charmed. Marian stood, rooted to the spot. Sounds struck her like blows, ringing through her. A chicken cackling. A baby crying. She thought, *If I died today, I would never see the twins.* A channa-wallah on the corner, rattling nuts into paper cones. Her father's footsteps.

"Tree viper." He picked up the snake by the neck, holding it far from his body. "Hanging down from a branch, just over your head."

Marian felt her insides begin to trickle away. Her father stood beside her, quiet and stern, and she did not know what to make of his expression. Her mother's face was easily molded to rage or sorrow; every mood another mask she might, without warning, decide to wear. But her father was another matter. His forehead was high, his jaw set, the clean planes of his cheeks smooth, with none of her mother's hollows and dimples. The only clue to his thinking was in his keen eyes, and frequently she found she could not meet his gaze for fear he would detect something lacking in her.

But his eyes were fixed on the snake; she could watch him freely.

"You can't see it until it's already dangling down. It hides right on the rib of the leaf." He flung the snake over the garden wall to the empty lot next door, and its body curled through the air in a slender green arc. The shape of a scream. Marian stared at the wall, vine-covered pink stucco that stood taller than her father. Thick green cords twisted in and out of the tilework that laced the top. She imagined the snake twitching to life in the rubbish heap on the other side, twining back through the openings.

"Is it poisonous?"

"Quite poisonous." Her father still faced the garden wall. "It strikes on the ear or the top of the head." The afternoon haze had pleated into golden rays. "Yes, very poisonous. How this thing came here, to our tree . . ." He seemed to be speaking to himself, but suddenly he turned, rubbing the back of his neck. "But it's nothing to go upsetting yourself about. This fellow must have been lost. They don't like the city, and see, the city is right on top of us."

He nodded toward the lot next door, empty for as long as Marian could remember, but now there was talk of a large new school going up. Different families of beggars sifted in and out of rubble piles there, making shelters. Marian wondered where the snake had landed. She and Simon weren't allowed in the yard, but they could see over the wall from the stairway landing.

Her father glanced quickly in her direction, then down at the hockey stick. "Better brush your hair properly before Mummy gets home. I'll be back in time for supper. Bring Togo upstairs with you and leave the hockey stick—tell Simon he's not to go near it."

"What if there are more?"

"There aren't," he said. Marian looked again at the debris at the base of the trunk, and her father gripped her shoulder so tightly that for a moment she could imagine him lifting her off the ground. She wanted to stay just like that, the bruising pressure of his fingers on her arm, until her mother and Simon and Martha were home. Until the twins were born and the new school built and all the snakes in the world shriveled to skins. She could not imagine a time when she would want to leave the safety of his grasp.

But before she could lean against him and ask him to stay, he relaxed his hold. "Go on, clean up now. I'm running late." He bent quickly to kiss her forehead, and she smelled his odor of damp white shirts, chikoo juice, and aftershave. She saw, for the first time, the glass face of his pocket watch, dangling down on its chain and flashing as it caught the light. A tiny crescent reflection danced in a jerky orbit around him, glancing off the packed-dirt path, prickling over grass blades. And then he was striding away from her, the watch bumping unnoticed against his trouser leg. The gate creaked, open and shut, the scrape of his slippers blended into the din. Marian watched, thinking, *Now he will notice.* His back was to her, his arms at his side, he reached the corner and swiftly turned. A wife calling a husband. Girls' laughter. Bird cries cluttering the cloudless skies.

It wasn't until Marian stepped out of the dress that she realized something had happened. She saw the stains, like iron, on the inside of the skirt; she turned the dress frantically over in her hands and saw the spots had bled through, and her first thought was that the snake had spit at her. Her thighs were sticky; she felt sticky between the legs. She touched her underclothes. In a spasm of shame, she realized she'd wet herself and ran to the bathroom. When she discovered the blood, her face drained of color. She held a rag to herself, thinking, *I've cut myself, I've only cut myself,* but the wound kept flowing. She rocked back and forth on the lip of the toilet, shivering in the heat. *Forgive us our trespasses.* She should never have taken the dress from the wardrobe. She knew that God was punishing her.

Marian never told anyone. She jumbled the dress into a ball, deep in the corner of her wardrobe. She washed her scraped knee and scrubbed her hands clean. She folded a rag inside her pants and changed into an old plaid dress. She watched for her family through the upstairs front window. Yellow breezes touched her cheeks, and without thinking, she began to braid her hair. Her mother arrived just as a pack of boys in blue shorts swarmed along St. Hilary Road, playing a cricket match in the street. They were shouting and laughing, as they did every evening, as if Marian herself was just now walking home from the Neddies', head ringing with the shapes of songs. Instead, she watched her mother push right through the center of the game, the belly of twins thrust before her like a shield. She looked up to the window with a quick, glad smile, and Marian waved back, another part of her heart sinking. It might have been a happy night.

The dress, crumpled in its corner, could not be scrubbed clean. Marian spent two more afternoons of sick Neddies, crying over a bucket and sponge. At last, she bundled it into a market sack and emptied it into the rubbish heap on Linking Road. The one near St. Jerome's was too close to home, and she didn't want the beggar children finding it. She had dreamt of a small girl with clay-covered hair wearing her dress—so long that it fell to her ankles—and the dark stain magically gone. In the dream, Marian's father turned and stared at the girl, at the leafy green bow. His eyes widened with sudden pride. Wait, madam, he called after her.

Marian kept the silver button, the shape of a flower, hidden deep in her pocket. On the morning of her tenth birthday, she pretended to be ill herself. Her mother didn't discover the dress was lost until just before supper, and Marian heard her berating Martha. Martha wept, protested, her mother stamped her foot and screamed. Marian closed her eyes so tightly that shots of color seared the darkness. The shape of her mother, crying when her father came home. "We have nothing to give her, Frank." Marian, silent, bled.

The next afternoon, Marian was given her grandmother's ruby ring. "My finger's gone too fat for it," Essie told her, pressing it into the girl's hand. "It won't fit you yet, but you're past ten now. Old enough to have it."

Martha returned to her village two weeks later. Her face was swollen and tired, lips closed over her smile, as if she had a toothache. Marian wanted to give her something, but had nothing of value that her mother wouldn't miss. In the end, she tied a string through the silver flower button and stuffed it into Martha's bundle. A new girl came the following week, a Catholic girl. Marian's mother let her keep her name, Lila.

For three days and three nights, Marian prayed, but her wound didn't heal until four days had gone by. Even then, it revisited every few weeks. God, she knew, had not forgotten. Five months later, when it came upon her during a visit to Bangalore, Aunty Trudy hugged her and laughed. "You're a woman now, *beta!* Hasn't your mother told you anything?" But even when she learned the truth, Marian knew there were things she would always carry with her, in hair, finger, and knee, in body and blood.

As for the snake, its tale grew like a vine through a pink stucco wall. Soon Simon was certain he'd glimpsed its mate;

soon Essie had witnessed the scene from the window. Marian must have been wearing her uniform. The snake was two meters or three. Her father sliced it in half with the field hockey stick. Even Marian, eventually, was not sure what she believed. Whatever actually happened to the Almeida family never seemed quite as real as the stories they told. Unless one of them worked to remember the facts, the truth of the matter might fall off to the side, like a shadow cast from a tree. And if no one took care to hold each memory and guard it well, the darkening years would swallow the shadow, and only the story would be left standing.

What You Call Winter

The first hint of trouble came when Roddy D'Souza saw his father floating past on a bicycle outside the gates of the house. It was January, the sky gritty blue through the haze. The guardsman, a sullen young man who always disappeared to the back to enjoy his forbidden cigarettes, came shuffling up the drive. "Namaste," he said. Roddy paid no attention. Through the wrought-iron bars of the gate he saw his father, coppery in the sunlight and wearing a brown suit. His feet, in the leather slippers Roddy still remembered, rose and fell evenly with the motion of the pedals. The bicycle was too small for him, but he sat up perfectly straight. He cycled past without turning to face his son, and then he was gone.

Roddy stared down the length of St. Hilary Road, to where a circus of activity obscured his view. The intersection was jammed with cars and autoricks, all dropping off schoolchildren. A bus rattled into their midst, disgorging more students. Roddy pressed his hand to his forehead, pinching the bridge of his nose. When he opened his eyes again, the street was clear of ghosts.

"What's wrong with you, always running off?" he said

absently to the guardsman. The fellow was either nowhere to be found or right at his elbow, smelling of smoke.

The guardsman didn't answer but made a great show of ushering Roddy through the gate and closing it behind him. Roddy ignored him. Down the street, children were shouting as they pressed into the school yard. Boys frisked at the edge of the crowd. The blank-eyed sun stared down. Nothing had been altered. Roddy set off in the opposite direction.

It had been sixty-five years since he'd seen his father, who died of a heart attack when Roddy was twelve. Dominic D'Souza had been sitting in the back of the Santa Clara Talkies theater on Linking Road on a Sunday afternoon. There had been several showings that day, lush Hindi films with song and dance numbers. Roddy never knew what flickering image had been his father's last. He and his brother, Eddie, had been forbidden to see films. "It's bad for young boys. Softens the brains," his father told them. The year he died, Roddy spent every Sunday during Lent in the darkness of the Santa Clara Talkies. He lied to his mother, who burst into tears at the mention of films and could hardly bear the trip to town for all the poster bills. He told her he was training for a footrace. For Easter she gave him a new pair of running shoes, and Roddy stopped going to the Talkies for good.

Roddy still remembered those Sundays. He went straight from Mass and sat in the last row, where he could see the backs of everyone's heads. The theater was warm and close, smelling of spicy nuts and hair oil. Babies fussed in their mothers' laps. All through the film there were coughs and cheers. The loud bursts of laughter felt like an assault. At intermission Roddy sank down in his seat and waited for the lights to dim again. He felt exposed beneath their glare and repulsed by the sight of those around him. How grotesque they seemed in the yellow wash of lights—their flashing teeth, the pores of their skin. He averted his eyes, as though the whole audience had been stripped bare before him and did not have the sense to hide their own nakedness.

He did not like the films. He watched them avidly, searching for what he could not name. A message, a lesson, a clue to his father's life or death? He saw mustachioed heroes and soft, pale girls. There were battles, love scenes, earthquakes, tigers. Dancing girls curved around pillars, trees, unyielding warriors. Roddy tried not to think of the dancing girls. When they twirled and beckoned he felt a kind of stirring that shamed him. He did not want his father to know about it, and he felt his father there, in the breathing all around him.

But he remained in the last row of the theater, waiting for a sign to send him home. Days passed, and nothing. Films rattled by, ghostly light, tinny music. Roddy waited, certain and then less certain that his father was still watching.

Every morning, Roddy walked three blocks to the Santa Clara Gymkhana, where he played cards with two other Catholic men and a Parsee. Rummy was their game. All four arrived just as the gymkhana opened, so they could secure their favorite table.

Roddy had worked in the Finance and Accounts Office of the University of Bombay. In 1978, in the prime of his career, he reached the age of mandatory retirement. It had happened so quickly. He had been serving on a number of boards at the time—the Unfair Means Committee, the Expert Consultative Group for the National Service Scheme, and the Banking Recruitment Association. His days had been full of politicians, luminaries, admiring students, seminars, ceremonies, and university dinners. Endless appointments. Every hour had its own heft, its own muscle. He was borne forward by their force.

Now time pooled around him, slack and stagnant. Some of

his old friends at the university had remained involved in that life. They'd called from time to time, urging him along to this meeting or that. Roddy often intended to go. "Yes, yes, I'll try to come," he told them, smiling to think of his welcome. It was a scene he often imagined—arriving a few minutes late, perhaps, interrupting the learned speaker and slipping modestly into his seat while all his colleagues jumped up to greet him. He could picture it so clearly that it felt like a memory.

But the journey from Santa Clara to town had begun to seem so long. An autorick to the station, the crowded platform, the train. The whole rigmarole back again, when whatever it was had ended. Roddy could hardly remember how he had done it every day, up at six in the morning and never back before dark. Now it seemed pointless to travel so far. The heat would be terrible, then the bother of finding a taxi. There was a cricket game on television, or his friends were waiting at the gym. One of them, Francis, had worked at the university also; Roddy found it more pleasant to remember such days with someone from his own generation, who worked as he had, in the old style, before the government and a new generation had changed everything. Eventually the phone calls stopped coming.

"And what's the sense of going if you won't get paid," his wife said darkly. "All the expense only, and none of the reward." Since his retirement, Annabelle had succumbed to financial paranoia and increasing bitterness, as if they were teetering on the brink of ruin and the university alone was responsible. "They never paid you properly," she cried. "And now see where we are!" She haggled over every purchase and accompanied the girl to the market to be sure every rupee was stretched to the fullest. She belonged to a Ladies Investment Club, where she discussed what to do with whatever she could shave from the household expenses.

Her latest scheme was to sell their plot to contractors, who would knock down the house and put up a flat building in its place. One by one, the neighbors were giving in, trading their family homes for a down payment and two or three of the flats. Annabelle had taken to bullying Roddy each time they stepped out of doors. "See this place? A nice enough place!" She spoke night and day of what she would do with the money.

Roddy had given up trying to argue with her. They had enough, in his opinion. He had shown her their accounts, in neat ledger books he had brought home from the university on his last day of work. He had taken a supply of twenty-five, one for each year until he was eighty. It gave him a shock to see only three blank ones left in the cupboard. He wished he'd taken more. He could not shake the feeling that a moment's impulse had the power to circumscribe his days—that through his own careless thievery, only three more years were meted out to him.

At the gymkhana, the boys were waiting. Roddy did not believe in ghosts, but the idea of his father cycling through the neighborhood could not be entirely overlooked. He had found himself stopping each time a bicycle came into view, shading his eyes, making sure. Delivery boys sped past him, a schoolgirl with a satchel, a stick-legged clerk. He shook his head and blew his nose vigorously into a yellowing handkerchief, as if to expel the day's lunacy along with the dust of the road.

They played on the upper veranda. Fans pleated the air, and young men smacked tennis balls on the courts below. Lulled by their lazy rhythm, Roddy began to relax.

"Another week and she goes," said Francis. At the gym he was known as "Frinkie," a concession to the Parsee, who had a strong accent. Frinkie's wife was traveling to America to visit their daughter. He had grandchildren in Ohio, a place Roddy had never heard of anyone living. Roddy's own son,

Stephen, lived in New York and worked in finance—a high-up, Roddy could tell anyone who asked.

"No troubles with visas and all?" asked Bertie, rearranging the cards in his hand.

"Just the hassle of it. They see we've gone and come back, so . . ." He shrugged.

"We can't get one for Mary." Bertie's daughter, Mary, had Down syndrome. Roddy could not remember the last time he had seen her, a large, dough-faced girl with thick lips and small eyes. It seemed to him he could more easily remember the time when she was born, the last of six. Bertie had said nothing until the child's baptism, when they had all seen for themselves. For a few months he had stopped coming to the gym and then abruptly, as if no time had elapsed, he had returned again.

"Why won't they give one to Mary?"

"Too risky, as far as they're concerned. She's older than most of these children last, no? Forty-three. They think she'll land up in a hospital and they don't want the aggravation." He tried to laugh. "Bastards. They're afraid she'll die there."

Roddy looked down at the table. He did not say what he was thinking, that it might be true of all of them. He imagined his last hours in the flat where Stephen lived, the swift and silent lift, the tops of buildings outside windows, and knew he would not go back to the States again. He was seventy-seven and his son could come to him.

"Tchah!" Roddy scowled. "I won't go with my hand out to these people with their precious visas. I could get what I want, but see how they treat us!"

Bertie picked up his cards but didn't look at them. "Actually Mary's been having trouble lately. Aching all the time and tired. We didn't know what was the matter and then doctor told us, she's doing too much. Running back and forth, involved in everything. She has her activities at the church and she likes to go to Puttu's school and help the little ones.

She lifts them up sometimes—heavy children, no? Four and five years old. And doctor says, 'You cannot let her do these things anymore. She's not like a forty-year-old. A girl like her, at this age. You have to think of her as old. She has the aches and pains of an old woman. You have to treat her that way now.' I tell you—" He broke off. "It's not what you prepare for, seeing your child grow old like that in front of your eyes. She is older than I am in her way." He concentrated suddenly on his cards. "At any rate, they won't give the visa."

No one quite knew what to do. This was not the usual tone of their meetings. They came to the card tables to escape such conversation, which waited for them at home. Here they spoke of sports matches, memorable club occasions, university days. Families were confined to the distant good news in letters: a grandson entering university or a daughter's new house. They kept to only the most general politics, topics upon which all would agree, and even their talk of the neighborhood centered on the way it used to be when they were influential forces within it.

"I know some people," Roddy began, then stopped. Whom did he know anymore? Stephen must have important contacts, but in another country where his position could not benefit his family.

Bertie shook his head, smiling his rabbity smile. His eyes were yellowed. "Don't worry. I told Celeste, our other children have left our house, but God has given me this child to keep. Go on, play."

Roddy leaned back in his chair. The room had begun to fill with other cardplayers. Their table attracted attention; he and Francis were among the gymkhana's oldest members. Roddy lifted his hand in greeting whenever anyone called his name. They played until the morning session was nearly finished, and then one by one the members stood up. Roddy stretched, ready for lunch, and made his way toward the door.

He did not see his father until he had nearly walked past him. Dominic was sitting at a table in the far corner, reading the newspaper. He turned the page, frowning, and reached for his specs.

Roddy stopped and stared. He dimly felt a hand on his shoulder, but he would not turn. He stared and stared at the image of his father reading the paper. "Do you see that?" he tried to shout to all the others. "Do you see him there?" He did not hear their replies, distant as if he had cotton in his ears. Darkness edged his vision and began to close in a grainy circle. Only his father was still in view—the black-rimmed specs, the huge knuckled hand. Roddy's limbs felt limp and boneless, as if he must either sink or float, and then the circle closed completely. The last thing Roddy remembered, magnified and terrifying, was the whispery sound of a newspaper page.

The fainting spell left him with a broken forearm. His hand had struck a table as he fell, and his arm folded awkwardly beneath him. He woke to searing pain and was taken to All Saints Hospital in an autorick. There was an operation to set the bone, and the next morning his arm was encased in a plaster cast. Someone's son, a hospital administrator, had recognized him. "Thank God!" Annabelle sat near his bed, feeding him dahl and rice. "He has taken you with no cost, and he called in the other doctors to see you. 'This is Roddy D'Souza,' he told them, 'one of our best university men.' " She glowed, transported by the memory. " 'Madam,' he told me, 'your husband will have every possible attention.' "

Roddy's throat was dry; he accepted the sip of water she offered. "Bertie brought you in the rick. Even after I arrived he wouldn't go. He waited with me until doctor came and Celeste brought us something to eat. Now she's gone to tell the girl what to make for tomorrow. Nothing too heavy. Maybe a piece of fish."

Roddy did not remember. The ride was obscured in a haze of pain and confusion. Had his father reappeared? Had Roddy called out to him? "Did I say anything?"

"What? When?"

"At the gym. When I fell. Or in the autorick?"

"Nobody said." She hesitated, and he wondered if he dared tell her. *I am having hallucinations,* he experimented silently. *My mind is going.*

But she was patting his hand, looking both eager and worried. "Did Bertie tell you his news?"

"What news?"

"He and Celeste have gone with a contractor."

"The whole world has gone with contractors."

"Three lakhs, and a flat for them, and another to spare. Big ones, he said."

"Annabelle—"

"Only think about it, Roddy. How long can we keep the house?"

Roddy tried to shift in bed. He was propped up against pillows but found it difficult to move without the use of his hand, and Annabelle leaned forward to help him. The hair of her scalp had thinned, he noticed. How had he not seen it before? Her arms were still strong, but the skin had begun to pucker. Her face was not wrinkled—she had looked after her face with a mysterious regimen of creams and remedies—but age spots had darkened to an insistent brown. He watched in fascination as she resumed her argument. The skin near her lips and brow stretched and tightened as she spoke. Her cheeks lifted, a glimpse of teeth, the spoon raised to his mouth once more. Each movement of her face and hands produced another, each word another.

Do you believe in ghosts? It struck him that he did not know even this much about his wife, this woman with whom his days had been tangled for more than fifty years. *Annabelle, do you believe in ghosts?* She might; it was just possible. He couldn't be sure. She was a silly woman at times, an unreasonable woman. She wore a Saint Christopher medal around her neck night and day for protection, on a string of green yarn that irritated Roddy. "Buy yourself a decent chain," he told her. She read the prophecies of Nostradamus and called Stephen after every unsettling dream. "Be careful, darling. I saw you at the bottom of a ditch last night."

Nest eggs, taxes, investments. She prattled on. How inevitable each word seemed, as inevitable as she herself seemed after so many years of marriage. He could form no words to interrupt her.

I saw my father today. He was riding a bicycle.

Of course Annabelle would know that he did not believe in ghosts. Of that Roddy was certain. He had kept no secrets—he had made his character perfectly clear. She would not, after so many years, feel obliged to wonder what he was thinking.

I don't think he saw me.

But a ghost Annabelle saw would have done something worth telling. She was not capable of such a bland fantasy. Even her most mundane moments were colored by a sense of lurking drama. Her ghost would have Dickensian flair, rattling chains and bearing messages.

"Promise to think on it. Promise to speak to Bertie." The pleading in her voice surprised him. Her cheeks were soft and flat, the soiled plate empty in her lap. This was his wife. There had been a time when he could not drag his fingers through her hair for its thickness.

He promised.

• • •

At night in the hospital he could not sleep. The pills dulled the pain in his arm to a diffuse ache, which he felt in his head and back and throbbing fingers. He could hear other patients in various states of sleep and wakefulness: coughs, moans, labored breathing. In daylight they seemed separated by walls and corridors, but at night these were lost in a brown film—not quite darkness—and he felt both exposed and alone.

He remembered a night long ago when he and Annabelle had slept, slumped in chairs, in a hospital room. Stephen was two and had broken his leg. Annabelle refused to leave him in a strange place, and Roddy stood by, not knowing how to stay or go, until the moment for leaving had passed and he found himself, for the first time, staying up all night with his son.

It had happened when they took him to a nearby park. Annabelle pushed Stephen on the swings while Roddy read his newspaper. After a time he had put down the paper and watched the mothers and children moving in front of him, as if they were figures on a film set. Outside the gate, men hoisted children onto ponies with bells and spangles, flowers drooping from their harnesses, and led them in slow circles around the park. *I can do that with Stephen one day,* thought Roddy. And then he heard a cry and turned just in time to see his son standing at the top of the slide. "Sit down, Stephen, down!" The panic in Annabelle's voice cut through the sleepy air of the park, turning heads. But Stephen jumped.

Later, after the screaming, the hospital, the surgery to set the leg, Roddy could not shake from his mind the picture of his son standing calmly at the edge of the slide. Did he know he would fall? Had he believed he could fly? The boy had always seemed inscrutable to him, a package Annabelle brought home from her mother's house in Bangalore, where she had gone to give birth. Roddy received a telegram, and eight weeks later his son came home. Every cry was a new mystery to him. *What does he want now?* Roddy wondered. *What's wrong with him now?* He did not expect to feel such fierce love or sadness; he looked on, helpless, while Annabelle took up the baby and rocked, or nursed, or murmured nonsense. How joined they were! When Roddy and Annabelle learned they could have no more children, Roddy felt he was only hearing what he already knew. How could anyone else interrupt the perfect understanding between mother and son? Even he was an outsider. Stephen jumped from the slide and Roddy watched, dumbstruck. It was Annabelle who crumpled to the ground, as if even then their bodies were one.

In the hospital, the baby slept badly. His cheeks burned and occasionally he cried out, eyes still shut. Annabelle soothed and petted him, singing songs that Roddy did not know. Just before dawn, Roddy left to bathe and change before work. Stephen had fallen into a fevered sleep, and Annabelle said not to worry, to go on, go. They would be fine.

After the accident, Roddy stayed close to home. He was given a sling and wore his left arm like a wing folded against him, but he needed Annabelle's help to put on his shirts and fasten his trousers. She stood a breath away from him, humming, eyes fixed on his chest. He lifted his chin as she reached the top button and her head bobbed near his shoulders.

He looked beyond the top of her head to their image in the mirror and remembered the first time they had danced, at their wedding. He had been surprised to feel her hand, so cold and small in his own, like a frightened child's. The match had been arranged; though both consented, they had met only four times before. He had wanted to tell her not to be afraid but did not know how to speak without feeling something stiff and steadying break open. Something was holding them up, some force propelling them across the floor. *Was this how my father felt?* he had wondered then.

Now he wondered how his father would have grown old. His mother had died slowly of cancer, the year Stephen was confirmed. By the end, she was in so much pain that she could hardly recognize the people around her. "Son," she whispered in a rare moment of clarity the last time Roddy saw her. "Son, water." He had poured a glass for her and held it to her mouth. Her lips were cracked and gray, and the water dribbled down her chin. "Sleep now, Mum. I'll be back in the evening." That morning he stood in the open doorway of the train, letting the foul air of Mahim Creek wash over him. He knew he should go back, but he let the stations slide away. Slum children squatted near the tracks, and men stared as the train went past. By the time he reached the university, Annabelle had called to say his mother was gone.

"There." Annabelle patted his arm. "All finished." He felt an urge to hold on to her with his good hand, but how could he explain such a gesture? And anyway, she had carried on with her morning business, leaving him dressed and alone in the mirror.

Over the next several days, Roddy saw his father frequently. Waiting in the queue at the chemist's, strolling on the seaside promenade along Carter Road, even in the shop where Roddy bought sherry, whose sweet, wiry taste he had always preferred to liquor. A week went past, then another. He was no longer agitated by the sight of his father but felt a growing sense of longing. He would have liked to call out to him, but he sensed that Dominic D'Souza was still beyond his reach. He did not feel haunted; his father had not even glanced in his direction. But he felt a circle drawn around his world, tightening.

Was he dying? Was that what the ghost had come to tell him?

He thought of consulting a doctor but rejected the idea. In practical moments, when the ghost had not appeared for some time and the sun shone so brightly that even the shadows seemed unmistakably clear, he realized he must be hallucinating. He could not bring himself to admit such a possibility to a doctor.

But when his father invariably turned up again, riding past on his bicycle or strolling near Sunset Park, Roddy knew what he was seeing was real. Otherwise why would Dominic D'Souza's tie be stained? Roddy did not remember his father in such a disrespectful way. Why would his father wear his reading specs on the road? Why, above all, had his father come and not his mother?

Beyond these questions were smaller, troubling ones. Accidents had begun to happen. Annabelle stumbled on the step and stubbed her toe badly. A crow flew over the balcony railing, flapping in desperate circles around the front room, until Annabelle drove it squawking from the house. A pipe burst, leaving a large rust-colored puddle on the bathroom floor.

"High time we make a change. This place is going to rack and ruin," said Annabelle. She had elicited an agreement from Roddy: they would meet with Bertie about the deal he had struck with the contractor. In the flush of this victory, she could no longer resist any opportunity to press her advantage.

Roddy was too distracted to argue. He could not determine whether the accidents were somehow the products of his father's arrival or the ordinary pitfalls of a household. It occurred to him that he was not in the habit of paying attention to what transpired beneath his own roof. "Is she always so clumsy?" he asked Annabelle when the girl dropped a platter of fried fish.

She sighed. "These girls, they've got their heads in the clouds," an answer so broad that he did not know what to make of it.

The night of Bertie's visit, Annabelle made lamb biryani, a rare expense that revealed her hopes for the evening's outcome. Roddy felt uneasy. The recent accidents preyed on his mind, and the dinner presented countless opportunities for mishaps. He had a horror of the ghost turning up during the dinner party, determined to wreak some new havoc. Roddy stayed home all day long, an occasion so uncommon that Annabelle asked if he were ill.

"We have people coming," he snapped. "I'm trying to prepare."

She laughed at him. "What will you do to prepare?" She was squatting on a low stool, peeling prawns, and flicking the leavings into an old red bowl. Her fingers were wet and specked with bits of shell, and she wiped her cheek with the back of her hand. The girl had left a battered tin pot on the flame and was chopping onions.

"Is that knife too big for her?"

"For Celia? What nonsense! Every day of the week she's chopping with it."

Roddy looked nervously at the prawns. "And these are fresh? You've smelt them?"

"What's the matter with you, Roddy? Go and pester someone else."

"Just take some care," he said with irritation. Throughout the day he wandered through the rooms of the house, finding danger in every corner. In the afternoon, when he lay down to sleep for an hour, he felt a coil of tension in his neck.

It was dark when they heard Bertie calling to the guardsman to open the gate. "That idiot," muttered Roddy. "Never there for two minutes running."

Annabelle smoothed her skirt. "Remember, you promised to listen," she said in a sharp whisper and opened the door.

"Hallo, hallo!" called Bertie, raising a hand.

"So good to see you," said Celeste, kissing Annabelle on each cheek. Behind her was Mary, in a shapeless pink dress with socks and sandals on her feet. She was smiling shyly. "Say hello, Mary."

"Hallo, hallo, hallo!" she shouted, then twined her hands and cocked her head to one side.

"Hallo, Mary! How pretty you're looking!"

Mary nodded, grinning.

Annabelle pretended to pout. "How long it's been since you've come to visit me! Where have you been hiding all this time? I think you've grown tired of us."

Mary shook her head violently. Hair slipped from her white bow, which reminded Roddy of a little girl's.

"All right, then, darling, come, come. Give me a kiss. There we are. You'll have a drink, all of you?"

"Rum for you, right, Bertie?" Roddy went to pour and found the level of rum in his bottle was well below what he remembered. But could he be sure? He was not a rum drinker; how long had it been since he had offered any to a guest? He stared at the bottle, trying to remember, until the sound of Annabelle's voice roused him and he hurried back into the front room.

Dinner was served without a hitch. Mary ate avidly, bent over her food with undivided attention, and when she had finished, she pushed back from the table and took her plate to the kitchen.

Bertie looked after her fondly. "Mary likes to help."

"Such a sweet girl," said Annabelle. "I see her every Sunday at St. Jerome's."

"Oh, they just love her in the choir. She practices those songs night and day, doesn't she, Bertie? She likes to put on little concerts for us. And the whole neighborhood knows her. When we walk down the street with her, I'm always astonished by how many friends she's picked up. At church, at the films. Everyone's waving!"

Roddy glanced toward the kitchen. Mary and Celia were laughing together over the sound of running water. Celia had a high-pitched giggle he had never heard before. He wondered what it would be like to have Stephen and his wife and children living nearby. What places would they occupy in the neighborhood?

"Now," Celeste began, "let me tell you how we came across this contractor."

Later, after they had gone, Roddy sat in his chair and listened to the thin trickle of water from the spout. The girl was nearly finished cleaning, and in the bedroom Annabelle was snoring. But Roddy felt too spent to get up from his chair. The waiting, all the fruitless worry, had exhausted him.

He fell asleep in the chair and woke with a start, some hours later, to the sound of laughter from the open window. He rose, stiff and aching, and looked through the iron bars. The night air was cool, and the guardsman had permission to burn a small fire. Sitting next to him was the kitchen girl, her head tipped back and a bottle to her lips. She sputtered and thumped the bottle to the ground, giggling. "Hssst." The guardsman put a finger to his lips, but this produced only more gales of laughter. He grabbed her bare ankle and tugged teasingly.

Of course Roddy had to put a stop to it. Celia was from a village near Poona, entrusted to them by her parents. It was Roddy's responsibility to look after her while she lived in their house. But that unpleasantness could wait until morning, he decided. He would leave it to Annabelle. For the time being he watched their play with an odd wistfulness, conscious that here was the explanation for the rum he had missed. The accidents were only that. His father had not come home.

The next day the guardsman was dismissed; the following week the girl was sent home to her mother. Roddy and Annabelle had a day girl in from the fishing village. At night they were alone. Roddy felt his life closing in smaller and smaller circles around him. Bertie was much occupied with his construction, and for the time being the card game was halted. Most days Roddy wandered to the gym to see who was about. When he was home, he watched cricket matches and napped more than usual.

Roddy's cast was removed, the skin beneath it pale and tender. A baby's skin, soft and wrinkled and oddly sensitive. He felt it tingling, newly exposed to dust and air, the first time he walked in the evening. By now the ghost appeared only sporadically—whimsically, it seemed to Roddy. Was he being teased? He saw Dominic's face in a bus window, or thought he did. He could not be certain that he spotted him in a wedding party. A figure disappeared around a corner on market day—was that his father's stride?

One day he went to see his parents' graves. Dominic D'Souza had taught mathematics at St. Gregory's School for Girls, three streets away from Roddy's house. He and Roddy's mother were buried side by side in the yard of the adjoining church, with a single stone slab that his mother had chosen.

It was at the grave that Roddy, for the first time, tried to summon his father. The courtyard was empty, the girls in classrooms. The school building buzzed like a hive. "Dad," he tried, though he had never called his father that. "Daddy!" The word rang against the stone. For a moment he stood, mortified by his own descent. How had he come to believe such things? But he stayed another twenty minutes, the hot sun pressing on his head and shoulders, until finally he turned away.

When he reached home, the telephone was ringing. It was

after eight and Annabelle had already gone to her investment club. Roddy answered; it was Stephen.

"So, Dad, it's come off at last! How does it feel?"

"Fine, fine."

"What did the doctor say?"

"I have to be careful still. It's tender. A bit stiff."

Annabelle chatted easily with Stephen, concocting one thing, then another, to report or suggest, offering advice about the children, but Roddy never knew what to say to him. He could hardly connect the strong, firm voice on the line with the child he had known, the narrow face and long, melancholy nose. The overbite they had paid to correct.

Once Stephen had come home with a cut lip and bruised cheek. After Annabelle ministered to him, she sent him out to the garden with a strap and told Roddy to see to it; he was the boy's father. Roddy had found the boy waiting for him just outside the door. He held the strap but did not offer it, and Roddy felt an unwelcome reluctance. Stephen's lip was pink and swollen, crusted with sugar that Annabelle had applied to stop the bleeding. The bruise on his cheek was beginning to darken. But his eyes were fierce as he faced his father, reminding Roddy of the heroes in films he had seen long ago. What had happened? Roddy wondered, but with no idea that he could ever really know. He felt a sudden jolt of anger that Annabelle should hold this boy responsible, this boy with his puffed lip who had already been wronged, and with that came the revelation that he and Stephen were allies at last. Roddy understood the boy when his mother could not; Roddy, not Annabelle, knew that this scene in the garden was a mistake, that Stephen had committed no offense.

"The lip is paining?" Roddy had asked, gently he hoped, and when the boy had jerked his head, no, Roddy felt a nearly unbearable tenderness for him. He had wanted to beg the child not to get hurt, not to put himself in danger. But he simply put an awkward hand on Stephen's shoulder and patted him there. "Go and tell your mother I've given you a shouting." Stephen had stared at him a moment; at first, it seemed, he did not understand. Then his gaze changed. If he realized that he and his father had become conspirators, he did not let on. He didn't smile, as a boy might after a narrow escape. But Roddy believed his son had been satisfied, that Stephen had looked at him and had not found him wanting.

Now Stephen was telling him about the children. Andrew in the seventh grade, Katie in the fifth. "Dad, Mum and I have been talking. Maybe you should think about a flat building. The house is so much for her to keep up at this age . . ." He listened to his son's voice streaming across long-distance lines: "money saved in case of an emergency . . . this thing with your arm . . . a wake-up call . . . a nice flat, built exactly to order . . ."

"My father built this house," he told Stephen. "He built this house for me and my brother, and I'm the only one left." He could see Stephen still, standing in the garden with his swollen lip and the strap in his hand. For a glorious moment Roddy saw the point of his father's visits—that they belonged here, in this place, even after death. His father, himself, his beloved son, a line unbroken. He felt a surge of joy. "This house will go to you!"

There was a long pause, and for a moment he thought the line had gone dead. "I know, Dad. But I live here now."

Stephen rushed to fill the sudden silence. Katie was studying India in school. She had made a collage full of pictures torn from magazines. Elephants, Roddy guessed. Andrew was doing well on his ice hockey team, but Stephen had to take him to practice at five in the morning. "It's pitch-black at that hour, and the wind comes barreling through the streets. But he still can't wait to get on the ice."

"We're having a cool winter as well," Roddy said.

"Dad!" He laughed. "What you call winter is nothing to us! It's like our summer."

Roddy felt a burning in his chest. Annabelle had wept when Stephen left India, but Roddy had not tried to stop him. He had let his son go. When had Stephen drifted so far? When had their seasons become his?

"This hockey business, is it dangerous?" Roddy asked suddenly. He saw the boy, Andrew's face recalled best from photographs, but with a cut and bleeding lip.

"Not too bad. They wear a lot of padding. There's nothing to worry about," his son told him.

Roddy went to the Santa Clara Talkies. A sign outside said the cinema would close in a few months to make way for the construction of an American-style department store. The theater would reopen farther down Linking Road. Roddy, who had not come to the Talkies since he was a child, felt a strange hollowness in knowing it would soon be gone.

He paid for a ticket and walked past the snacks counter, where children were splayed against the glass, choosing sweets. The hall was dim and close, filled with people smoking cigarettes and waiting in queues for the W.C. He had come at intermission, but he pushed against the crowds on their way to the lobby and climbed the worn steps to the balcony. His seat was in the last row, and he could see the heads of the people in front of him. From behind they might have been anyone, a dark knobby head, a wiry gray one. His father and mother, who had died so many years apart. His brother, who had slipped away to the Gulf and then to death so unobtrusively that Roddy could scarcely register the shift, from gone to gone, until the years had hardened his absence into something unyielding and permanent. Stephen and Jess and their little ones, trying to stand in the bucket seats to see the whole of the room, suddenly exposed beneath the intermission lights. A few rows farther, a woman with a bun held an infant over her shoulder, and even the baby's face was so soft, so impressionable, that it might have been Stephen staring back over the years. He could not remember much of his son's features as a baby, only the feel of him, the span of Roddy's hand over his chest, the weight of his head.

The lights blinked, calling back the crowd. Roddy had not felt so lost since the weeks after his father's death. His mother had spun her grief into fervent prayer; his brother, young enough still to crawl into his mother's bed without feeling ashamed, had cried on her pillow. Roddy found no comfort in either place. He had come to the films, in a fury of rage and sorrow. *You see, I am here, where you were, where you forbade me to go,* he thought fiercely, as though he commanded his father's undivided attention even then. He sat in the back of the theater, twelve years old, and thought of all the nights his father had made him afraid. A folio of students' work open on the table and Roddy with a book in his lap. They worked in silence. Roddy's neck and shoulders ached.

"Sit up straight. How can you learn, slumped over like that?"

His father's voice made him jump and Roddy eyed the clock with dread. Words on the page dissolved as he read them; he turned back a page.

"Are you ready?"

His father's eyes were sharp and unrelenting. Roddy stumbled through answers he knew. "Wait, wait . . ."

"You know it or you don't know it. Go back again and tell me when you know it."

It was what Roddy remembered best of his father, those evenings of study, that keen-eyed gaze. For weeks, he could not imagine the world without those eyes pinning him to his book and forcing him up again. He could not imagine a world in which he could suddenly watch films one day after the next. He could not imagine a world, any world, beyond his father's reach. As Lent passed, he waited with mounting desperation to be driven from the theater. Easter brought nothing. The footrace with which he had deceived his mother, finally run and lost, and the days flattened—broad, unruly, all his own. He moved into them knowing his father had left him.

The lights dimmed again, and the reel flapped for a moment until a picture took hold. The film started abruptly where it had left off. All the dark heads in front of him were silhouetted against the screen. They were not his father or his mother, not the grandchildren he hardly knew. He was alone in the theater and suddenly frightened. When had he become so alone? How was it possible? Roddy D'Souza, a dutiful son, a family man. He had married, he had raised a child, he was a man with friends and connections; what had happened? He saw the guardsman and the village girl joined hand to ankle by the fire; he saw his wife reaching out to the baby boy at the top of the slide. He saw his life shrinking, cinched in closer and closer by the slow, calm circles of the ghost on his bicycle.

Air thickened in his lungs, the circles tightened around his rib cage. His breath came in gasps and he struggled to his feet, pushing past knees and thighs, fighting his way to the aisle. His hand slid onto someone's shoulder, and he grasped it tightly—"What's wrong with you? Sit down!"—as he stumbled past to the end of the row. He leaned against the back wall and drooped forward, slack as a puppet, trying to breathe the stifling air. Was this the story of his father's death, drowning in the darkness of the theater, alone? His breath rasped in his throat, sharp and whispery. *Annabelle. Stephen.*

And then a peal of laughter startled him. Sitting on the aisle, two rows ahead of him, was Bertie's daughter, Mary, laughing out loud and clapping her hands. Roddy glanced at the screen, where a tearful mother in a widow's white sari was begging her son for something or other. The whole of the theater was caught up in this drama, hushed, enthralled, but Mary raised her hands high over her head and cheered. She was attracting attention. People turned to stare, and Roddy could hear others begin to laugh. Were they mocking her? He looked for Bertie and Celeste but couldn't see them anywhere.

Mary swung her head from side to side, nodding and grinning at all the people around her. Some were smiling kindly, he could see now, sharing in her pleasure. A small child stood upright in his mother's lap and pointed, and Mary pointed back at him, thumping her hand on her thigh in delight. "So sweet," he heard a woman say. A middle-aged man lifted his arms, encouraging Mary to go on with her clapping. *Sssccccchhhhttt,* hissed a younger man, but Mary paid no attention.

Roddy was breathing more evenly now; the bands around his chest had eased. He neither looked for his father nor wondered if his father looked for him. When the scene changed, and the son in the film pushed angrily past his mother, Roddy moved next to Mary. There were no more seats in the row, but he stood just behind her in the aisle and waited for the film to end. Her laughter spent itself eventually, but she rocked back and forth, smiling at some secret pleasure until Roddy surprised her and walked her home.

The Santa Clara Talkies closed two months later, and construction began on the department store, a development Annabelle followed with great anticipation. She had been to department stores in the States with Stephen's wife, Jess—the stacks of shirts in every style and color, the endless rows of children's shoes. And she was ready with money to spend. Roddy had struck a deal with the contractor.

"And he's given me a gold chain, son. For my Christopher medal, just think! Your father!"

When it was Roddy's turn to speak, he cleared his throat.

"If I can get a visa . . . you know, it's difficult at my age . . . after the winter . . ."

He handed the telephone back to Annabelle when his son said, "We can't wait, Dad!" He imagined Katie holding up her collage to show him, shy little thing, and the pictures Roddy might help her add to it. He could go to the ice rink with a blanket for his knees and watch Andrew skate.

Roddy still saw the ghost from time to time: his father tall and stiff on the small-sized bicycle or standing legs apart, hands linked at the back, to stare out at the sea. When the ghost finally did turn to stare back at him one day, just three weeks before he was to go to the States, Roddy found that the weight of his father's gaze was not what he'd remembered as a twelve-year-old. Not at all, and he was not afraid.

The Bold, the Beautiful

The procedure to remove Grace's cataract was originally scheduled for the week before her elder daughter, Colleen, came to visit. But Grace developed a chest cold, and although the doctor felt perfectly confident that he could move forward, Grace herself was not convinced. She allowed her younger daughter, Bianca, to keep the appointment, she let Bianca drive her to the doctor's clinic in neighboring Santa Cruz, she waited until she had been admitted to the examination room. But once there, Bianca reported to Colleen, their mother refused to remove her sweater.

"I don't know, I don't know." Grace looked up at the doctor's assistant helplessly. In her hands was the thin cotton garment that she had been instructed to wear. "I have a cold, you see. Will this be enough?"

The assistant, not equal to the task of persuading her, had called Bianca in from the waiting room.

"Mummy doesn't want to change," she said.

"And that was it?" asked Colleen. It was after eleven, the hour when Colleen knew she could reach her sister at home.

Bianca lived with her husband and children in a flat just above her mother's.

"No, no. She waited to see the doctor. Embarrassing, actually. His waiting room was full of people, and there's Mum calling him in to have a chat."

"What did he say?"

"Oh, you know how she is, doctor this, doctor that. I think she only wanted sympathy. She went on and on about her cold . . ."

"She's been nervous about the procedure," Colleen said. "Every time I call, she tells me how anxious she is."

Bianca snorted. "She'd have no reason to be anxious if she'd let us take her to the doctor a year ago. When you come I'll give you the whole story—but she's known for months she's had a problem. Now the doctor says she's left this so long that the cataract has hardened."

"You like this doctor, Biddy? He's good?" She used the old family name for her sister.

"He's fantastic with her. He listened to all her questions, and finally he said there was no point going forward until she feels comfortable. So we've rescheduled for the end of next week. Such a nuisance, Colls. I wanted it finished before you came—"

"It's just as well this way. Now I can help. You can't be running back and forth with her all day. You can't miss that much work."

"And can you believe—I have to go to Bangalore for two days at least. I can't put it off." Biddy ran her own business out of an office in the ground-floor flat. She exported silks.

"Why put it off? I'll be there; I can look after her."

Biddy seemed unconvinced. "There's a whole regimen of drops. Six times a day, and you know she won't put them in herself. I've got the instructions, but there's all sorts of bother, one has to be refrigerated—"

"I can do it," Colleen said. "Just leave everything until I

come." Her sister didn't answer, she noticed. Instead she turned the subject to flight times. It would take Colleen an hour to get through immigration and customs, she guessed. Biddy's husband, Lionel, would be at the airport to meet her.

The trouble with Grace's vision was discovered by accident.

"God knows she didn't breathe a word of it—not to me, at any rate." They were sitting on Biddy's terrace. Colleen was to stay with her mother, but she'd arrived so late that the sisters decided not to wake her; she could move down in the morning. Colleen had shed her thick sweater and was having a beer. Biddy looked elegant even in the small hours of the morning: rings and bangles, a silk scarf knotted perfectly, long legs stretching to the railing. She had kicked her heels carelessly to the floor, and Colleen saw that her toes were painted vivid red. "I should have figured it out. She's been squinting at the television. But I thought that was the onions. She's taken to doing kitchen work while she watches—from her chair, mind you."

Every afternoon at three, the hour of Christ's Crucifixion, Grace sat in the armchair that had once been her husband's favorite and said the prayers of the rosary. At three thirty, her prayers completed, she took careful aim with the remote control and tuned the television to her favorite program, the daily broadcast of an American soap opera.

"Such nonsense, *The Bold and the Beautiful.* Mum's totally devoted—we get an earful if she has to miss a day. And while she watches, she's chopping." Biddy's voice rose in complaint. "She keeps the cutting board out on her lap and in the middle of her program, she's sawing away at a tomato. She takes half an hour at least for each onion—every slice has to be absolutely perfect—she won't even let the girl do it. 'They must be even, babe,' she says, 'or the smaller pieces will burn.' "

Colleen laughed.

"So she sits there crying away, from the TV or the onion, God only knows, with her fingers wet and slippery, and this cutting board perched on her lap—I tell you, she'll cut herself to the bone one of these days—and nobody noticed that she could hardly see the screen." Biddy mimicked her mother, leaning forward and peering across the street at the dark form of another flat building. "But you know, every day you're in and out, you don't notice these things that happen gradually. I only realized when I came down one evening and found her sobbing. And there was Uncle Frank standing beside her chair, looking positively miserable to find himself in the midst of all this waterworks, telling me, 'Mummy's upset.' "

Colleen had to put down her beer; her sister could make her laugh as no one else could. She felt instantly, entirely at home again, as though all the hours of the flight had wisped away.

"When Mum realized she was having trouble with her vision, she didn't say a word to me. What was she thinking—I'm right upstairs! How many times a day do I see her? But she decided she'd better confide in Uncle Frank."

Uncle Frank was their mother's eldest brother. Decades ago, before Uncle Frank had married, their father had bought three plots on St. Hilary Road: the biggest for himself, to be inherited by Frank; a second for his youngest son (the middle boy, a priest, would not be in need of property); and a third as a dowry for Colleen's mother, Grace. Ten years ago Uncle Peter had torn down his house to make way for a flat building, and three years ago Grace had done the same. But the family still lived all in a row.

"So Uncle Frank says not to worry, he knows just what to do. Now. You remember Abdul?"

"Of course." Abdul ran a medical stand among the street

vendors on one of Santa Clara's main shopping roads. For years she had seen it as she passed: its three flimsy walls, the size of a refrigerator crate; the stained and yellowed eye chart hanging from a tack; the sign proclaiming, WELL VERSED IN MEDICAL SCIENCES in English and Hindi. It stood between the mochi's stall, where she used to have her slippers resoled, and the sugarcane cart, where she bought glasses of sweet cloudy juice when her throat was dry from the bus ride home. She had been gone only ten years; the streets were caught in her memory as in a shaft of clear, hot light.

"He died a few weeks ago actually—a pity we can't go over and shake him. Uncle Frank took Mum to see him."

"Oh, Biddy!" Colleen could see it all: Uncle Frank, ushering her mother to see his old friend and standing by, determined to hide his concern in a series of gruff instructions that the eye is to be fixed, no matter what the cost—he only is paying. Her mother standing before the doctor stand, rubbing her eye furiously, as if she might yet dislodge a telltale bit of dirt, perhaps prompted by Uncle Frank to describe the way the people on television seem to move behind a cloud, no matter how close she brings her chair.

"It is a dead eye," Abdul announced after the examination. And then to Uncle Frank, "What can I do, my friend? What can be done? Some die suddenly, some die a piece at a time. The eye is gone."

"Oh, no!" Colleen laughed.

"Poor thing. And I think Uncle Frank felt as bad as she did. So he brought her home with this death sentence, and that's how I found the pair of them. That jackass Abdul! And even after they broke down and confessed, I had the whole song and dance from Mum—'No, no, I don't want to be trouble, I don't know this doctor, let me see if there's someone who so-and-so-who's-ninety-three knows, I can't go during my program, maybe next week is better, he's looking too young, babe'—I've had a hell of a time getting her in there." Biddy turned suddenly; the door to the flat had opened.

"Lionel?" But he had poured the beers and gone to make up Colleen's bed. "Who's there?"

"I heard the lift." Their mother's voice was more quavering than Colleen remembered. And then she came into view, peeping through the doorway, her face hopeful.

"My God, Mum, what are you wearing?" Biddy had begun to laugh. Grace had pulled a pair of elastic-waisted trousers on top of her nightgown and wrapped a shawl over her head. "You look like a Russian peasant!"

"This night air, babe, and with my cold!" She laughed at herself then and even did a little pirouette, one hand above her head and the other on her hip, before hugging Colleen. "Hi, darling, hi, hi! I was waiting for you to come and then I must have dropped off."

They sat up laughing and talking for nearly an hour, Grace holding Colleen's hand in her own lap and patting it occasionally, until Lionel cleared away the glasses and told them hush, they would wake the children.

Colleen stayed with her mother and got up early, her hours reversed. There was a kitchen girl who came in the mornings, Colleen knew, but she hadn't yet arrived. Colleen made herself a cup of tea and surveyed the kitchen. The bottom of the frying pan had burnt black, she saw, scraping at the carbon with a spoon. There was a new tea set, but the chipped mismatched cups she recognized from years past were still on the shelf. She chose one and went to sit on the terrace.

The yard had been landscaped. A row of spindly young trees lined the wall, and a tiled path led to the concrete drive, neatly creating two small squares of grass. A clump of bougainvillea mounded the pistachio-colored wall. Colleen had left India before her mother decided to sell to contractors. It was a sensible decision, Colleen knew. Her mother had been sharing the house with Biddy and Lionel, who had two children by then and were expecting their third. Flats would mean a place of their own. Lionel did all he could, but the house was in need of repair and updating at prohibitive costs. And even if such improvements were possible, the house itself had become a liability, susceptible to a recent batch of heritage laws. The family would have been obliged to maintain it in pristine condition while paying exorbitant taxes for the privilege of living in what had become a piece of history. The old bungalows, their roofs slanting low over the verandas like sharp-knit brows, gave way to blank-faced flat buildings with lifts and the promise of new pipes. The cement mosaic floors were easy to clean, Grace had told Colleen, who mourned the lost tile. Her mother found Colleen's nostalgia amusing and puzzling and of course, Colleen knew, yet another proof that her daughter was bright enough but lacking common sense. Colleen and her brothers had been given flats as well; they tumbled down toward her mother's in birth order. Her brothers had rented theirs to tenants, but Colleen had promptly sold her rights to Biddy and Lionel, who took over the ground floor for Biddy's silk business. The title to the land had gone, and the flat below Grace's served as payment to the contractor, who made a nice profit selling to a Hindu family. "Actually they're very quiet," Grace reported with a note of surprise that irritated Colleen. But Grace insisted on the right to name the building and to choose its pale green color. She called it Shamrock Lodge: a tribute, she told Colleen, to the Irish priests who had come through Santa Clara on tours of Catholic India, or stayed for longer stints to study or serve in the schools and parishes, and in whose honor Colleen herself had been named. It was a Father Joe from County Kerry, with whom her mother still corresponded—"such a gentle man but with a mischievous look"—who had given Biddy her nickname. Colleen wondered how Father Joe had received the news that his two years in Santa Clara had inspired this remarkable new address and perhaps the even more remarkable sign that Grace had commissioned, its lettering encased in a three-leaved border of wrought iron. "I wanted Leprechaun's Lair, but the signmaker says the word is too long. He could split it with a hyphen—but that would not be very pretty, do you think? He says something shorter is better." Colleen, given the circumstances, had agreed with the signmaker.

When Colleen came in again, her mother was at the table with a cardigan buttoned over her nightgown and shabby bedroom slippers on. She was squinting slightly and smelled of Vicks. "Hi, darling," she murmured, putting a hand to Colleen's cheek. Her hands were plump, the wrinkles soft.

Her mother had been slender as a young woman, with hollows beneath her cheekbones and a delicate jawline, but she had not aged the way Colleen expected. Her father had been tall and fair, with the broad face Colleen had inherited and the same wide-set eyes and thick bridge of the nose, the same cheeks, flat and even. When he grew older, his hair had gone the color of iron, his skin yellowed, as though a page of old newspaper, and his large hands seemed larger, more flapping, as he slowly lost his strength. He was nearly twenty years older than her mother and had died eighteen years ago after several years of heart complaints. But her mother had gone spongy, like something left too long to soak. Her hands reminded Colleen of overripe fruit.

"Up so early, babe?"

Colleen saw the dark pouches beneath her mother's eyes. "Go and rest a bit longer, Mum. I heard you coughing."

"I'm always up at this hour. So I can see the girl when she comes." She refused the cup Colleen offered her, one of the new set. "Only the two of us—we can use the old and save these nice ones. Babe? Should I just show you where my papers are? We don't know what will happen with this surgery . . ."

"Mum, it's a common procedure. You should be in and out in a few hours."

"No, babe, you don't know what doctor's told me. The cataract has—what's the word he used—*advanced.* It's very serious."

"But not dangerous, Mum."

"I'm telling you what he said! Biddy was there, she knows. Doctor says this is very rare."

"That's because you left it so long. You should go for regular checkups, Mum. You shouldn't wait for one of us to have to push you."

"What pushing have you done? I didn't ask you to come and push! I'm happy to look after myself. You don't have to do a thing."

Her mother had raised her head indignantly; now she dropped her gaze and concentrated on her teacup, her hand quivering.

"That's not what I mean. Of course I want to help." Colleen paused. "But let's finish this off and then we can enjoy the rest of my visit."

Grace smiled slightly.

"I've got some things for you, too," Colleen said. "A good pan, nonstick."

"I have a pan." Grace looked up.

"You can use a new one—that one's covered in black. It's not safe to cook like that, Mum."

"It's perfectly safe. A little stained, that's all." Grace frowned as she put a hand toward the kettle, then allowed Colleen to pour her a cup. "So . . ." She stirred a careful spoon and a half of sugar into her cup. "You've heard Toby Fernandez is engaged?"

"Biddy told me. To Violet Rebello, is it? I went to school with her sister."

"Yes," her mother said, in a tone that suggested all was not necessarily certain. "She's an older girl, of course."

"Younger than Toby."

"Older than you, I mean. And not so pretty. Her face is too lean. And the mouth is big. A wolfish face."

"Mum! You're terrible!" She laughed.

"I'm only saying what I see!"

Colleen resisted the temptation to point out that her mother's vision was impaired. "I don't remember anything like that."

"Well, you see only what you want to see." Grace sipped her tea and put it down with a certain smug pleasure at having answered her daughter so neatly, and with the stylized innocence that was her usual guise when masking some deeper anger or worry.

"I'll have to try to come for the wedding." Colleen made a point of speaking lightly. "It'll be this Christmas?"

"Yes," Grace said tightly. Then, unable to restrain herself even when she had decided to be cool: "Of course they'll be in a rush. This Violet must be nearing forty."

Colleen said nothing. Her mother's mood at such moments could be tipped in too many directions—fury, despair, relief, triumph—to make conversation safe terrain.

"Even if they married tomorrow, he might very well be cutting off his chance for children."

"He must know that. Perhaps they don't want children."

"Tcha!"

Colleen made her voice as gentle as she could. "I'm very pleased for them, Mum."

Grace sniffed.

"I am. We're friends, but not that kind of friend. I've told you."

She had not told her mother everything, naturally; she had

not told her mother that before she left India, Toby had made her an offer. But perhaps her mother guessed as much. And Colleen could guess, too, how much her answer had cost her mother. She could be living right down the road. There might have been grandchildren.

"You were so well suited, babe," Grace said, and Colleen saw that this time—as was perhaps the case too many times in her company—her mother had tipped toward sadness.

Colleen had bathed and dressed when she heard footsteps on the stairs. The door of the flat was open; Biddy's children sometimes came down to greet their grandmother in the mornings. Grace had dressed but returned to the table and her teacup. "It may be Sachi—she doesn't like the lift," she said to Colleen, then called into the corridor: "Who's there, who's come?"

A girl came in, a young married woman wearing salwar kameez and rubber slippers.

"Hallo, hallo," she said in a voice that seemed loud. Colleen and her mother had still been talking in an early-morning hush and here, with the girl's arrival, was day breaking over them like a wave.

Her mother looked delighted, as if the girl had come to pay a visit. "Sachi! This is Sachi."

"Hallo!" Sachi said again. She had a round yellow face, dotted with tiny moles near the hairline. Her hair was in a knot at her neck. She smiled at Colleen and tossed her head in a satisfied nod. "Here is baby!"

"This is my older girl," Grace said, and then to Colleen, "See how strong her hands are! She rubs my neck, just there, when I have a headache. Or she gives very nice foot rubs with oil; she can give you one later. She comes when she can, sometimes two times a week, sometimes three." She began chatting to Sachi in Marathi, a language Colleen had never picked up well. They were speaking of arrangements for the day's meals.

"Oh, my girl—" Grace broke off and turned to Colleen. "Your first day, and Sachi can get some nice pieces of chicken. We should put off this eye nonsense."

Colleen was prepared for this. "You can't keep changing. It isn't fair to the doctor. Biddy says he's been very good."

"He's a nice man," Grace conceded. "Let me speak with him directly; he'll understand when I've explained—"

Biddy came bustling in with a plastic bag in one hand and a large leather purse with brass buckles. Her lipstick was dark red, making her face appear even more mobile than usual.

"What's this? Is she backing out again? Coward!" She kissed Grace's forehead. "Oh, God, Colls, running late again! What's the matter with me—"

"I am not a coward!" Grace said, but Biddy cut her off. She handed Colleen the bag.

"Here's everything the doctor's given us—" One of the children was calling down to her. "One minute! I'm coming!" she shouted up the staircase. Then to Colleen: "He's written everything out, the procedure, all the prescriptions. Then we have to choose which lenses to buy—"

"What's the choice, babe? I want to choose for myself."

Biddy ignored her. "Just check and see. She's not supposed to eat for some time beforehand—Mum, wait, don't eat that 'til we've read this—"

"See, Sachi, how these girls treat me! Not even a banana!" Sachi laughed and brought out a cup and saucer before disappearing into the kitchen. "There, Biddy, I've had half only. Now have some tea."

Biddy clicked her tongue impatiently. "Not now, Mum, I'm running late. I'll never get these kids off. Coming!" she called again. "I'll just take them to school and stop by Santa Clara Medical on my way back. I can pick up the drops."

"Why go?" Colleen said. "You're in such a rush already. I can get the drops."

"No, no, not you," their mother said. "Let Biddy go."

Biddy looked from one to the other. Her gaze settled on Colleen. "If you don't mind, it would help—"

Grace spoke firmly. "No, babe. Better for you to go. They know you there."

Colleen tried to keep the irritation from her voice. "They don't need to know me, Mum; they need to know the drops. Of course I can go."

"Yes, but," her mother murmured, "if there's any trouble, then suddenly Biddy has to take something back . . . Babe, you have the time if you go now."

Grace stared at Biddy, wide-eyed. Finally Biddy turned to Colleen. "Never mind. I'll go."

A look of weary resignation passed between them.

Colleen tried to keep her voice light. "You see, Biddy—she doesn't trust me even to run your errands."

"No, darling!" A rusty laugh that jarred Colleen's nerves. "Only it's better for continuity if Biddy does everything from the start. She'll be here when you've gone." Grace turned to Biddy: "You have to go overnight? Your sister's just come."

"I *know,* Mum. I'm trying to get back. I've cut it down from two nights actually. I don't know how I'll finish." A voice called from above and Biddy flung herself toward the door. "Oh, God, these children! Come and say good-bye, Colls—they won't budge 'til they've seen you."

The waiting room was small and crowded, with a harsh light overhead. In one corner was a young couple with a baby, not more than a year old, who was trying to get a foothold on her father's chest. What could have gone wrong already? Colleen wondered. Why would such a little thing need an eye operation? He lifted her high and the baby laughed.

Colleen was called into the room where her mother had consented to put on the cotton gown. Over that Grace had rebuttoned her thick cardigan, and over that, she put on her shawl.

"Doctor," Grace began in a sweet voice. "Oh, here's my daughter!" She smiled in relief. "Now, you can tell her what you explained to me? Only using your words—I don't know exactly how you like to put it. I've told her my case is different from most other people's."

"Nothing to worry about, Mrs. Lobo. It only means we may need to use a slightly different procedure. But I promise you, in five years of practice, I've never had a patient with complications."

"And then one other factor, Doctor, this cold. The moment I lie back my head feels—" She put both hands to her temples and pressed. "Then, you know, I have difficulty breathing—"

"That's only the congestion. That won't interfere with what I'm doing."

"Oh, if you think so," Grace said, holding the ends of her shawl together. "But this tightness in the chest. I still have a cough."

"Not to worry, Mrs. Lobo. That won't interfere with what we're doing." He was a young man with a large square jaw and easy smile. He glanced at Colleen conspiratorially. "Your mother is very curious, isn't she? Very thorough."

"Oh, yes."

"I like to know things." Grace lifted her head.

"Good for you," the doctor said. "Then have you made a decision about the lenses?"

"Tell me again."

There were three types. A cheap type, which he did not advise; another for 25,000 rupees, which was usually considered sufficient, he said carefully; and the most expensive variety, 32,000 rupees, which came with a UV coating. "That's only useful if you spend a lot of time outdoors," he said. "Otherwise the midlevel lenses are just as good."

Grace frowned. "But this UV—" she began.

"Never mind, we'll take the highest quality," Colleen told the doctor. Biddy had already taken her aside: Just get the very best, even if she doesn't need it. It will make her more comfortable.

"Right, then, very good," said the doctor. "You can take care of that with Amrita outside. I have lenses here, so you'll just be buying them from me—that way we don't wait another day for the lenses to come. We can go straight ahead."

"Cash only, Doctor?" Grace sounded doubtful. "Darling, you have enough? Or we can come back tomorrow to pay the rest, Doctor?"

"I have it, Mum!"

He smiled at them both before leaving. "Nice boy," Grace said. "His mother is a Menezes, she's on St. Vitus, I think."

Someone came to take her blood pressure. "Why?" asked Grace. "Is there any trouble?"

"This is standard only," she was assured.

The doctor came in again, overrode the assistant's request for Grace to remove her shawl, and as he left, suggested that she lie down. It was difficult for Grace to climb up on the high, narrow bed; she leaned on Colleen and bore down, a surprising weight. The doctor laughed when he reentered.

"Mrs. Lobo, you're doing acrobatics in here? We could have cranked the bed down for you! Never mind, you're too spry for that, aren't you?" He helped ease her onto the mattress, and Colleen, who had just spotted the lever to lower the bed, felt a fool.

"You'll wait in here with her until we're ready to go? That's not usual, Mrs. Lobo, but what did I tell you? You're a special case. Very good, then. In a few minutes we'll be under way."

The room had two beds and no chairs. After a bit, Colleen perched on the second bed. Her mother was unusually quiet, until other people came into the room and prompted a new line of questioning.

Now Colleen looked at her mother, who lay very still, face to the ceiling, waiting like a docile child. Her body seemed flattened, the long throat, the arms limp at either side: a small body after all.

Grace coughed, a dry little sound, then raised herself up on an elbow and coughed again with more drama.

"You're feeling all right, Mum?"

She lay back down, smiled slightly. "Just a little hungry."

"We can get something in for dinner. Anything you like."

"But Sachi has gone to get chicken!"

"The chicken, then. But see how you feel. You may not feel up to eating afterward."

They were silent.

"I'll miss my program," Grace said.

"You can catch up tomorrow."

"You can get the main flow, but there's always some little thing you miss if you don't watch."

Colleen looked at her mother's hand, at the wedding ring she still wore though her father had been gone more than eighteen years. "Vanessa watches *The Bold and the Beautiful.*"

Grace coughed again, and Colleen was annoyed with herself. Why had she said such a thing? Of course it was a lie. Her roommate had no interest in soap operas. "At least I think she used to once."

The assistant reentered with the anesthesiologist, who wore green scrubs and slippers. His answers to Grace's questions were clipped and efficient.

"Can my daughter stay?" Grace suddenly asked him.

"No, we're ready to begin. Doctor is coming."

"Babe?" Grace sounded frightened and Colleen took her hand. "How long will it take?"

"The procedure should last ten minutes. But you'll be sleeping for at least an hour or so. You can go and get a snack," the anesthesiologist told Colleen.

"I'll be right outside, Mum," she said. "I won't go anywhere."

Colleen was thirteen years old when she went to her father and told him she was having trouble seeing. He had looked up from his papers, surprised. He took off his own specs and drew her closer. She leaned against him.

"Seeing what, baby? Things far away or close at hand?"

"Far away," she answered promptly. For the past week she had been squinting at the board at the head of the classroom, waiting for her teacher to notice.

He gave her a book from the pile on his desk and she read the first lines without hesitation.

"Now—" He turned her gently. "Tell me what is on that shelf there."

She stumbled through the contents of her mother's shelf, a jumble of dry goods, jars of pickles, dusty bottles, vitamins. "A box." She frowned terribly. "No, a bag, a brown bag."

"You have headaches?"

She did not know the answer to this. "Yes . . . sometimes . . ."

"And how long have you had trouble seeing? A long time?"

"No . . ." She was nervous.

"You didn't want to tell anyone? I see."

Colleen looked at him without understanding. By then her father was in his sixties, the age of her friends' grandfathers. His hair was dark but sparse, combed in fine lines. He had a wide, square face and large hands. He stroked her head absently and Colleen waited.

"We must get you a pair of specs, I think," he said, and then, misunderstanding her jerk, he kissed her forehead. "Never mind, girly. I wear them too. We'll be two of a kind."

The second time she met Vanessa for dinner, Colleen told her the story of feigning eye trouble when she was a girl. At first it was an anecdote, a funny trick she'd played as a kid—isn't it funny, the ideas you have when you're a kid?

"I thought they would make me look smart. Another girl in my class had them and I thought they were wonderful."

Vanessa laughed, as Colleen had hoped she would. But almost at once, Colleen was ashamed of herself. "There wasn't a lot of money. It must have pinched, the doctor's visit and the cost of the lenses."

It had all been so far from what Colleen had imagined: tests, trips to the doctor, consultations. Perhaps her father would have to take her to town. She pictured her face transformed by glasses, glasses that made her look interesting and bookish. She's such a reader, her father would say proudly.

Instead her mother had come to find her in the bath, cutting through Colleen's embarrassment with the sharp order to turn around. Colleen didn't like it, but she didn't say so—not because she was afraid of her mother but because she worried it was unnatural, a daughter ashamed to be seen by her mother. So Colleen let her mother take a brush to her. Her ankles, her spine, the back of her neck—her mother scrubbed as if Colleen were a dirty window, then looked right through her when she had finished. "Now your knees. Hold still." Her mother crouched on the floor before her and Colleen had to brace herself, one hand against the wall, as she rocked from the pressure on her legs. She could see the line of her mother's part, sharp as if she'd used a blade. "We're going to town," her mother told her. "Wear your good skirt. I want you to look presentable."

When she had dressed, Colleen was sent to wait in the garden while her mother spoke with her father on the veranda steps. She watched as her father peeled bills from a thin fold.

"Is it enough, you think?"

"I don't know. Go and see. If we need more, we can pay the difference later."

Colleen stamped at the shaggy shell of a coconut, cracked open and rotted.

Her mother joined her a moment later, sternly checking the contents of her pocketbook. Her father went to the back of the garden without saying anything, without waving.

"Come. You've cleaned your teeth properly?"

"Dad's not coming?"

"I'm taking you."

They set off. The street was hot and dusty, crowded with people, and Colleen's feet felt heavy in socks and shoes. Her mother's silence made her nervous. They met neighbors with shopping baskets, but Grace didn't stop and linger in her usual way. Colleen wondered whether they were late, but didn't risk setting her mother off by asking. Grace was barreling through the crowds, pulling Colleen along beside her, until they had to stop at a junction.

"We'll get the best we can," she said suddenly, her grip on Colleen's arm so tight that Colleen could feel the pressure of each finger even after her mother had let her go. She imagined the marks as something permanent, something anyone could see if she rolled up her sleeve.

Colleen looked up at Vanessa. "We searched for hours in two different shops. The shop owners were furious with us—Mum looked through every single tray, as if she would suddenly find the one good pair she could afford. But all she could find for the price were ugly, cheap things—huge, with thick rims—I think they were men's glasses, actually—and in the end we had to buy them. I just managed to keep myself from crying right there in the shop.

"Anyway, that was that. I was stuck with them. Mum had gone to my teachers to be sure I wore them in school. I kept up the pretense for months. I couldn't bear to tell my parents it was all a lie. Finally I went to my dad and put on an enormous act. The glasses had fixed my eyes, I told him! I could see without them. 'Is that it, baby? All better?' "

Vanessa smiled.

"He tested me with a book from so many paces and I read it perfectly. He didn't say another word, only took the glasses and kept them in a box. 'In case your eyes go weak again.' "

"I remember feeling so relieved; I thought I'd been totally convincing. Later my mother took a strap to me and I didn't know how she found out I'd been shamming." Vanessa was watching her and Colleen felt unsure where to put her hands; she wrapped them around her glass and took a sip of wine. "Of course she had every right. I mean, she was usually very fair, and it wasn't as if things were bad between us. This was a punishment. But Dad was angry with her over that. He never shouted at her, but he did over that."

Later her father had come in to wish her good night. Her shame was so great that she had tried to feign sleep, but instead (a new shame) she began to cry. He sat with her until her sobs had subsided, patting her hand, while Biddy, who shared the bed, looked on with solemn interest. "Say a little prayer," he told Colleen. "God forgives anyone who comes to Him." She had tried to concern herself with God's forgiveness when it was really theirs she wanted: her father's and mother's. But for months afterward, she had risen early to hear daily Mass at St. Anthony's, in case God's forgiveness might satisfy her after all.

Still, she could hardly bear to think of her father's face that night: the eyes sad and knowing, his disappointment bound so closely with love that perhaps they were inextricable.

"Stupid little thing, wasn't I?" Colleen tried to smile and

failed. She had not meant to drag the whole wretched business into the light, but when she looked up, Vanessa had not turned away. Her eyes were steady, alive with sympathy and interest. Colleen felt suddenly that Vanessa—who was no one she could speak of at home, not even a friend yet to mention to Biddy—had the power to forgive this deception, long past and in another country.

"Your father died?"

"A long time ago." This came back to her too: his face when he had no longer recognized her.

Vanessa reached across the table to take Colleen's hand. After a moment, during which she began to brush her thumb lightly against Colleen's fingers, she smiled.

"So, are there pictures of you in these awful glasses?" she asked, and Colleen, relieved as a girl, began to laugh.

The procedure, Colleen phoned Biddy in Bangalore to report, had not gone smoothly. The cataract had been left too long and hardened to such a degree that it could not be removed without an incision. Then, at the critical moment, just as he told her to be completely still, Grace coughed.

"I guess it happened just as he was cutting."

The pressure inside the eye went very high for a moment. "Even I was alarmed," the doctor told them when he came to speak with Grace. "Wanted to give me a shock, didn't you? You were out to break my perfect record! Well, it worked—you gave me quite a fright. But not to worry."

"Apparently if any of the blood vessels had burst, she could have lost sight in that eye," Colleen told Biddy. "But the doctor was able to control it."

"Thank God!"

"It meant the operation lasted forty minutes instead of ten. So they had to keep giving her shots of anesthesia—that will make her feel ill. Also now she'll have to take something stronger for pain, and the doctor's given her medication to very gradually relieve the pressure in the eye. But only very slowly—he had to put a large air bubble inside the eye to keep it pressurized enough for healing."

"Okay, okay . . ."

"So her sight will have a haze or black cloud for the next two weeks. But after that she'll be fine."

"And now?"

"Very groggy still. I've given her the stuff for pain so she can sleep through the night."

"Christ," she said, "I can't believe it."

"Don't worry, you haven't missed a thing. She's made me wrap up the cataract in a tissue and bring it home for you to see."

"No, not really!" Biddy began to laugh. "How disgusting! You really have it?"

"It's rock hard."

"Oh, God, Colls!"

"I thought I was going to be ill, right there in the doctor's office. Honestly, I almost was. I nearly brought shame on the whole family. But Mum was so earnest, what else could I do?"

Biddy was home the following day in time for tea. She came clicking up the stairs in her heels, too impatient to wait for the lift, and dropped her bag at the door.

Grace was leaning forward in her chair, watching the last of her program. Colleen had not permitted her to chop anything until her vision had cleared, and sat at the table, cubing potatoes and receiving instruction on the characters of *The Bold and the Beautiful.*

"See this fellow, with his wicked look. He has hatched a plot to marry that girl against her family's wishes. Sweet-looking thing. She should marry this other person. Wait. He'll come soon. He has a gentlemanly quality."

"Hi," she greeted Biddy with some relief.

"Hey, Colls. Mum! How are you feeling?"

Grace smiled up at her daughter, a brief concession to Biddy's concern and the pleasure of having her home.

"Mum!"

"Hang on, darling, one minute, this is almost finished. You see"—she threw the remark in Colleen's direction—"what a villain he is! You see how he is convincing her?"

Biddy clicked her tongue. "Mum! Turn off that nonsense!"

But Grace was too engrossed to pay attention. The suitor she favored had appeared on the screen, and she smiled in satisfaction, pointing so Colleen would see him. "There, you see, he's come. That's where it will end." She turned from the screen. "Hi, babe."

Biddy clicked her tongue. "What are you doing, watching television when you've just gone in for your eyes?"

"I missed yesterday, babe."

"She insisted."

"Stubborn, stubborn," Biddy said absently, inspecting her mother's bandaged eye. "You've changed the dressing?"

"I am not stubborn. I know my own mind. That is quite another thing."

"Before bed tonight, the doctor says. We have to wait at least a full day."

With no immediate tasks to claim her, Biddy relaxed. She sat near her sister. "This suits you," she said, adjusting the shoulder of Colleen's dark shirt. "But you need a bit of color. Maybe a scarf."

"She looks nice as she is. Simple and neat. What color does she need to chop potatoes?" Grace asked.

"Oh, the queen of nightdresses speaks!" Biddy teased.

"You see this one, always harassing me," Grace said to no one in particular, as though explaining yet another character in her soap opera. "I've put on these today." She wore a flowered blouse, untucked, and a sturdy cotton skirt with an elastic waistband.

"Good, because Father Addie is coming to check on you. I'll just run and wash up."

"What have you finished, babe? Potatoes aren't done? We can put out something for Father Addie. He likes bhel puri. I can get up and do it if the potatoes aren't ready."

"Sit, Mum! I'll do it."

Grace winced.

"It hurts?"

"No, just my head a little."

"You want the medicine, Mum?" Colleen put down her knife. "Or a cup of tea? What can I do?"

Grace smiled weakly. "Ask Sachi to come. She can rub my head for a few minutes before Father arrives."

Father Adalbert was a few years younger than Grace and had come to the parish directly out of seminary. He had known Colleen, Biddy, and their elder brothers throughout their childhoods. He was not unusually tall, but he was solidly built, robust, with a strong, ringing voice (ideally suited to the pulpit, Colleen had always thought) and large hands that he lifted high in greeting. He wore a leather jacket over his clerical collar and rubber-soled loafers that squeaked on the floor. When he had kissed Colleen, and called "Hallo, hallo, here we all are!" to Biddy, who was just coming down the steps, and gone to press Grace's hand, peering at the bandage and announcing that already he could feel she was much, much happier with the surgery behind her—isn't it? yes?—looking around affably, certain of the affirmation he sought, he finally settled on the sofa and crossed his legs, beaming at them each in turn. Colleen felt both disconcerted by the stir of his entry and grateful for it; she had not realized into what quiet patterns she and her mother had already fallen.

"You'll have sherry, Father? Or tea? We'll have a fresh pot. Babe?" Grace waved faintly toward the kitchen, a gesture her daughters understood to mean, Put on the kettle.

"He'll have a sherry, won't you, Father? Or what about a shandy? Come on, I'll join you." Biddy had already busied herself with glasses.

"Yes, yes, shall we?" Father Addie rubbed his hands together, a butcher's hands, Colleen thought. When he held the Host up for the congregation to see, the bread looked frail and brittle, bone-white in his thick fingers. It was then, and not in contemplation of the crucifix above the altar, that Colleen had found it possible to imagine an emaciated Christ, pale and broken.

When he had inquired about the surgery and learned the details of Grace's near escape—Biddy rising up out of her chair to veto a viewing of the cataract in its handkerchief shroud—he turned his attention to Colleen.

"You're looking very good, very happy. Blooming with health! Living in the States agrees with you, isn't it?"

Colleen glanced in her mother's direction but admitted this was so.

"Keeping busy?"

This, also, was true. She worked for an international aid organization, writing grants and appeals.

"Good for you," he said. "I tell you, I don't know if I could do it. A fresh start in a new country?"

"This one was always bold," Grace piped up. "Such a girl for running, I don't know how I kept up with her."

Colleen thought of Biddy: her bright red lipstick and ringing voice, the business she had launched.

"That was only as a little girl," Colleen told her mother.

"No, no, no, you were always bold. Can you imagine? She

went with two suitcases only. And she was gone almost two years before she came home. So young-looking—she always had a baby face."

"And you don't find it lonely?" Father asked.

"I've made friends. Mark and Rowena aren't too far away, and I have cousins nearby."

"And she has a roommate, Father." Colleen looked up in surprise. "A single girl, Vanessa is her name." Grace pronounced the name carefully, so that each syllable received equal emphasis. "She sent me a card for my operation."

This was the first Colleen had heard of a card. *When,* she thought in confusion, *had Vanessa sent it?*—as though that were the point about which to wonder. She telegraphed a quick question to Biddy, who raised her eyebrows and shrugged in a pantomime of ignorance.

"It's a nice card. I have it just here—" Grace was digging into the pile of papers she kept on a nesting table near her chair. "Here, here it is. See?" She held it up for Father to admire: an off-white stock with a four-leaf clover embossed in gold. "The inside is blank," Grace said. "Sometimes they put little verses, but not always. So she has written: 'The best of luck for your recovery.' The four-leaf clover is for luck, you know." That was not all Vanessa had written, Colleen could see immediately. A letter was folded inside, but Grace had removed this to pass the card to Father Addie, who said what a thoughtful girl and smiled at Colleen in approval.

The week before she left India for good, Colleen went to confession. She had been baptized at St. Anthony's, a member of its parish her whole life, but the airline ticket locked in her mother's cupboard at home had cast all the neighborhood in a new and startling light. She was struck, suddenly, by the church's beauty. The church was cream-colored, gold in the late-afternoon sun. She passed through the heavy doors. The walls were a meter thick, meant to sustain a chalky cool, but rows of fans hung down from the blue arched ceiling on long, rigid poles that rocked with the motion of the blades. She dipped her fingers in holy water and walked slowly up an aisle. It seemed to her that she was walking in a track of her own footsteps, worn through years of moving easily from one Mass to the next, one week to another. Now, suddenly, she wanted to notice the niches for the Stations of the Cross, the statues with their white-painted faces and startling red lips, the gilt-edged robes of Mary and Saint Anthony, who each presided over a side of the nave.

The confessional was on Saint Anthony's side. Colleen had not expected to hear Father Addie's voice; the parish was sizable enough to require many priests and he had risen to a position of some authority among them. He seldom heard confession anymore, she imagined, and of course he would recognize Colleen—for a moment she considered bolting. But he had begun, the rhythms so familiar: how long had it been since her last confession. She answered, two months, and then, having spoken, she knew she would not run away.

She confessed to fits of temper, to various acts of frustration and pettiness. To fear, to lack of faith.

"In God or in yourself?"

She did not quite know.

"He is your strength. You can lean on Him, wherever you are, whatever your worry." Colleen thought briefly of how it felt, as a child, to lean against her father's legs. It was hot and close behind the drapery of the booth; she felt suddenly near tears or illness.

"What else, my child?"

Colleen hesitated. She could not put into words what she knew to be the truth, nor could she go without trying to name some portion of the pain she caused and carried. She thought of Toby, shifting in his seat when she had given her answer too quickly; she thought of Biddy and the two nephews she adored, wheedling her to stay with them; she thought of Grace.

"I am hurting my mother. I'm hurting her badly."

"How?"

She caught the note of surprise in his voice, and it undid her. She began to cry and could not answer. He waited.

Then, quietly: "What is it you're doing to your mother? How have you hurt her?"

"I'm leaving."

There was a pause before he answered. "That's not a sin, my child."

She cried even more, unable to explain what was, and he did not press her. Again he waited, and then he began to pray, in a strong, firm voice, until she felt that she could join him.

Before Father Addie left, Grace suggested that he lead them in a prayer of thanksgiving for her eye. They joined hands. Colleen stood between her mother and Father, with Biddy winking irreverently at her until it was time to bow their heads. "You begin," Father suggested to Grace.

It was past the time for her pain medication, Colleen realized suddenly. Her mother seemed small and defenseless, the bandage over her eye the sign of a terrible wound.

"Thank you, Lord, for returning to me this gift of sight," her mother said in a quavering voice, and Colleen realized the essence of Abdul's diagnosis had not been lost on her mother. Her mother understood full well—the power of a life of faith behind her—that her eye, once dead, had been resurrected.

The next day, when Biddy was downstairs in her office, sorting through piles of embroidered silk, when Lionel was at the bank and the children at school, when the hour of three had come and gone and prayers were at an end, Grace switched on *The Bold and the Beautiful* and Colleen came to join her.

"What's happening, Mum? Who's this one?"

The program lurched forward, scene after scene. "He

won't tell his wife that he's gone to dinner with that girl, and see, she'll suddenly discover. Then he's caught in a trap!" She shook her head at this bit of stupidity.

The mother of twins does not tell her husband he isn't their father. "There again, you see? For one night only she made a terrible mistake and that was because of an earlier misunderstanding. Maybe he would forgive her, but." Colleen marveled at this habit of her mother's, to end a thought firmly with "but," as though nothing more needed saying.

A brother plots to take over his father's business.

"This boy is always scheming and the father is a good man, he doesn't see the truth. All of them are hiding this and that. Then the secrets tumble out and everyone's plans are upset."

When the program was over, Colleen gave Grace a teacup and she accepted it, the soft hands shaking slightly until the cup was steady in her hands. She breathed deeply, letting the steam warm her face. The strain of watching her program had tired her, and she closed her eyes for a minute or two, keeping their sight locked safely in the papery skin of her body for a little longer, a little longer. Abdul had said his piece; she knew her husband had been gone for nearly as many years as they had spent together, she knew that she too had grown old. But the next day the mother may confess; the decent man may win the girl; the prodigal son may repent. And Grace will have eyes to see it.

"Sleep a little while, Mum."

But Grace only rested her eyes until her tea had cooled. By then, Colleen had brought a package in from her room. She unwrapped the new frying pan she had bought for her mother. She did this in front of Sachi, who accepted the new pan with pleasure, and in front of her mother, who frowned when she saw what was happening but decided to let it go.

The Crow and the Monkey

On the day of the New Year's party, Jude was invited to go next door and help his cousin Neil and Uncle Peter make the old man for the bonfire. It was a mild season in Santa Clara; the sun was not too hot to spend afternoons outdoors. But his mother insisted that Jude lie down for an hour first. He was recovering from a cold, and she did not like the sound of the cough in his chest.

Jude did not usually mind his afternoon sleep, but the lure of this invitation was too powerful to endure a wasted hour and he could hear tantalizing activity next door. The channa-wallah had been calling, his voice adrift as he made his way down the street, and Jude heard Uncle Peter stop him at their gate. Already he had missed a treat of spiced chickpeas.

"You've had your lunch," his mother said and jerked his sweater over his head. "Now go to sleep or you'll be dropping like an old man yourself at midnight."

Jude strained to listen. Uncle Peter was not alone outside; Jude could hear Neil's voice, high and excited. Clearly Aunty Freddy had not imposed a nap on such a holiday, although Jude knew better than to point out this distinction to his mother. Just a few days ago she had called Aunty Freddy crazy as a crow after Aunty Freddy came to borrow her old blue coat. "For what, I'd like to know," his mother had said. "For a trip to Delhi she has no money to take?" Uncle Peter, Jude heard his mother say, had lost his shirt; he wondered if Aunty Freddy was giving him a coat instead. If so, he agreed that she must be crazy—Uncle Peter would not want a lady's coat. He was tall, with a loud, ringing laugh that made Jude think of parties. He did not have a job in an office the way Jude's father did; he had trips and meetings instead. When he was home, even in the middle of the day, he played cricket with Neil and the other boys on St. Hilary Road. Uncle Peter taught Jude's older brother, Simon, to bowl, and before Simon went to boarding school he was best in all the neighborhood. He had come home for the holiday; Jude hoped they all might practice once the old man was finished.

But Jude didn't mention this possibility either; he knew the sniffing noise his mother would make if he brought up Uncle Peter's cricket matches. Instead he promised that he did not feel ill, not one bit. And since it was nearly a new year, he would soon be six, old enough to miss one nap.

"Old enough to stop whining." Jude did not like the smell of the Vicks his mother spread on his chest. She rubbed so vigorously that Jude felt his skin sliding along his ribs like a piece of washing against a board.

He would sit down while he worked, Jude offered. He would be resting the whole time. Otherwise the old man would be finished before he could so much as stuff a leg.

"Enough!" His mother gave him a warning look. When she had gone, his older sister, Marian, came to the door and smiled at Jude as she put up the netting; the mosquitoes would not be out so early, but she knew he liked to sleep beneath a tent or a ship's sail. "Just lie quietly if you can't sleep. It's only an hour."

Jude started to count, but seconds became minutes so slowly that he despaired. He could feel another day surging past him while he was trapped in a dim room. His chest reeked, a fly buzzed. The overhead fan did not become a propeller. Some days it gained speed until the whole roof lifted off and the bed hovered above the rest of the house, but today it was just a fan, dull and stupid, its blades sluggish as clock hands. His mother had closed the wooden window guards, but slivers of midday sun fell across the floor and one, wire-bright, reached the bed. Jude moved his toe idly in and out of it. He could hear Uncle Peter and Neil below him in their compound; their words were muffled, but their voices had the serious pitch of workmen deep in collaboration. Birds kept up a constant chatter and someone argued with a fruit vendor. Briefly Jude imagined it was a giant crow, dressed in his mother's old coat but with Aunty Freddy's red leather pocketbook. Then he heard the unmistakable creak of his own gate swinging open and the sharp clownish blast of a bicycle horn. Simon was off somewhere, free to do as he liked because he was fourteen. Jude kicked the folded coverlet at the foot of the bed.

"How's he coming?" Simon called from the road.

"See for yourself!" Neil's voice rose, triumphant. Progress must be brisk. Jude ached to think of all he had missed. He wished he was fourteen, he wished he had a crazy mother. He did not dare to speak either hope aloud, but he made the declarations firmly in his head, where God could read them if He chose. Jude didn't care! Let God even see Jude, parting the curtains of netting and slipping through them, walking softly across the cool tile to the window.

Two minutes later his name rang out like a clap of thunder. His mother's face was like water with a fast wind moving over it: sudden sharp furrows and danger.

"What is the meaning of this? You want to stay here all night and miss the party?"

Jude clambered down from his perch by the window. He had never conceived of such a terrible punishment; he had been looking forward to the New Year's party nearly as much as to Christmas itself—the tree and the gifts, Simon's return from school, Jude's solo in the children's choir.

"I was only looking . . ."

"Looking, looking! You should be looking at the back of your eyes. Go and lie down, this instant." She waited until Jude had climbed back through the netting. "Now. One more sound from you and you won't be looking beyond this bed until the year is finished. Do you understand?"

He nodded, his hair bristling against the rough pillow.

She frowned—"One hour, one full hour, from this minute"—and left him.

When he awoke, Jude was cold. Someone had been in to cover his legs and he pulled the cotton coverlet to his shoulders. The golden glow outside had faded and the cracks of light through the window were thin as milk. Crow calls sounded lonely, as though the sky had tipped and emptied itself of everything but birds. Jude felt stiff and out of sorts. He could not hear his mother or sister, could not hear any voices. But noises from the kitchen reassured him and he pushed aside the netting to get up. Only then did he remember the old man and go rushing to the window.

The yard next door was quiet. Uncle Peter and Neil were no longer in sight, and although Jude could not see the old man, he knew it must be finished. Disappointment flushed through him like a swallow of something nasty—a sip from his father's glass or a dose of the cod-liver oil his mother forced him to take each evening. He thought that nothing, not even setting the old man alight, could make up for this loss.

In the kitchen he found Rosa rolling out dough. "Awake, baba!" She smiled but did not stop, her shoulders rocking. "Come and see."

Jude did not go to her. He was too angry to give in to anyone who conspired to let him sleep—even Rosa, who had been with the household since he was small and whose leaving he dreaded.

"Ooh!" She wrinkled her forehead and pouted, an imitation of Jude that she could not maintain for long. She had a round face with small, dark eyes, as narrow as caraway seeds when she laughed at him. These days Rosa was always laughing. A match had been proposed for her, in a series of English letters that she kept beneath her blanket even though she had trouble reading them. "God knows I tried to teach you," Jude's mother had sighed over her when the last one had arrived. Then she turned to call Jude. "Come. You can both practice!"

Jude obeyed, slowly. He did not like the letters, nor the sessions they inspired: Jude and Rosa sitting at the table, the terrible pages spread before them and Jude's mother standing over his shoulder to supervise the lesson. Jude could read printed words, but these had a rainy look to them, shaky and windswept like trees in the monsoon. Rosa peered at the letters from one angle and then another, as though by shifting her eyes she might dislodge their secrets, and Jude struggled through the handwriting with his mother sharply supplying the tails of words he sounded out too slowly.

The last letter had come with snapshots. One was of the boy's face and one was his whole body, taken as he stood in front of a closed door. This is his house, Rosa said. See, this is where I will live. She rapped her knuckle against a wooden stool as though to imagine someone knocking on her own door. You will visit, yes? No, Jude told her. He spoke in the reproachful tone his mother used when she wanted something changed, a voice Jude himself seldom dared to cross, but Rosa only caught him round the neck and knocked on his head until he fell across her lap.

Now Rosa's fist sank into another lump of dough and for

a moment Jude was tempted to put aside thoughts of the old man and help her. But she took up her roller again and shooed him away. "Dirty, dirty! Go and clean your hands."

Jude forgot his campaign to be so good that Rosa would forget her pictures and stay. "My hands are clean," he said and left her.

He passed quickly into the bedroom again and found his slippers. Rosa was occupied in the kitchen, his mother was gone—probably to church with Marian and Simon. His father was safely asleep, having his evening nap. Jude could risk a quick peek into Neil's yard to see the old man. Perhaps even now he could contrive some way to add on to him.

The stairway ran along the outside of the house, on the side opposite Uncle Peter's compound. Over the wall, Jude could see movement behind the piles of material left there by a builder whose permits had been held up in court. Some families had come to live in the lot. Every few months they were cleared away by the builder's security men, but as soon as the site was unguarded they drifted back like flies. Jude's mother complained that the squatters were making the road unsafe, and Jude was not allowed out on his own without permission. So he carried his slippers in his hands until he had reached the last step, then crossed the garden and opened the gate so slowly that it didn't creak.

He expected to feel free and powerful once he made it to the road—the way Simon seemed whenever he mounted his bicycle, standing high on the pedals and with a few easy pushes surging halfway down St. Hilary Road. Instead Jude looked nervously to the squatters' lot and then past there to the large paved courtyard of St. Jerome's, where his mother might at any moment appear. He hurried through Uncle Peter's gate, forgetting to check the yard first. There, against the thick stucco wall that separated the Almeida brothers' plots, leaned the old man. Bent over its straw chest was Aunty Freddy.

She looked up, startled. For a moment Jude imagined her flying away like a bird, hunching her shoulders and flapping her printed cotton sleeves. But she only fixed her sharp eyes on him. "Well, what is it? Where's Mummy?"

Jude felt foolish. He made a faltering gesture toward the old man, then let his hand drop. "I came to see," he said.

"Speak properly, child! None of this mumbling."

"I came to see the old man," Jude said again. He wished his cousin would come and supply a reason for his sudden appearance. He wondered if Aunty Freddy would scold him herself or call his mother. Her face was tight with something he thought must be anger.

"Neil's gone off with his father. They're buying firecrackers for the party. You should have come earlier."

The unfairness of such a remark and his disappointment at yet another missed outing—he could picture, so clearly, Neil choosing a rocket-size firecracker—nearly drove Jude wild. "Earlier I wanted to come, but Mummy said I had to sleep!"

"Oh, yes, your mummy has her rules, doesn't she? Always a right way and a wrong way."

Jude did not know what to say to this. Surely all the world was divided into right and wrong, not just by his mother but by priests and God and even by his own queasiness now, knowing he was where he should not be.

Aunty Freddy looked at him. She had a narrow face with small, sharp features whose quick, flicking movements seemed restless.

"Keeping your mouth shut. Very good. Just like the Almeida men, aren't you?"

"No."

"Oh, you're not?" Aunty Freddy laughed, a rough sound.

Jude shook his head. His father took the train to Churchgate Station every morning and walked across the Oval Maidan to his office in the Rajabai clock tower, at the university where Jude would go someday, his mother told him, if he only kept reading. Jude was not sure he wanted to go with his father, swallowed up into a crowded train each morning and expected to read and read. He guessed that was what made his father so quiet, a life of words that need never be spoken aloud. (His mother's hand on Jude's shoulder— Don't move your lips, son.) Behind the clock face and its great churning hands, Jude imagined that papers flew like swallows, sweeping upward with creased beaks and pages fanned like tail feathers, circling in a windy rush, some diving sharply and some fluttering down with rustling coos until they settled, at last, on his father's desk. His father, Jude realized, was always reading: letters, reports, notes from meetings, books with no pictures. At night, as soon as he had eaten his supper, he tucked the *Times of India* under his arm and went to the Santa Clara Gymkhana to meet his friends, where Jude supposed they all sat in foursomes and read together. There were contests, Jude knew, and his mother scolded his father when he lost.

Jude was not so interested in reading, though he did not tell Aunty Freddy this in case she shared his mother's views. Nor did he want to be in business, which was Uncle Peter's job.

"When I grow up I'll be a captain. Or a pilot." He had not decided yet. But it was clear to him that he would not be like other Almeida men, none of whom had captained anything.

Aunty Freddy snorted. "Good for you. Get on your boat or your plane and go far from here." She turned toward the old man, still muttering. Her hair had recently been cut short and looked ruffled in the back. The cotton dress she wore was large and wildly patterned with black and red, reaching nearly to her ankles. Jude's mother had a similar robe for home, but when she went outdoors she wore skirts and blouses like most of the Catholic ladies of Santa Clara. Jude wondered if Aunty Freddy had been napping, if she too had missed the chance to help make the old man.

"Is it finished?"

"Come and look," she said, her voice less impatient than it had been.

Jude stepped closer. The old man was slumped on his side, the way Jude had often seen beggars sleep across the doorways of closed shops on Hill Road. His stuffed-pillowcase head was cinched at the neck like a balloon, and an old brown hat was jammed on top. He wore a waistcoat over a cotton shirt with bristles poking out from between the buttons and bunchy drawstring pajama pants. His hands were just thatches of straw, rough as twigs, and his feet lumpy sockfuls. One flopped out from the leg like a dying fish, and Jude wished he could nudge it back into place.

"Well. What do you think?"

"He's big." Jude looked ruefully at the bundled thighs he'd had no hand in making. "He's fat at the bottom."

A quick appreciative bark from Aunty Freddy encouraged him. "But you see what it's missing?"

Jude's eye fell again to the feet. "Shoes?"

"Shoes! That would smell to high heaven when he burns. No, he needs a face, doesn't he? I should give him one."

Jude felt his hopes rising. "I could help."

"Yes, yes, of course he needs a face . . ."

Jude spoke more loudly. "Aunty, can I help?"

She turned, surprised. "Help?" She looked at him as if he had just that moment arrived in her garden. "You're my godson, did you know that?"

He nodded. He did not tell her what his mother always said: if there had not been such a rush to baptize Jude, she would never have agreed to Aunty Freddy. Blame your father, she insisted. Jude's father, when questioned, shook his head and frowned. Tcha, how can I remember all these ins and outs? Jude's mother had encouraged him to think of one of her own cousins as a more suitable choice. This can be your godmother in spirit, she told him, and the spirit godmother sent five rupees on Jude's birthday, which Aunty Freddy had never done.

"And I'm godmother to your sister as well."

"Not Marian," Jude said. He knew Marian's godparents. Aunty Freddy meant the other, the twin his mother and father never mentioned. Jude knew the name because Simon had told him. Theresa.

"No, no, not Marian. I wasn't married when Marian was born. I hadn't come here to live. I used to live in a beautiful house in the south. I had a room all to myself and my father gave me paints. I painted flowers all along the walls, and birds in trees, and a monkey swinging from my window." Her voice sounded far away, as though the garden she'd painted was real and the one where she and Jude stood was a dream. Then abruptly she returned. "I was very good with my paints."

It was difficult to believe a child could be permitted to paint on walls. In his house, even small drawings on paper were considered a luxury; tablets were expensive and intended for writing. "What's on your walls here?" he asked. He had seen the insides of his cousins' rooms, of course, and it was a point of envy that Neil and Angela each had a cushion in the shape of an animal, but he could not recall having been in the bedroom Aunty Freddy and Uncle Peter shared.

"Here! When would I paint here? You think there's a minute to spare? And who the hell would look at it? Not your uncle!"

Jude stepped back, alarmed by this outburst and the mention of hell.

"I tell you, if my father had known the kind of life he was sending me into . . ." Aunty Freddy kept talking—the way other people shouted, though not as loudly as that. She no longer seemed to notice Jude but bent over the old man, her hands moving as quickly as her tongue. She propped him up so that he was sitting against the wall, shoulders drooping, legs splayed. Jude watched, transfixed, he did not know for how long. Aunty Freddy's voice had a low, screeching sound to it, like a bird gone hoarse. She was talking about her mother and father, who had died only a few months apart, when Marian's voice rang out, calling Jude's name, and both he and Aunty Freddy turned to see her coming in the gate. She was still wearing her church clothes, a blouse and a pleated skirt.

"Jude! Why did you run off like that? Mummy's worried!" She took Jude's hand. "Hello, Aunty. Sorry about all this."

"All what? He's perfectly safe with me, whatever your mother thinks."

"Oh, no, no, Aunty, it's not that! But he didn't say anything to Rosa or Dad—we had no idea where he'd gone."

"It was for a minute only, just to see, and then Aunty said we can make the face. Everything else is finished, that's all that's left!" Jude tugged his sister's hand, trying to communicate the urgency of this last chance. Now that she had come and Aunty Freddy had stopped her ramblings, the old man's allure had returned.

"No, we have to go," Marian said firmly. "We'll be back soon for the party."

"Is that what you're wearing tonight?" Aunty Freddy's eyebrows rose. "Well, stay far from your uncle. He has an eye for all the pretty girls."

Marian flushed and led Jude away. He turned back once to say good-bye, but Aunty Freddy was already leaning over the old man and Marian jerked his arm to hurry him.

"Not so fast!" Jude complained, but Marian did not say sorry or anything at all until they'd reached their own gate.

"Don't repeat what she said," she told Jude.

"What?" Upstairs, he knew, his mother waited, displeased and ready to punish him. The world seemed full of scoldings and rules and stupid directions, a web from which he could not tear free. He pulled his hand from Marian's. "What thing she said?"

"Never mind. Nothing."

"Anyway, you don't know everything yourself," he said, thinking of the monkey Aunty Freddy had painted on her walls and that at last, like Marian and Simon and all the grown-ups he knew, he had a secret. He hoped she would beg him to tell, but she only called him crosspatch and told him to run upstairs before Mummy shouted at them both.

Until the last minute, Jude didn't know if he would be permitted to go to the party. After a first hail of scoldings, his mother had said, "We'll see" and "Don't pester" for most of the evening. At last she called him, her face so stern that Jude knew to fear the worst.

When she had elicited a wavering apology, she shook her head. "See how badly you've disappointed us all. I asked Rosa to make kulkuls to surprise you and instead you ran off."

This was a blow. Kulkuls were Jude's favorite sweet, small curls of dough, pressed against a clean comb to give them ridges. Jude loved to help with the comb and to roll the golden nuggets in powdered sugar when they had been fried. His eyes felt hot and full.

"Just let the boy come, Essie," his father said impatiently. Jude looked up in surprise, but his father appeared to be struggling with his necktie.

"What does this have to do with you? He disobeyed me! You want him running all over the city on his own? You want him kidnapped?"

"Tcha!"

"You want to help, you can go and speak to someone about

these vagrants next door. They're turning this road into a wilderness!"

She waited until his father had gone back to the balcony, where he looked out over the railing at the activity on the street. Even from the bedroom Jude could hear enough voices to form a parade, the parade of lucky people who could go to a party. His mother considered him with an expression so hard and searching that he could not guess what she would decide.

"Very well. Go and wash your face."

In the bathroom he took special pains to scrub so well that no one, not even his mother, could find fault. Rosa found him there and caught him from behind. "Don't feel sad, baba." She had saved some dough for tomorrow, she told him, smiling at his face in the mirror. He could help her with the comb. He could eat his kulkuls piping hot.

St. Hilary Road was alive with lights and laughing people. Street banners wished everyone Best Compliments of the Season and a Happy and Prosperous New Year. Guests from town parked in a long, crooked line of cars, and those with drivers pulled up to gates to let off their passengers. Children in party clothes laughed and argued and hopped one-footed in shoes they mustn't scuff. Some pretended to climb garden walls, and others held with two-handed reverence the gifts or dishes of food entrusted to their care.

Jude held his mother's hand. He wore a sweater at her insistence, though the sleeves scratched his arms, and shorts with socks and shoes. His hair had been combed back damply from his forehead. Simon had gone ahead with their father, but Marian had lingered to walk with Jude and her mother.

In only a few hours Uncle Peter's yard had been transformed. The garden was hectic with lights. Streamers ran from the compound wall to the guava tree, forming an airy pinwheel; more were looped along the gate and veranda. Someone had raised a flag of India, and the illuminated stars had been switched on, twisting slowly and scattering light like confetti to the packed earth near the veranda steps. Two toddlers were stamping the chinks of light and screamed with laughter whenever the light darted out from under their footsteps. Jude saw people he recognized: Aunty Grace was carrying her new baby; Neil and their cousins, Mark and Ian, were jumping off the second veranda step; and Neil's sister, Angela, was twirling with three others, tumbling to the ground in fits of laughter. Jude's cousin Colleen was encased in Uncle Louis's arms, waving a sparkler in front of her and surrounded by a pack of envious children waiting their turn. Simon and some of his friends stood in a tight circle, flicking a football to one another with their feet and heads. "Careful, boys. Not near the food! Not near the little ones!"

Jude did not see Uncle Peter anywhere, but tucked into a corner of the garden was the old man's pyre of wood and brush. The man itself had been mounted on a post, its back turned to the party. Paper sandals were strapped to its feet.

"You see, godson! I gave him shoes for you!" Aunty Freddy swung toward them the moment they arrived. She wore bright red lipstick and a yellow chiffon salwar kameez with one side of her dupatta trailing nearly to the grass as she bent to seize Jude. She kissed both cheeks and pinched his chin tightly. "So sweet, this fellow! I could eat him up!"

Jude submitted briefly to this affection, then returned his attention to the garden, determined to stake his claim early in the matter of firecrackers. "Where's Uncle Peter?"

Aunty Freddy tossed an impatient hand. "Blowing up his balloons somewhere. Marian, darling, you're looking lovely! Such a beauty!"

Marian had worn a plain cotton salwar kameez, the scarf cutting stiffly across her shoulder. "Thank you."

"Oh, God, none of this mumbling, I can't abide! And no false modesty! What is the point of it? You are young and pretty, enjoy it while you can! God knows it doesn't last—am I right, Essie? Come, later on I'll put some lipstick on you, and something for your eyelashes. And such a complexion, we must play it up. We'll have a fabulous time. Come, you want to come now?"

Jude's mother interrupted. "We've brought sweets, Freddy. Where can we put them?"

"Ooo! Kulkuls, my favorite!" She popped one in her mouth. "Now take them away or no one else at the party will have them!" She waved her hand as she moved away. "Keep them far from me! Go on!" She seemed to have forgotten Marian's lipstick. They watched as she went skittering through the party.

Jude's mother handed the platter to Marian and pointed to a table near the veranda. "Good girl," she said suddenly. Then she turned to Jude and took his chin in her own fingers, wiping off Aunty Freddy's lipstick with her wet thumb.

"Happy now? You're at your party at last, hmm?"

"But where's Uncle Peter?" Jude asked her. "He needs me for the firecrackers."

"Uncle Peter can manage without you for a few minutes." She swatted him on the bottom. "Go. Run and find your cousins and play."

By eleven thirty the party had reached its peak. Jude saw his father sitting heavily on the steps of the veranda, a glass near his legs. His mother was in a circle of other women, all sitting in folding chairs, which seemed precarious on the uneven ground. Jude's cousin Colleen and three or four other children had collapsed at the base of the guava tree in their party clothes. Aunty Grace spread a blanket over them and smiled at Jude. "Such a big boy, wide awake in the middle of the night!"

Jude wandered inside the house, where Uncle Peter was playing the piano to a crowd of people. Even with all the windows flung open, the room was hot and close. Uncle Peter had rolled up his sleeves, but the back of his shirt was damp. A girl Jude didn't know shared the narrow wooden bench, singing with her mouth open wide.

Jude could see Simon and Marian at the far end of the room, but he went to stand beside Uncle Peter. For a moment he hesitated. The room seemed to throb with noise and people and Uncle Peter was at the center of it all, banging out chords. His hands were huge on the keys and even his knees seemed to be jumping. Jude felt suddenly shy. But then his uncle turned his head and grinned as if he'd been waiting for Jude all along.

"Where've you been hiding?" he called. "Come on and sing!"

"Uncle Peter, is it time?"

"What?"

Jude leaned closer. His uncle's face was slick; he smelled of cologne and sweat and smoke.

"Is it time for the old man?"

The girl on the piano bench laughed. "Better go, Pete! Your public is waiting!"

Uncle Peter shook his head, smiling, though Jude did not see why. He reached for his drink with one hand, but the other lingered on the piano keys. "What's the time?" he asked.

Aunty Freddy's voice rang out from the doorway, where Jude hadn't seen her enter. She stood holding Angela, who was four but almost as tall as Jude. "You've got twenty minutes still. Give us another!"

The girl slid up from the bench. "Come and sit, Freddy. You sing the next one."

"No, no, I'm very happy here. And you two—such lovely harmonies!" She kissed the top of Angela's head. "Come, sleepyhead, come, baby. Wake up." She looked over the child to Uncle Peter, her eyes bright and fierce. "Daddy's singing for you."

Uncle Peter suddenly put an arm around Jude. "You, sir! Come and sit with me." He slid over and pulled Jude onto the bench, where Jude could feel the heat from his uncle's body. "Just a quick one," he said, and began to play. At first everyone joined in—the girl with the wide-open mouth, Simon and Marian—even Jude knew the words. But soon Jude could hear Aunty Freddy's voice above all the others, clear and strong, and in the end it was only she and Uncle Peter singing together, for that song and then one more. She had tears in her eyes, Jude saw, though the songs were not sad ones. Uncle Peter started another, and just as Jude was about to tug his arm to remind him, Aunty Freddy raised her voice over the cheers and clapping to call everyone outside: they did not want to miss the old man.

A council of uncles and cousins gathered near the bonfire pile. Neil was hopping from one foot to the other. Jude went to stand near Simon.

"Look what I have for his pants!" Uncle Peter held up a firecracker. "Come, let's get this fellow in the fire!"

He and Uncle Louis lifted the old man, still on his pole, and slowly turned him. For the first time Jude and the others saw the banner draped across his chest that read 1962, and the face Aunty Freddy had painted. Simon's head jerked up and Ian took his father's hand. Only Jude spoke.

"It's Uncle Peter!"

Simon knocked his shoulder. "Be quiet, you!"

"But it is!" Jude wished he dared to kick his brother, but a strange silence had dropped over the whole assemblage.

Uncle Peter was still holding the pole, so that the old man stood upright.

Uncle Peter laughed again, but this time it was a feeble sound, trailing away like smoke. When he stopped, the pillowcase continued to smile its thin brown smile. Aunty Freddy's sketch was outlined in only one color and was slightly lopsided on the knobby pillowcase head, but it was unmistakable. Uncle Peter's wide painted jaw sloped to his painted chin. Uncle Peter's painted forehead arched back into his crisp painted hairline. Uncle Peter's painted eyes, pinched close to his painted nose, stared back at the Almeidas. Rising above the sound of the party came Aunty Freddy's cawing laughter.

Uncle Louis cleared his throat. "Peter—"

"No, no, it's fine. Fine. Maybe she had a bit too much of the holiday spirit! Let's just forget it. The children want their fire. Come, Neil, help me get him up here."

But Neil had gone very quiet. He stared up at his father in confusion.

"Come on!" Uncle Peter gave the old man a little shake. A few bits of straw drifted to the ground. When Neil didn't move, Uncle Peter seemed to droop as though he too had a post and had just been lifted off it.

"Not to worry!" Uncle Louis said. He was a tall man, with all his hair already gray but thick and springing and a gentle wiry smile that seemed to match his spectacles. "I know just the thing!" He slapped all his pockets until he'd found a pen. "Hold it steady, Peter. There. See, Neil? See what I'm doing?" He drew a fierce black mustache with curling ends and then—Jude came closer to look—he drew a beard right on top of old-man-Peter's chin.

"There. You see, nothing to be sad about." Uncle Louis put his hand on Neil's shoulder and called him son even though Neil was his nephew. Uncle Peter was standing just as quietly as Neil, as if each was waiting for the other to move first.

"We'll be waiting here 'til next year!" called Aunty Freddy from the center of the crowd. "Does the old man have a wristwatch?" A cloud of good-natured jeering rose up from the people as Freddy careened toward the old man. "What's this, you've covered up my masterpiece?"

"Freddy . . ." Uncle Louis raised his hand as if to call a halt, but Uncle Peter interrupted him.

"That's enough from you. We are doing this."

"Well, get on with it then. Everyone's waiting!" She looked around at all of them, lastly Uncle Peter. "What's the matter with you? It's just a little paint. Right? Right, darling?" She had caught Neil from behind and bent playfully to kiss him, three, four times. Her lipstick had faded to a drier color, cracked in places like a riverbed in the dry season, but still she left a small smudged blot on his cheek. "I might be taking up painting again in the new year. It's time to have some fun! You have your fun, don't you, Peter? But the children may like it. We can paint together, right, my darling baby, all the lovely things we see."

A shout rose up around the yard. Uncle Peter had set the old man alight, and the flame crept along the hem of the trousers until it found its first snatch of straw. Soon the whole leg was snapping. Neil stood stock-still near the edge of the fire, right where Jude wanted to be, though Marian had caught hold of his hand and pulled him back from the spitting embers. Then Uncle Peter told Neil to stand back, looping an arm around him so that he was held just out of reach of the fire. Behind a veil of smoke and flame, Jude could see the thin brown eyes that Aunty Freddy had drawn. In a matter of seconds the pale cotton cheeks were singed, the chest and arms roaring. The old man's hat tumbled off his head, showering sparks and scattering the women.

It was over soon. The old man crumpled to a common bonfire, the adults sang "Auld Lang Syne." Neil broke from his father's embrace and went running after another cousin. Simon was setting off firecrackers. Marian was talking to a group of girls from her school, and Jude's mother was helping other women carry empty dishes into the house. Jude turned and turned but could not see his father. The ground was covered with silver stars and tiny gold banners spelling Happy New Year. Jude wanted to catch up with Neil, but he didn't feel like running. He sat at the base of the tree.

"Another song!" Aunty Freddy called. "Come, everyone join in!" She had her arm tight around her daughter's shoulders. The singing resumed and Jude lay down. Stars thick as confetti, the sound of voices. He slept.

When he woke, the singing had ended. The other children at the base of the tree were borne away to bed, heads on their mothers' shoulders, shoes dangling against their fathers' belts.

"Your daddy was ill," Uncle Peter told Jude. "Mummy's gone home with him and Marian said she would take you, but I said not to wake you, we would keep you for the night. You can sleep with Neil."

"I set off a firecracker," Neil said when they were in bed. "You missed it. It went up like that." He snapped his fingers, a reminder that Jude had not learned how.

In bed, it seemed to Jude that the party had not ended but twisted into some new form. People in and out of the house, clatters from the kitchen, laughter exploding like firecrackers. Aunty Freddy opened the door and a tilted square of light came swinging over Jude's bed. He kept his eyes squeezed shut while she leaned over Neil. "Good night, my son, good night, my darling boy." When she had gone, Jude realized that no one had closed the wooden shutters. Mosquitoes would come in. The breeze was chilly, and no one had said anything about Jude's cough. Jude wanted his own brother. He wanted to go home.

He put his foot against Neil's leg, and Neil kicked it away.

"Don't pull the blanket," Neil told him fiercely.

It was well past breakfast when Jude woke alone in the bed. Angela was sitting dully in a chair with a book in her lap; Neil was nowhere to be found. A woman with fuzz on her lip and pewter-colored hair came in and told Angela to wash and dress herself properly. "You must be a big girl now, a brave girl." To Jude she said, "Your sister is coming to get you."

Jude went outside without washing his face or teeth and found Neil in the garden. The air smelled of smoke. Tiny foil letters glittered in the dust, and someone had stacked folding chairs in a corner. Neil wore his school uniform, although it was a holiday, and he was crouched in the grass, picking up the confetti piece by piece. Neil kept his back to Jude, but Jude could see that he was crying with sudden shuddering breaths. He scraped his nails through the grass and dirt until another woman—a different woman, the house was full of women—came to call them inside.

This is what Jude remembers best of that tumble of days before Neil and Angela came to stay several weeks with his family: the wide-open eyes of the old man as he burned and Neil bent over in the yard, picking up bits of confetti. In the confusion of the first afternoon, when nobody knew where Aunty Freddy had gone or that she was gone for good, it was Jude's mother who thought to hunt for the coat Aunty Freddy had borrowed. The coat was missing, along with a suitcase and all of Aunty Freddy's gold, an odd assortment of clothes and toiletries, and her paintbrushes. Uncle Peter had called in the police, and the beggars who lived in the abandoned lot were questioned to rule out a kidnapping. One of these, a woman who spent a sleepless night suffering from stomach cramps, reported that she had seen a woman marching down the road. When she passed beneath a sprinkling of

Christmas lights, the woman came into clear view. She wore a coat and was carrying a suitcase. No one was with her. The following morning, Uncle Peter came over with a telegram, which Jude's father read without speaking. Jude wondered what it said, but his mother did not give it to him for practice.

A few minutes later Jude saw both of them leaning over the balcony, looking out at the road and not at each other. He sidled near and leaned against his father's leg. His father was the older brother, he knew, but Uncle Peter was taller. Jude tried to imagine catching up to Simon.

"They can stay here for a time . . ." his father said. He had put his hand in Jude's hair and was rubbing. "In a little while, she'll settle down."

Uncle Peter said something Jude did not hear and his father frowned. "What trouble? Tcha!"

Jude ducked out from beneath his father's hand. He wanted to find Simon, who would be going back to school in only a few days, but Simon had gone off on his bicycle.

That was the day that Jude's mother had talked in a high, angry voice about her coat, her old coat, her coat that was not so old after all but really her second-best, the coat she intended to give to Rosa when Rosa married. Angela and Neil had not yet come to stay with them, but they were in the garden with Marian, who told them their mother had gone on holiday, to see their uncle. Everyone likes a holiday, she said. When they had grown up, they also might want to visit the house where they'd lived when they were small. Jude thought of the monkey Aunty Freddy had painted, swinging down from the window to greet her.

Jude ought to have stayed in the garden, but his cough was bothering him. He went to the kitchen to find Rosa instead. She offered to let him make kulkuls later, but for the moment he just sat in her lap and leaned back against her, as though his weight alone might keep her there.

Half the Story

Before they'd even checked their bags everything was an adventure to Vee, a lark or a joke, a proof of her new daring self. She clutched Marian's arm while they waited in line, her nails manicured a bright, hard pink. "Can you believe it? Can you believe I'm really doing this?" Marian could not, quite. All afternoon she had been listening to Vee tell everyone they met that this was her first time leaving the country. "I could never do it without you, honey, not in a million years." She had bought a three-piece set of leather luggage with an extra bag folded inside for all she planned to buy. "My God, the fabrics! The colors! I'll go crazy, I know I will. We'll have a ball."

Marian smiled. They were the same age, but Vee's gushing made Marian feel older—indulgent and, at times, cautioning. Vee was the one to suggest late lunches downtown, shopping sprees, grandiose plans for field trips and fund-raisers. It fell to Marian to remind Vee that the children would soon be home or that she couldn't afford what Vee could.

"I'm buying a carpet." Vee's face tightened briefly. "Maybe three or four carpets. I can ship, can't I?"

But Marian had been the one to propose this unlikely

journey—Marian, who had gone to pick up Vee for a committee meeting and found her sobbing at the kitchen table three weeks after her husband had left her. "What will I do?" Vee asked again and again, until it sounded as if she were begging for something.

Marian had not known what to say. After a moment she slid into the seat next to Vee and took her hand. All around them the kitchen gleamed, newly remodeled and sparkling white. It had been a point of envy for Marian, who had pored over tile samples and cabinet faces with her friend and tried not to think of the almond-colored refrigerator she herself still had to contend with, the oily carpet she longed to rip up. But now this: Vee in her silk blouse and a slip, bare-legged. A bowl of oranges on the table. Cody in his diaper, unnaturally silent. He stood in the doorway with his father's Reds hat in his hand and stared dolefully at Marian.

"Oh, that hat!" Vee cried. "For God's sake, give me that fucking hat."

It was Marian who picked Cody up when he began to bawl. "It's cold in here, Vee. Just let me put something on him." She dressed the baby and put him in his playpen. He watched her, still holding the hat, as she called the school. "Mrs. Wallace"—she glanced at Vee as she used the name—"Mrs. Wallace and I have to cancel the meeting. Can you leave a message that we'll reschedule? No, no, I'll be there at three to pick up the kids." She heated a kettle of water and gave Vee a mug of hot tea. "Drink this. You'll feel better." Vee in her slip, her long, pale legs. "Are you cold?"

By now Vee had stopped crying, but the skin near her eyes was pink and strangely naked without makeup. "I'm fine. I'm fine now."

"What happened?"

"I'm sorry. I'm fine." She held the mug with two hands, the way Cody would. "We can still make it if we hurry. I just need—"

"Vee." Marian shook her head. "Maybe you need to get away. You could take the boys to Florida for a few days."

"Not Florida. Not my parents." Her eyes filled with tears.

"Somewhere else, then. Could your parents take the boys?"

"You've traveled before. I never have. I don't want to go alone." Vee stared at Cody, naked-eyed. "He really loves that filthy hat, doesn't he?"

Marian peeled an orange, urged Vee to eat. "Where would you like to go?" she asked, and then suddenly, without thinking, "Why don't you come home with me?"

In the airport Vee bore no resemblance to the half-dressed woman eating sections of orange with her baby. "I bought a water filter," she said happily. "And chocolates for the flight. And a silk robe for your mother. What do you think?"

Marian's own suitcases were battered and inelegant, strapped shut with cords. Her younger daughter, Tara, sat on them when it came time to latch them. Inside, folded among her blouses and tucked into her shoes, were packets of soup, cake mix, oatmeal, vitamins, a family-size jar of Metamucil, a touch-tone telephone, a shower curtain with plastic rings, a radio. "It's 1983," her husband, Daniel, said. "You can buy radios in Bombay." He was what Marian called an American, although she too had a U.S. passport now. His family, which he called Irish, had not lived in Ireland for three generations, and he had never been there. He did not understand the boxes of pasta she brought home to her mother every other year, the Black & Decker iron, the dresses from Macy's.

"They're cotton." Daniel laughed. "They're probably made in India."

"But they can't buy this quality there, I'm telling you."

Flattened at the bottom of the case were packets of photographs and manila envelopes filled with report cards, Tara's art projects, Nicole's book reports. Both children had written letters at Marian's insistence.

" 'Dear Grandma and Grandpa . . .' What should I say?" Tara had demanded. " 'School is fine. I am halfback on the soccer team.' Do they know what halfbacks are?"

Nicole sealed her letter without giving Marian a chance to look it over and added long strips of Scotch tape over the seam.

"What did you say?" Marian tried to ask lightly.

Nicole shrugged. "Why do you need to know?" She chewed her fingernail, and Marian fought the urge to brush her daughter's hand from her mouth. But she could see Daniel staring at her pointedly. Their last night in a month, his raised brows told her. Don't spoil it.

Marian's face tightened as she met his gaze. Why is it always my fault? she wanted to ask him. Instead she looked at her elder daughter, the narrow face, the hair hanging past her shoulders in long, thin sheets. Marian preferred her daughter to clip it back—"let us *see* you"—but Nicole wore it straight down over her ears, flat against her cheeks, like curtains drawing shut on a stage. She was twelve and suddenly tall, at sea on her own legs. She tripped up stairs and disliked wearing skirts.

Nicole folded and refolded one corner of the sealed envelope, waiting, it seemed, for her mother to say the wrong thing.

"I don't need to know," Marian told her, annoyed. "Here, put it in."

"I'm going to India," Vee told the woman who took her boarding pass. She grabbed Marian's arm and hung on, giggling. "What do you think of that? Just a couple of girlfriends, ditching their families, off to India!"

Marian slipped out of Vee's grasp. She felt strained, her

smile wavering as it did when she waited for the snap of a shutter to release her from some uncomfortable pose. She never liked to contradict, but the trip Vee described was not the one on which Marian was embarking. On St. Hilary Road, in her parents' house, her mother's alarm clock would be set to go off in the middle of the night—a ritual her mother insisted on every time Marian came home. "I just say a quick prayer and go right back to sleep," she promised. "What are your connection times?" Marian knew the alarm would ring for her departures from New York and Frankfurt too, and that for the last nine hours her mother would not sleep at all. She would pick at her food, too excited to eat, and fuss with a whisk broom, and nag her father into wearing his good pajamas. "Go to sleep, Frank. Otherwise you'll be dozing off when they come—I know how you are." She would keep the servant up late into the night. "Just make sure we've got the good cover on her bed, not the old one with the stain, the pretty one." She would set the alarm for eleven o'clock but shoo Marian's brother, Jude, out beforehand—"What if they're early, these headwinds, tailwinds, what have you?" The shelves freshly dusted, the floors swabbed, the lights in every room blazing. The alarm would ring into her waiting hand—there, landed!—and then she would wait for her daughter to come home.

Her father slept on a narrow bed he pulled to the front balcony: to escape all her mother's ring-ring nonsense in the middle of the night, he explained brusquely to Marian every time she arrived. But she knew he slept where the sound of the car after midnight would rouse him, to be sure he was up by the time the gate was open.

"Here we go!" Vee squeezed Marian's hand as they moved into the jointed tunnel that led to the aircraft. "Honest to God, Marian, I feel like I've been waiting for this my whole life. You know what I mean. Just picking up and going someplace."

But for Marian, India was not an impulse of escape or delight; it was the clock set in the middle of the night, the pull from sleep, the prayer. She felt a tremor of loneliness, swift and unsettling—she was not fully seen, she was not understood. It happened sometimes with Vee, even with Daniel and the children. Some essential part of her was out of reach, turned away like the far side of the moon no matter how they moved around each other. She wondered if Vee realized that. She suspected not and all at once was flooded with love and pity for this friend who did not yet know they were traveling alone.

"Who is this girl you're bringing?" Jude asked when they spoke on the phone. He had not been to visit Marian since they'd left Massachusetts and moved to Cincinnati six years ago; he had never met Vee.

"Vee, she's called. Virginia. Her older son is in Tara's class. You know, I've mentioned her before." She stopped, confused. Over the years she had learned to navigate between two worlds, but she still found it difficult to reveal one to another. "We're both class mothers. We're in the Junior League together." But what did Jude know of Junior Leagues? Marian thought of the lunches and museums, the car pools and barbecues, the country club where Vee and Gordon were members and invited them to swim. Vee's son, Mickey, led the girls to the snack bar all day long for cheeseburgers, ice creams, large Cokes that no one finished. Nicole and Tara ate their french fries, wide-eyed. Vee waved away the money Marian tried to give her. Later, when Vee had gone for a dip, Marian pressed some bills into Mickey's hand and he looked up at her, amused and puzzled. "We just give them our name," he told her. "We don't use money."

Finally she thought of Vee's face, the large, loose mouth, the generous features. Her eyes were round and blue, the lines at their corners barely visible beneath her makeup. Her blond hair done up in a twist or tied back with a scarf. Gold hoop earrings, large enough for a baby's bangle. "She's fair. Scandinavian-looking, very pretty. She towers over me."

"But what's she like?"

"Oh, friendly, very sweet. And now her husband's treating her so badly—I don't know, it was a spur-of-the-moment thing, inviting her. I didn't really think—"

"What? You didn't think she'd come?"

"Well, no. But listen, she's a lot of fun. Very sweet, really."

"You sound nervous."

"No, no, nothing like that. It's only that she can seem a little loud before you get to know her. A little brash. You know, American. Of course Nicole adores her." Marian meant it as an assurance, but aloud, the words seemed to sour. "Anyway, you'll meet her for yourself."

"What will she think of it here?" Jude wondered. Marian could not begin to guess. "Tell me about your home," Vee had demanded, again and again—another translation Marian did not know how to attempt.

Once the mediators had given up on conventional methods, Vee and Gordon were told to meet at ten on a Tuesday morning in the house they had shared. Mickey was in school, Cody at a neighbor's. Each party was encouraged to invite a friend or family member for support. Vee chose Marian; Gordon brought his brother, Stan. A mediator would oversee the proceedings; at two the lawyers would arrive to finalize the arrangements. This was two weeks before Christmas. The larger matters had been settled; convertible to Gordon, house to Vee. Every other weekend to Gordon, weekdays to Vee. Christmas to Gordon, Easter to Vee.

Marian pulled into the driveway just as Gordon and Stan arrived, so she waited in her car, engine running, until they had gone inside. She thought of Nicole and Tara at the country club food counter, trading Gordon's name for onion rings, and did not know what to say to him.

They started in the living room. Gordon won the toss.

"So he can take whatever he wants?" Vee asked, so loudly that Marian flinched.

"He has the first pick, and then it's your turn," the mediator explained again with exaggerated calm.

"Relax, honey. I'm taking my time," Gordon told Vee. He spun slowly, a single finger extended, and finally pointed to the grandfather clock that had belonged to Vee's grandmother. "That."

Vee took the portrait of the boys she had commissioned for Gordon's birthday, the year Mickey was seven and Cody was one.

Gordon chose the coffee table. "I can't stand those fucking couches."

Vee tried to take both the couch and the love seat—"They're a set!"—but the mediator gave her one and made her wait until her next turn for the other.

They trailed through the rooms of the house. Gordon got the dining table and five chairs; Vee took the remaining three.

"What will you do with three dining room chairs?" Marian whispered.

"What will he do with five?"

Floor lamps, end tables, chests of drawers. Vee picked the king-size bed.

"Can I have the mattress?" Gordon wanted to know, but the mediator decided the bed and mattress were a single unit.

"Take the stereo," Stan advised.

Marian stood slightly behind Vee, not saying a word, not wanting to look up. She felt she was involved in a strangely intimate ceremony and wondered why she had agreed to this.

"You're out of your mind," Daniel had told her flatly the week before, when Vee first approached her.

"But she's asked me," Marian said. "How can I say no?" She thought of mornings spent on her kitchen stool, television muted, watching Donohue running soundless up and down the aisles while she listened to Vee cry into the telephone. Standing up for her seemed a matter of loyalty, nothing more.

"You don't know what he's put her through. He's fighting over every little thing."

"Divorces can be ugly. That doesn't mean you should get involved."

It astonished Marian that he couldn't understand. "I'm not getting involved, I'm her friend. I'm going as her friend."

They had not quite argued over it. They were cleaning up after a dinner party, the children asleep, the dishwasher running. Daniel sorted the silver. Marian put serving dishes in the cupboards, one inside the other. The room smelled of hot, soapy water and frying oil laced with masala and onions, and they opened a window to the sharp, dark air. "You know it wasn't easy for me to come here. It wasn't easy to—" She broke off, shook her head. "Vee was my first friend."

Daniel stopped, turned to face Marian. He had put on weight since he quit smoking, had cut the sideburns that once made her laugh. His hair, so much lighter than hers, was beginning to gray. She tried to remember what it was like to look at him before she'd begun to imagine a life together, but all the choices that had led her here—choices that felt like accidents, choices that had once seemed impossible—now felt inevitable. He looked tired, she realized, and with a pang she thought of all that had not been easy for him either—the trips to India when there was no money to send her; the nights he had come home to see her crying over letters; the first year of their marriage, when her mother refused to acknowledge him. For a moment she tried to imagine her father helping her mother in the kitchen, and it came to her that Daniel did all he could with what was within his reach, that he tried every day to make what was hard easier. She wished she had found a gentler way to explain herself.

He shrugged. "Just don't expect this to be easy either. That's all I'm saying."

"I don't," she told him.

But in her kitchen, her belongings so inextricably bound with Daniel's, Marian had not known how to prepare herself for Gordon's clock and Vee's couches, for the commandeering of dining-room chairs or the moment the whole party paused outside a door with "C-O-D-Y" spelled in colored wooden letters. A plastic fireman's helmet hung off the doorknob. The mediator glanced up. "This is the younger one, right?"

"Just leave it," Gordon said.

Vee said nothing.

"You both agree?"

Yes. Yes.

They stood in the hallway while the mediator consulted his list. There was still the study to go, the family room, the kitchen. Marian felt nauseous.

"What about Gordon Junior? Anything in his room?"

"We call him Mickey."

Marian could hear that Vee was close to tears, and she stepped forward to touch her arm.

Gordon pushed his hands in his pockets, head down.

"Keep it together, buddy," Stan told him. He slapped Gordon's back twice before clapping his hands, a sharp call for action. "Let's keep this show on the road. Gordy. What do you say? VCR?"

Gordon toed the carpet beneath his feet—one that Marian had brought back for them from India—and suddenly raised his head. "Is it my turn?" He looked directly at Marian, eyes blazing, and she remembered the first night they'd met, at one of Vee's parties. He wore a blazer with brass buttons, shoes without socks. His face was a dry baked red that reminded

Marian of clay roads at home, but his hair was thick and sandy, falling over his forehead when he took a sip of vodka.

"So you're from somewhere—hang on, Vee told me—I'll get it in a minute—"

"Bombay," Marian supplied quickly. She had no interest in becoming a party game. She wore dresses as a child in India, a uniform skirt to school every day, but now, in the States, she preferred Indian clothes for all but the most casual occasions. That night she had worn a long silk kameez with churidar pants.

"Got something on your face there!" He waved a finger near the bindi on her forehead and laughed, a short bark of a laugh to go with the dog-shake of his hair. "So, India. Huh. How'd you end up here?"

"I came first as a student and then I met Daniel." She smiled to see Daniel, locked in conversation at the other end of the room.

"Sure, sure." He nodded vigorously, not looking at her, as though in tune to some song she couldn't hear. "Well, that was a stroke of luck, right?"

"To meet?"

"To end up here. I hear India's rough. All that poverty—and disease, am I right?"

Marian began to think about a second glass of wine.

A woman with large, pale eyes had cut in. "Oh, but India is known for its spirituality. I mean, of course there's the poverty—I don't know how you handle that, I never could. But there's such intense spirituality too. Have you ever been on a pilgrimage?"

Her family in India was Catholic, Marian explained. But her mother had once gone to Rome and had an audience with the Pope.

The woman seemed disappointed, but Gordon was clearly encouraged by this news. "The Pope? Well, then, you won't mind if I ask you something—what's up with the cows? They can walk on the roads, right in front of cars, wherever they want. I've seen it on TV." He eyed her with sudden keenness. "That happen where you live?"

There were cows in Santa Clara, Marian confirmed. But there was more to India than beggars and cows.

"No kidding!" Another bark of a laugh. "I mean, from a strategic standpoint, these people are pretty fucking important. You know what I'm saying. They have the bomb. It's scary—there's no telling what will set them off."

We're a volatile bunch, thought Marian, trying to catch Daniel's eye across the room. The pale-eyed woman wondered if Marian believed in reincarnation.

"I do!" Gordon winked at Marian. "Why not take a few turns, right? Maybe next time it'll be you and me."

In the house, with the mediator, Gordon was in no winking mood. He stared at Marian, his face hard and set, the rug she had given them beneath his feet. She wanted to shrink behind Vee, and her own cowardice shamed her. Marian thought of her mornings on the kitchen stool, light pouring through the windows and Vee's voice on the phone; she thought of her secret pride in being chosen to witness this last humiliating spectacle. It occurred to her that she deserved the weight of his stare.

Gordon dragged his shoe across the carpet and addressed the mediator directly, not bothering to glance in Marian's direction again. "I'll take this."

For the first few years in Cincinnati, it was Marian who needed Vee. They met before Marian learned to drive. She was struggling back from Kroger's, two shopping bags pushed into the bottom of Tara's stroller while Nicole, six years old, dragged on her hand. Nearly a mile in each direction and long past naptime, but Marian had nobody to look after the children. Daniel's department had sent him to a conference, and after four months, only a few neighbors had rung their bell. The houses stood shoulder to shoulder and guarded their occupants, windows winter-tight, doors sternly shut.

Nicole began to whine. "Just a little longer, darling." The sidewalks were rough. The stroller bar hummed beneath her hands, the wheels jerked. Tara had fallen asleep, with her head bumping against a bag of apples, a thin patch of plastic sticking to her cheek.

A horn blast startled Marian, and she looked up to see that a car had stopped. "What in the world!" a woman had laughed. Her hair bright, her smile wide and open. "What in the world!" As though she'd never seen such a thing as Marian in her plain white cotton kameez, pushing a stroller. But she spoke without the wariness that Marian had come to expect after her first weeks in Ohio, without the suspicious glances at the bindi on her forehead, her children's skin.

And without any further conversation, "Come on, I'll take you. Get in."

"I'm just down the road. Really, I can manage."

"Don't be silly! I'll take you." She laughed again, and for a moment Marian was transported back to St. Hilary Road, to her mother conducting conversations from the middle of the road. Marian stared at the laughing woman in the wide American street and felt a surge of longing for neighbors whose voices calling from one garden to the next strung their lives together.

"Are you sure?"

"Of course I'm sure!"

This is what Marian would want her brother to understand: the power of Vee's frank, laughing gaze, the command of such a welcome. But Jude had never left Santa Clara to live elsewhere. Marian thought of the week her father suffered his first stroke. It was minor, Jude assured her; there was no reason to come. But Nicole was only two weeks old, so Marian was frequently up tending to her at just those hours, she imagined, when her father might be sitting up in his hospital bed to eat the lunch her mother prepared; or waiting for the doctor's daily visit; or asking someone—whom?—for a glass of water. Was Jude at work? Was anyone there to give it to him? She rocked the baby in a dark room. Eventually Daniel appeared at the door, drowsy and disheveled, to take his turn, and then, before exhaustion overtook her, Marian lay in bed and tried to recall the Bible verses she had memorized as a girl—as though they were a mantra, something to transport her back to the days when her father was strong. The verses came back to her in fragments; she fumbled for missing words, broken rhythms. Sometimes they came in a rush, words tumbling into one another, too slipshod to resemble the tightly woven faith she had known as a child. *Pray, pray for Dad,* she told herself. But God seemed anchored to that other place, to the bright daylit hours where her father ate and slept—so far away that even the silence when Daniel returned to bed seemed pitiless.

Jude knew nothing of such hours; his days and nights were fixed in place. How could he understand the shock of Vee's horn blast, the gift of her bright face framed in the car window? Kroger's bags tucked beneath Marian's sleeping baby, her daughter exhausted beside her, a buckling sidewalk, and suddenly a cheerful voice calling.

"Come on, get in!"

Shy, proud, grateful, homesick nearly to death, Marian had obeyed.

"Just move whatever's in your way," the woman said easily, and turned her attention to Nicole. "And aren't you the most beautiful girl in the world!"

Nicole smiled, already in love.

Marian tugged the apples out from under Tara's arm

and looked up swiftly. "Say thank you, Mrs.—" She paused, questioning.

"Vee, honey. Just call me Vee."

The first miserable winter seemed to slide away once Marian met Vee. For the first year, before the money came, Gordon and Vee lived only two blocks away. Vee seldom bothered with telephones or doorbells. "Are you there? Marian, are you there? Let's go to the movies, let's learn Chinese cooking, let's start a book club." In the middle of December she brought roast duck, French bread, red wine. "Let's eat with our fingers." The children sat cross-legged on the floor, greasy-faced, drinking grape juice. Spring came, a gentle, grassy spring, so unlike the streaks of mud and ice Marian had known in Massachusetts. A tree on their front lawn turned out to be dogwood and announced itself in creamy white blossoms. Houses relaxed their tight grip, and they met the Powells, the Resnicks, the Owenses, the Grants. Daniel built a deck. Tara and Mickey drummed on nails with their fat plastic hammers and Nicole turned cartwheels in the yard. Marian sewed ribbon to the cuffs of the girls' overalls and Vee used a sequin gun on the pockets—an idea from a magazine. "Let's go to the zoo, let's go for ice cream, let's take the kids swimming."

"You must come in the summer, Dad," Marian said brightly on the phone, in that edge of time when her night was her family's morning. "You'll like it here." This was when they still spoke in terms of his visiting, in the years when they were only waiting for this or that before buying his ticket. A bit more time for his leg to improve. A few more months to get a visa.

One rainy afternoon, Vee asked to try on one of Marian's saris. "Oh, my God, the colors! This purple, this green!" She pulled hanger after hanger from the closet, slid the silks onto her arms, stroked the stiff gold thread.

Tara was napping, but Nicole, underfoot, wound a dupatta around her face like bandages. "Look! I'm a mummy!"

Vee stood completely still while Marian dressed her, her arms held away from her body. The choli blouse strained at the shoulders.

"Don't worry," Marian laughed, tucking the sari at her waist. "You can move, it won't unwind."

"Look," called Nicole. "I'm a princess."

When Marian had finished, Vee walked in small, careful steps to the full-length mirror. "Well? Am I ravishing?"

The sari was silver and pink, cool pearly colors that Marian seldom wore. "It suits you. You should keep it."

"Really? Let's take a picture! Hang on, hang on, not like this. Nicole, help me take off my socks! And I need a necklace! Something fabulous, Marian!"

"I'm a nun," Nicole informed her, already kneeling, the dupatta draped over her hair. They combed through Marian's jewelry and Vee found earrings, bangles, a heavy silver choker. She gazed longingly at herself in the mirror. "Someday we should go," she said, then turned to Marian, looking suddenly shy. "There's so much I want to see."

Nicole snapped the photo, the dupatta trailing behind her like a veil, a rack of her mother's bangles crashing from wrist to elbow as she lifted the camera. They stood arm in arm, Marian in slacks and Vee in the sari, slightly off center.

A few weeks before the trip to India, Gordon took the boys to spend Christmas with his parents. Vee came to spend the holiday with Marian and Daniel. She arrived on the morning of the 24th, wearing a dark fur coat, high-heeled boots, and a frosted clip in her hair. Nicole had been looking out for her.

"Why don't you help Tara with the cookies 'til she comes?" Marian suggested.

Nicole scowled, looking remarkably like Marian's father. "I'm not waiting. I'm just in here." But she joined Tara in the kitchen.

Marian lingered near the window. The house smelled of butter, citrus, and pine, but the yard outside was raw and sodden. She wondered what her father would think of the life she had built here: the children, the house, the snow melting in patches on the lawn. Had he ever seen snow? Her mother and Jude had come to visit several times, but after her father's stroke he was reluctant to sit on a plane for so many hours. His left leg still gave him trouble, he said.

A movement outside the window caught Marian's eye, and she saw Vee in her dark coat, the collar thick and high. Her hair bright and twisted up with a clip. The cream-colored Buick, pale as unfrosted cookies. Vee was tugging at the back door, and for a moment Marian thought maybe Gordon had left the boys with her after all, or even just Cody. But no, the door gaped open and Marian saw that the back of the car was filled with parcels wrapped in silver and gold.

Old snow lined the side of the road, filthy and ice-pocked. Vee leaned gingerly into the car, trying not to dirty the bottom of her coat. Marian thought of the pure white drifts of cotton her mother spread over the branches of an artificial Christmas tree. Marian and Daniel had brought the tree to Santa Clara years ago, the branches laid out carefully in the bottom of a duffel bag. The first year, her father spent an afternoon piecing the tree together and eventually, her interest in sweets and gift wrapping spent, Nicole drifted over to help. She sat cross-legged on the floor, frowning in concentration. Had her father been pleased when his granddaughter joined him, Marian wondered? Neither spoke much, except to announce the completion of another branch. The "needles" were odorless—far too green and the texture of garbage bags—but the "snow" was thick and perfect. "No clumps!"

Her mother passed out rolls of cotton to the girls. "And not too thin either. You people with your winters, you should know how it looks."

Outside, the snow rose nearly to Vee's knees where the plows had banked it, dark as factory smoke. She emerged from the car with two large boxes clutched to her chest. For a moment she tottered on narrow-heeled boots, her face bent down to the packages, her body lost in the dark panels of her coat. Marian watched her pick a stumbling path over the snowbank.

"Nicole," Marian called, "Vee's here! Go and help her!" A minute later she watched the scene through her window, soundless and bright: her daughter, pole-legged, half running, half skittering down the driveway to where Vee waited. Vee was no longer struggling. She was transformed again to the friend Marian had always known—gracious and golden-haired, smiling her generous smile, welcoming, even now welcoming, as though this moment with Marian's daughter in Marian's driveway was hers to invite Marian into.

"Daniel, she's here! Tara!"

For a moment Marian had tears in her eyes. There was something grand and tragic about Vee, so lovely in her rich, dark coat as she greeted Nicole, and something small and hopeless about the bank of dirty snow. Was she meant to be in this place, this mud and ice, this patch of land just above the straggling hemline of the Ohio River? It had always been Vee's home—Marian was the one who felt out of place, the one with every reason to question how she had landed up here. "It's not forever," Daniel had said when the offer came for a three-year appointment.

But Marian knew how easily one thing and then another became forever. "Only five years," she'd told her parents when she left for graduate school in Massachusetts. "It's not forever." Daniel was a year ahead of her, and they met at a department coffee. He had a small blue Chevette with fake sheepskin on the front seats. They began to go for drives together. (*Dear Mum and Dad,* she began again and again, afraid to commit to paper what they must already have suspected. *We'll visit as soon as we can* was what she offered them in place of *It's not forever.*) Later she and Daniel would call the Chevette their first car. They would sit with Vee and her friends in the Blue Moon Saloon, Erie Avenue, Cincinnati, Ohio, and laugh about those sheepskin seats. By then Marian had come to enjoy this life she could never have envisioned: the car she had learned to drive, the sharp fall mornings on the sidelines of the girls' games, the coffees and parties and planning meetings, a world Vee had helped open up for her.

But Vee? Marian looked at her and thought beaches on the Riviera, casinos and nightclubs—places made, as Vee was made, for money and pleasure. Nicole, she realized, looked at her and thought Cincinnati. With what longing she thought it, with what raw young need: America! Marian watched them, framed in the window: her daughter, adoring and coatless in the cold; the mound of Christmas gifts left in the car; Vee in her fur and slender heels, her bravado nearly as sustaining as courage.

Vee kissed Nicole, tumbled the packages into her arms, looked up to the window where Marian stood, and waved with her whole arm, as broadly as her coat allowed.

"Let me tell you something, sweetheart." Vee peered at Nicole, her eyes wide, her voice solemn. "Never settle. I'm telling you this as your friend. When it comes to men, never settle."

It was Christmas afternoon. As usual, Vee embarrassed Marian with her extravagance.

"Oh, well, I don't have daughters to buy for!" Vee lifted a

sheet of Nicole's hair away from her face. "You have a beautiful face, sweetheart, beautiful cheekbones. You need to show them off."

Nicole blushed and clipped her hair back with the rhinestone barrette Vee had just given her. Vee had also bought her a pair of Guess! jeans with zippers on the ankles, the *Ford Models Guide to Beauty,* a makeup kit, and her first razor.

"Here." Vee handed Nicole a cloth bag. "Here's some of my old makeup to practice with. The colors are all wrong for you, but at least you'll get used to putting it on." She caught a glimpse of Marian's face and held up both hands. "I know, I know. She doesn't need it. You really don't, sweetheart—your bones! But it's fun and"—turning to Marian—"she has to learn sometime."

"On special occasions," Marian said. "And not too much." She watched as Vee fastened a small plastic cape around Nicole's neck and kept a mental tally: eyeliner, mascara, lipstick. "I don't think she needs that," she said when Vee pulled out her blusher. "She has enough color, don't you think?"

Now Nicole sat on the edge of the tub, her skirt pulled up, her bare legs covered with lather.

"Always use shaving cream, never soap. Soap dries your skin." Vee handed her the razor.

Marian's arms were folded against her chest, as if to hold herself back. "Are you sure you want to do this? Once you shave, you have to keep going."

Nicole looked pained. "Mom, I told you."

"I know, I know. All the girls do it. Shelley laughed at you in the locker room." She smiled ruefully at Vee. "In India we wax. That's still what I do. It's so much easier, darling, you only have to do it once a month."

"She heats it on the stove," Nicole told Vee. "The wax smells gross."

Marian lifted a shoulder in acquiescence and Vee nodded to Nicole.

"Okay, sweetheart. Start at the ankle, very gently. Long, smooth strokes. Up to the knee . . . that's right. A light touch." She was kneeling by the tub, watching the progress of the razor. "I mean it, now. You should never, ever settle. Boys are going to come after you. Maybe not right away"—she paused as a drop of blood beaded on Nicole's ankle—"but eventually. Just you wait. And then, the important thing is, don't settle. I did, and look where it got me."

"Vee—" Marian shook her head slightly, frowning.

"Of course your mother knows this better than anyone. I mean, she waited, didn't she? She waited for just the right person, and then she followed her heart, no matter what anyone else thought. It's so romantic—they practically eloped!"

Marian sensed her daughter's discomfort. Nicole, she realized, did not like to think of her parents in such terms.

"I know your dad might not seem like the most exciting guy, but believe me, the exciting ones can be a real dead-end." She turned to Marian, rolled her eyes. "You know he bought a powerboat?"

"Careful, darling, you'll gash yourself!"

"No, I won't!" But small nicks bloomed along her leg.

Vee took her hand and guided the razor. "Just promise me you'll always listen to your mother. She knows a good man when she sees one." Nicole concentrated on her knee; Vee pressed on with a stagy wink in Marian's direction. "Listen, sweetheart. I need to ask you a favor. A big one."

"What?"

"While I'm gone, Gordon's gonna have the boys for a week. In the house." She turned to Marian, eyebrows raised. "Nice, right? His place isn't ready."

"Vee, I don't want her getting involved in all that—"

"No, no. Of course not. Not *involved*."

Marian saw that Nicole's face was tight with anger and indignation. She imagined how her daughter would protest if Vee were not in the room. "Go ahead, I'm sorry."

"Well, you know, the boys love Nicole—they really do, sweetheart—and since she's usually the one who sits for them, I thought maybe she could just be available. I mean, if Gordon needs to run out for something. Or whatever it is he does with his time . . ." She rolled her eyes. "Anyway, the boys would be with someone I trust."

"Sure," Nicole said quickly. She straightened up on her stool, eager for any adult commission. The makeup made sharp edges of her lips and eyes. "I can do that."

"Oh, Nicole, I don't know . . ."

"Mom! It's only babysitting."

"But you won't feel strange?" She thought of Gordon, hard-eyed, dragging his foot through the pile of the carpet.

"No!"

"Maybe Dad can go with you—"

"Sure," Vee said quickly. "That's fine, sweetie. You might feel better—"

"But I don't need any help. What would Dad do? That would just make everything weird. Gordon would think Dad was checking up on him."

"She's right." Vee looked at Marian. "She's absolutely right."

Marian smiled weakly. Her daughter was right. How had her daughter come to understand such things? She thought of herself at twelve, such a younger twelve than America permitted.

Then Vee held up her hand. "But your mother's right too, sweetheart. If you feel at all uncomfortable doing this—"

"I don't. I feel fine. It's no big deal."

"And Gordon's very fond of you, darling. If he calls, you just go and don't get involved in any discussion of what's happening. Understand?"

Marian held up a warning finger.

"I *know,* Mom."

"Of course she knows." Vee put an arm around Nicole's shoulder. "She's growing up so fast, isn't she?"

Marian remembered a day when her daughter was four and found a sheet of adhesive bindis. Nicole stuck a constellation to her forehead and the rest on her dolls. A year later Nicole asked for blond hair for Christmas. Marian looked at her daughter—the lips glistening, the lashes thick and painted—and she did not know what to say that would not disappoint them all. So she shrugged and smiled, feeling she had surrendered more than she intended.

When it was time to pick Vee up to go to the airport, Marian was still rushing through the house. Her tea mug was half filled on the counter, its contents cold—she swallowed it down on the way to the sink. Lights were on in the bedrooms, though sharp winter sunlight poured through the windows—she snapped them off, glancing at the state of the carpets, the unmade beds. She wished she'd had time to vacuum.

"You'll turn out the lights when you're not using them? Tara! Don't forget!"

Daniel beeped the horn.

"No wearing makeup while I'm gone," Marian warned.

Nicole's face hardened.

"You think your father won't notice, but he'll notice."

"I won't. I told you already."

Marian hugged her, and for a moment it seemed as if Nicole's body yielded in her arms. "Try to eat something decent every day, will you, darling? Don't let Dad just bring you pizza. Tara, come and give me a kiss."

They stood in the doorway as she left. It was cold and Nicole hugged her arms to her chest. Tara was solemn and round-cheeked, baby-faced still. They looked lonely—two small figures on the wide front porch. Everything was wide in the Midwest, even in the suburbs. The yards, winter-yellow, and the smooth-paved roads. The sedans and station wagons. The flattened vowels and broad-backed casseroles. Only the wind had a narrow edge. Marian looked up at the sky, the tatters of clouds and the hard blue overhead. Tree branches scratched up at it, bare and ridiculous in all that space. She turned again to her children and felt a sudden pang of doubt.

"We'll be fine," Daniel told her. "It's only a few weeks." He reversed out of the driveway and paused for a moment, lifting his hand to wave as if he were the one leaving.

"Wait!" Marian could see Nicole was calling out to them. "Hang on. Roll down the window!" She leaned over Daniel to hear. "What is it, darling?"

Her daughter had pushed her hands in the pockets of her jeans; her shoulders were hunched against the cold. "Tell Vee I said good-bye."

"She adores you, you know."

Vee was staring out the window. In Frankfurt, the plane had filled with Indian families. A meal had been served, a movie shown, the lights dimmed. Around them, sleep crumbled to coughs and restless movements. The engines droned in the plane's haunches, a thrumming Marian felt in her back and legs.

"She really does, she adores you," Marian said. She did not say the rest of it, that there were things about Vee she did not want her daughter to adore. They had never exchanged such truths before; this was not the terrain of their friendship. But in the semidarkness of aisle lights and lavatory signs it seemed possible that they had left even that behind them. Outside was darkness, and below was darkness that might have been land or sea. Time waited for them in one place or another—her mother's alarm clock, her father's bed pulled to the balcony, her children, running or reading or sleeping—but for now, the plane had slipped loose of such moorings. The moon was rounded but not full, the heel of a foot turned elsewhere. "Sometimes it worries me."

"Oh, she's in a stage. You know, you remember what that's like. She'll grow out of it." Then, sadly, seriously. "I love her too, Marian."

"I know. I know you do." What could Marian say? Whatever else was between them would remain unsaid, a dark stretch of earth the plane passed over. She could not even name what it was. She thought of the day Vee called her—"I've thrown my wedding band down the drain," she'd announced. "But now I'm scared to run the disposal. Remember that day when Mickey set the microwave on fire?" Mickey, nine years old and alone in the house, heating up his pizza in foil while Vee spent three hours at the hairdresser's. But what was the point of saying such things? Soon they would land.

"You're good with her, Vee."

"Well." She paused. "I should have had a girl." It sounded like an apology. She turned to face Marian. "You're her mother," she said.

That day, the day Vee's wedding band lodged in the drain, Marian and Daniel came over to take apart the disposal. He set the blades on a sheet of newspaper; they were dark-stained and cruelly curved.

"Cool," said Mickey, a boy generally fascinated by how things came apart. He had been permitted to save the microwave he had melted.

Daniel rolled up his shirtsleeve and gingerly reached down the pipe, head cocked to one side.

"What will I do with it, anyway?" Vee giggled. "Throw it in the river? Run over it with the car?"

"Put it on the railroad tracks," suggested Mickey. He had

also been the one to put the fire out, with an extinguisher he found in the garage. "We do that with pennies. They flatten out, splat."

"Do they, angel?"

Marian glanced at Mickey nervously; she didn't consider this a healthy conversation for a nine-year-old. He kept the misshapen microwave in his room, near a large green fish tank. But despite his attachment to his father, Mickey seemed to take a cheerful interest in the fate of his mother's wedding band.

"I should give it to Nicole," Vee said loudly. "A warning. A—what do you call it? Talisman."

"Don't be silly, Vee," Marian said quickly.

"Oh, I'm only kidding!" She snatched up Cody and covered his face with kisses; the little boy squirmed in pleasure. "Your mama's only kidding, right?"

The next week Gordon would arrive at the house with his brother. Marian would sit in her idling car until they had gone inside. The dining chairs would be distributed.

"Got it!" Daniel dropped the ring onto the newspaper with the blades of the disposal, and Mickey leaned close to see. "Watch out for those, buddy."

But Mickey picked up the ring between two fingers and examined it carefully. "Do you think it would melt?" he wondered.

Within a year Mickey will begin to set fires. Small Boy Scout experiments at first, twigs crosshatched into a kind of housing with paper in its center. An abandoned birds' nest; his gym clothes doused in turpentine; Cody's old crib. He will rip down the rotting walls of the tree house his father built him, leaving the floor as a lookout platform. He will wait for a dry night and burn those too. He will return to the house and carefully bathe, and even then his hair and fingertips will smell of thick black smoke.

Vee will meet a man in Florida, an older man who announces he wants to take care of her. He will not mind the idea of Mickey and Cody (until Mickey ignites a slick of oil in the swimming pool). When she talks about Del, she will laugh at nearly anything, her voice high and brittle. She will move the boys to a house outside Orlando that Marian and Daniel will never see. "He likes me to tell him if I'm going out," she says, laughing. "He likes to know who I'm calling. He's so attentive." One day, years later, Marian will pick up the phone and hear Vee's voice.

"I got your letter, honey. I've been crying and crying. But you know I'll come. Del will understand if it's serious. He can spare me for a couple of days if the doctors say it's *really serious.* Just tell me when you have the surgery. It must be soon, right? Very soon. They'll want to take care of that tumor *right away.* You just tell me and I'll come."

"Next week," Marian says cautiously. She is in perfect health; all the letters she sent in the first few years were sent back, unopened, and she has long since stopped writing. Rumors twist through parents' groups and dinner parties; some of Vee's old friends think Del has ties to the Klan. Marian motions to Daniel to listen on the other extension. "Vee, if you want to come, you can stay here—"

"I'm coming. I'll be there. I wouldn't let you go through this alone. You don't have to worry about *asking me to come.*"

"Thanks." Marian's voice is shaking. "Please come, then, okay? How are you? How are the boys?"

"Oh, they're fine, fine." She laughs, a sound almost like crying. "I can't wait to see you. You know it's hard for me to get away. You know, right? But I'll be there, I will. I promise."

"Vee—"

"I have to go now. I can't talk long . . ."

"What's your number, Vee? I'll call you. I'll call you back—"

"No, no, I'll call you. I'll call tomorrow."

A week goes by, another, another. A month, a year. The phone doesn't ring. Cody, a teenager by now. The last they heard of Mickey, a special school. There is nothing she and Daniel can think to do.

Nicole will not miss Vee as much as Marian worries she will. She will do as she promised and babysit for Mickey and Cody while Vee is in Bombay. Gordon will come to the door, sleepy, disheveled, rubbing his stubbled jaw. It seems longer than three months since she's seen him. "I've missed you, squirt." He grins, a familiar grin. "Go on up, Mickey's waiting." A few minutes later he calls upstairs. "I ordered a pizza, okay? Money's on the table." She hears him leave. Cody falls asleep with an old baseball hat in his hand, and she and Mickey watch an R-rated movie on the VCR.

"Are you sure we're allowed?"

Mickey laughs but not unkindly. He has a round, merry face and laughter seems its natural function. "I do it all the time. C'mon."

They stretch out on the top of his parents' bed—Vee's bed. Nicole has seen R-rated movies before, whenever she babysits in houses with HBO. But she feels strange with Mickey beside her. He lies on his belly, feet in the air, and seems to find nothing unusual in the naked woman draping herself over the naked man. Nicole watches carefully, as though someone might be watching her watching. She is very still and keeps her face set. When it is over they play cards, War.

"Come over tomorrow," he offers when they hear his father at the door. "If you want."

Gordon drives her home in his convertible. The top is down although it's January.

"Cold?" he calls. He is wearing loafers with no socks, she notices. He has a leather jacket.

She pulls her parka closer around her. "No."

"It's great, isn't it?"

The wind cuts into her face, making her cry. She has put on lipstick and a touch of mascara, and worries that tears will smudge her makeup. Gordon is taking the long way home, driving fast, faster. He pulls to the curb at the house where he and Vee used to live, two blocks from Nicole's house, before they moved to the rich part of town.

"Remember this place?" He runs a hand through his wind-stiffened hair.

"Yeah."

"What do you think? Maybe we should have stayed in this place."

"I don't know."

"Maybe it would have made a difference."

"I don't know . . ."

"You're cold, squirt. Come here." He puts an arm around her and pulls her close, rubbing the sleeve of her coat. He smells like medicine, she thinks. His breath bitter as the taste of pennies. His voice thick and slow when he tells her how pretty she looks. His hands cold.

Later she will lie in bed with her parka on top of her pajamas. She will stare out the window of her bedroom at the same sight that she has stared at since she was a little girl, a pine tree rising above the roofline of a house down the street. She will mentally shave a single protruding branch down to size over and over. She will remember Kurt Hollander at Peggy Newman's pool party the summer before, the way he ducked his head swiftly to hers right in front of Janey Price. She will tell herself fiercely, *This is not the first kiss, this is not the first kiss.* Later there will be other fierce thoughts, one after the other, stubble and whiskey and wind. Hands. For the rest of her life, parts of her will be too fierce and others parts too soft. She will hold them away, dark craters and fine colorless dust.

This is not the first kiss—the only thought she permits. She misses her mother. She is cold, still cold, and wears her parka to bed. *This is not the first kiss.*

That is her half of a story, the half Marian never knows.

They have landed in Bombay. Vee is rumpled, nervous. The air settles on them, heavy as sea water. Vee unpins her hair, brushes it, and repins it as they wait to disembark.

"It's so hot!"

"This is nothing. It's the middle of the night. Wait until the sun is out."

"Will your brother be here?"

"He'll be right outside customs. No one's allowed to come inside."

They move through immigration and enter the large hall for baggage claim.

"What's that?"

Vee points to the observation deck, an overhang encased in plastic where people meeting flights are permitted to catch a first glimpse of their families. Marian scans the wall of faces pressed against the Plexiglas.

"Look! There's Jude!"

"Where?"

"That one, there!"

Vee waves, a huge extravagant wave. "Jude! Hi, Jude!"

Other families have turned to look at Vee, laughing.

"He can't hear you. It's soundproof!"

"Oh, who cares? Hey, Jude! We made it!"

Marian was sure that Jude would be embarrassed by this display, but he is laughing in a way Marian recognizes from late nights of old jokes, after the kids are asleep and sometimes even her parents, when they are free to remember just what they like. Suddenly, through her exhaustion, Marian is buoyant. She thinks of her father, pretending he has not fallen asleep, rising from his vigil to clap his hands in welcome. She can imagine them all unpacking the suitcases together when they reach home, drinking tea at two in the morning, unearthing the food, the phone, the radio, passing around the photographs. She sees now how the ritual will expand to include Vee—Vee and her chocolates, her water filter, the silk robe that Marian's mother will try on at once, the sweater her father will pull on over his pajamas. The report cards and art projects, the pictures Vee has brought of Mickey and Cody and an old one she has unearthed of herself in a sari, standing with Marian.

Jude remains on the observation deck until the first bags emerge through the flaps of the luggage belt. Then he catches Marian's eye and points; he will meet them in the wash of smoky air outside the door. Vee has found a cart and is asking questions about customs.

Marian is thinking of the letter Nicole has written to her parents. She would like to read it. She knows that nothing of real importance will be revealed beneath those long seams of tape, but she would like to see the handwriting, the words her daughter chose.

Home for a Short Time

Toby came home from work to find his father alone in their flat.

"Back already?" His father looked up from his reading, clearly surprised to find the sun was setting. "Oh, I see. What's the time?"

"Just past seven." Toby shuffled through some mail without picking it up. "Where's Michael?"

"At Regina's for a drink. Someone's come by there, I've forgotten. He says he'll be back to eat."

"He's left all this out?"

The dining table was covered with loose pictures and old cracked albums. "The walls are so bare," Michael had complained the night he arrived from America for a three-week visit. "What about hanging a few photos at least?"

"He hasn't finished," his father said mildly. "He wants your help with it, actually. Just past seven . . . then I've got another hour before dinner, yes?" He returned to his book.

Toby did not ask what assistance his brother required. Whatever it was could wait. Instead he passed into the empty kitchen and poured a beer into a glass. He glanced out the back window to find Neelam, their servant, down in the compound doing her washing.

The flat was dusky. A single lamp shone at his father's desk, but Toby didn't bother with lights. He switched on the ceiling fan in his bedroom, stood at the window, and drank deeply. His throat felt rough, his skin gritty. It was nearing March and even the evenings were hot. The train had been crowded and air from the open doors stank of exhaust, factory smoke, dried fish, sewage. He had spent forty minutes pressed into the backs and shoulders of other men, smelling their breath and hair oil.

"I'll just have a quick bath," he called to his father.

But he stayed at the window, reluctant to launch any new course of action. Beyond the compound walls, other commuters were making their way home. The new construction across the street was nearly finished, six stories high, thick-walled, built slap up to the road despite the zoning codes. The contractor was experimenting with color, and stripes of pink, beige, taupe had been hastily painted on one wall to test their effect. The workers had stopped for the evening and were tending cooking fires around the rubble heap where the car park would be. A woman with the tail of her sari tucked between her legs threw some rubbish in the street gutter.

Toby heard Neelam return and the hiss of a gas flame. His beer was gone. Soon Michael would be home; soon dinner would be ready. He moved into the bathroom and switched on the hot-water heater, then examined himself in the mirror. His own face was never what he expected; he still carried an image of himself just on the edge of manhood. But here he was in the glass, middle-aged. His face had been a long, bony affair when he was a boy, all nose and jaw and Adam's apple; now there was a heaviness beneath the eyes, more flesh to the cheeks. His forehead had always been high, his eyes large and wide-set. The lines at their corners sometimes made him seem tired. But his mustache was the same as ever. His hair was still thick, and he carefully blackened whatever went gray—an attempt to keep himself recognizable. It hardly seemed credible that he was nearing fifty.

He had taken off his shirt when the phone began to ring. His father looked up from the desk as Toby hurried to pick it up. His sister, Regina, announced that she and her husband, George, would drop in after dinner.

"Since when do you have to call? Just come."

"Listen, you, that isn't all. Michael's coming just now with Jean."

Instantly Toby felt both foolish and exposed—as though an actual person had caught him on the way to the bath.

"She's in town?"

"Overnight. Tomorrow she goes to Bangalore. She had a drink with us, and Michael said he'd bring her over to say hello to Dad."

"Now?"

"Yes, now! Go and put a decent shirt on." Again Toby sensed his sister could see him: barefoot and bare-chested, a towel around his neck. By the time he realized she was only attending to his manners, he felt he was stumbling to keep up.

"But hang on—how is she?"

Regina paused, a rarity. "It's so sad, isn't it?" Without giving him time to answer, she instructed Toby to hurry up, get ready.

Toby risked a quick bath, jumping in and rushing out, listening to hear if anyone had yet arrived. "Out in a minute, Dad! Just see if there's wine." He ran a rueful thumb over his chin; there was no time to shave. A hand-clap of cologne, his watch, the cross on its gold chain replaced around his neck. He chose a shirt Michael had brought for him, stiff green cotton, and tucked it carefully. His good slacks, a dark leather belt neatly buckled. He was still trim, still fit. His shoes were a bit scuffed, but he wiped them with the black-stained polish rag; perhaps it helped. Still no sign of them? It had been thirty minutes at least, and Regina and George lived just around the corner, on St. Peter Road. Where could they be?

He ducked his head into the kitchen. "Neelam? You can put out some glasses. And a bowl of snacks—what do we have? Almonds?" Neelam was new to the household; Regina had found her four months ago. Toby rarely questioned his sister's hand in such arrangements, but he experienced a pang of doubt when he met Neelam: a widow with wide-spaced knees and toes, short gray hair that bristled at her neck, and arms shrunken nearly to bone.

"She's strong enough for a broom and some cooking. And you can't have a young woman around, a bachelor like you. It doesn't look right."

"But that's ridiculous. You never said anything about Manjari." Manjari was younger, also unmarried, though promised to a boy in her village. She had left the family to take up a high-paid post as ayah for a family in Delhi.

"Manjari was here ten years, and when she came I was still living downstairs. That is the difference. And another thing, sir: nobody thought you'd go on being a bachelor." This was a common refrain and Toby had no interest in hearing more, so he welcomed Neelam without another word. She was given a small room near the lift bay and settled in with them well enough, Toby considered. Her cooking was adequate, her kitchen clean. At times he worried the work was too much for her; sometimes, in the evenings, she would stand very still before taking her next step, or sway with fatigue. But he had no wish to put her out of a job, so he kept quiet about these episodes to Regina.

Once, when he helped Neelam remove a pile of wood and bricks from the compound wall, she told Toby about her son, who had gone to earn money in the Gulf. "Oorjit is his name. He is coming back to buy a house for us," Neelam said. "He will marry when he comes back and have many sons. He has always been lucky." Her voice sounded like something charred, her teeth pebbly, the color of ash. "He also helps me to carry," she said when they had nearly finished, and Toby realized she had mentioned her son as a gesture of thanks.

Now she appeared with a brass bowl of nuts. She was wearing a sari with one end tucked through her legs, Koli style, in a bright pink best suited to young girls and over-sweet candies. The tail of her sari, flicked over her shoulder, was wet and wrung—perhaps with washing up, Toby thought.

"And wine, Neelam." She had not attempted to make order of Michael's photo project, but had pushed what she could to the center of the table to clear a space for the glasses, and as Toby uncorked the bottle she brought him, he glanced at a picture. Regina stood in her school jumper with a bow pricking up from a mass of curly hair; Michael, a stocky boy, clearly itching in his collar; Toby small beside them, a spindly support for the youngest, Louise, to lean against. She was barely walking, just a year, he guessed. Their mother died a few months later, and the last baby with her. But in this photo Louise already seemed motherless. Toby tucked it beneath a picture of his father in a suit and checked his watch. Nearly eight. Jean and Michael must have stopped off somewhere.

Toby's father emerged, unrolling his sleeves, to join Toby at the table. He saw the wineglasses and asked, "Someone's coming?"

"Jean Colaco. Kapur, that is. Jean Kapur."

"Really? She's here?"

At that moment Toby heard the tinny music of the lift as it jangled to their floor. He and his father waited, in an oddly formal silence, until Michael drew back its caged door, alone.

"Hey! What a reception!"

All that was taut in Toby went slack.

"Where is Jean, then?" his father asked.

"She wanted to pop over, but she was feeling too sleepy. She's just come in last night—totally jet-lagged. I walked her back to Ruby's place." Ruby was one of Jean's sisters, still in the neighborhood. "She's coming back in a week or so—I'm sure she'll stop in. So! Shall we have a glass of wine?"

"You have," Toby said. He went to the kitchen to pour himself another beer and tell Neelam not to delay dinner any longer; no one was coming.

Alfred Fernandez ate in the old style, sweeping the fingers of his right hand from the plate to his mouth in quick, tidy motions. Toby and Michael used forks and knives, which Neelam laid out like stiffly posed couples in the middle of their plates.

Michael had been heavyset as a child; now he was a jogger with a meaty face and solid chest. He ate in large bites, tearing bread into chunks and pushing food on top with a knife. "Terrible business, this thing with Jean's husband. I knew it was his heart, but she told us he was in the kitchen making breakfast for the kids when it happened. He just collapsed, right in front of them. Dead by the time she ran downstairs. It must have been a massive attack."

Toby thought of her sons, whose ages he could not remember. Little fellows, the last time he'd seen them: two dark heads bent over their handheld video games. They wore matching shorts and sandals, their hair neatly parted.

His father shook his head. "He must have been young."

"My age exactly. Six months' difference."

Neelam had made a fish curry. Toby felt a bone in his throat and took a bit of rice. "How did she seem?"

"I don't know. She was tired, of course. Can't be easy to talk about this business, but I suppose the shock's worn off by now."

His father considered, fingers poised over a last mouthful of wet rice. "She's a strong girl. But she hasn't any family nearby, does she?"

"Not in Pennsylvania. Unless the husband's people are there."

"Poor child." He glanced toward the kitchen. "See if the girl has more fish there."

He always spoke to Neelam through Toby, in the same way that he had once deferred to his wife and then to his daughters in matters of the kitchen. But Neelam didn't wait for Toby to put the question to her; she got up from the kitchen floor and offered the platter of fish to Toby's father, who examined each piece before he picked one. When he tipped his head in acknowledgment, she turned toward Toby. Her eyes were red and tired.

"Give Michael another helping, and then you take what you want," he told her. "Go and eat." She did not smile, but her head drooped and he sensed her relief. Michael had begun to discuss his plans for the photographs with alarming energy, and Toby found he too was relieved to think of Neelam moving toward the end of her day—and to think of the day itself nearly ended.

Toby's bed was in the front of the flat, and he found himself staring out into the darkness toward where Jean once had lived. He could dimly see the shape of the new flat building. Balconies without rails jutted out like ledges, and on the roof steel wires bristled through concrete posts.

Toby turned from the window and tried to put Jean out of his mind, though he often thought of her before sleep. Over the years the sharpness of such thoughts had gentled, from pain to longing to a kind of wonder about the life he might have lived. He was no longer kept awake by these questions, but he returned to them at night, a habit he could not name except to suppose he still missed her.

Twenty-four years before, they had been engaged, both families in favor of the match. Toby knew Jean's parents had approved; he was a neighbor, practically part of the family already, with a good place in a solid Bombay business—and he would take their daughter no farther than across the road. It was the life everyone had wanted for them, the life Toby had wanted.

Jean grew up playing with Toby's sisters, and as they grew older they were all in the same gang of friends. Then in their second year of university, Toby asked Jean to a New Year's party. He had meant nothing significant by the invitation. He usually teamed up with their friend Colleen for dances, but she would be out of town and everyone must go in some pair or other. But instead of laughing and nodding, instead of teasing him or slinging an arm around his shoulder, Jean blushed and let her gaze fall to her hands.

"Yes, thanks."

Years later, Toby was humiliated to recall that this—the merest suggestion of interest—had been enough to change the way he saw her. Could all that had followed have hinged on so little? When she looked up again, a glance both more brave and more timid than he had encountered from a girl before, he felt immersed in something new and perilous.

That was the first night he had gone home and lain awake thinking about Jean, not beautiful but striking, with strong dark brows and eyes the color of river water, not quite brown nor gray nor green. She resembled her father, and then all at once she resembled no one at all. Within a matter of days, Toby could not remember what it had been like to look at her before. The change was as wholly transforming as a landscape flooded, and in her presence he felt both the shock of buoyancy and the danger of being swept away.

What would have happened if he had not seen her blush? If in that instant he had looked away, would he still have loved her? Perhaps the idea would never have occurred to him; perhaps nothing would have come to light if Colleen had been in town—and Toby would have gone on happily as he was. There were nights when he believed that he and Jean were inevitable, a secret she knew first but one he was bound to discover. There were other nights, long and bitter, when he decided that what angered him most was not what she had ended but what with a silly blush, a reckless blush, she'd so carelessly begun.

Two days later, Toby was enlisted to help bring the ladder up from a ground-floor storage bay. It was too big for the lift, so they had to carry it up four flights of stairs, swinging around corners and landings until at last it was set up in the back bedroom. Large metal shelves lined three walls, with cartons, trunks, and old suitcases stacked to the ceiling.

"We should take them all down," said Michael. "They're just collecting dust up here." He stepped up another rung. "This is disgusting. You should clean this once a year at least."

Toby said nothing. Such instructions were a feature of Michael's visits. He sailed into town on a wave of zeal and duty, hunting out whatever Toby had failed to do and tackling it with a self-righteous vigor that was all a bit fishy, Toby felt, since Michael came only when it suited him and then required Toby to leave work early to hold the ladder.

"We can sort through them and get rid of what we don't need."

"You can't just start throwing out Dad's things."

"These are family things." Michael coughed. "Here—here are the albums. Careful, they're heavy. I'm telling you, this is just unhealthy. You're living in filth."

"I'm living down here."

"But seriously, when's the last time you cleaned out these shelves? You should do more to keep the place up."

"I do work, you know. I have a business to run." Toby looked at his elder brother, who had climbed to nearly the top of the ladder. To grub around with dirty boxes Michael wore stiff dark jeans with a braided belt, a button-down shirt that strained over the packed flesh of his stomach and chest, and brown loafers with leather tassels. Michael had left India when Toby was still at university; he had landed a job with an international food company that was expanding into Asian markets. He had gone first to Germany, where he met his wife, and then to a post in the States. It had been years since Toby had visited. He remembered quite clearly the carpeted rooms; the table laid, bright and glassy, for the inevitable dinner party; the strong black coffee his sister-in-law brewed every morning and the dark lipstick stains she left on her mug. But these glimpses left him unable to fully envision the life Michael and Sabine conducted. Did his brother climb ladders in his town house? Were there boxes? Dust?

"Do you ever see Jean? In the States, I mean?"

"Jean? No, not really. A wedding once. She's outside Philadelphia and we don't get out of D.C. much. Why?"

"You're both over there, that's all."

"It's a big country, Toby."

Michael spoke with an amused superiority that made Toby want to shake the ladder. "I'm meeting people in a few minutes," he said. "How many photos do you need anyway? You could cover every wall in the place."

"I want to choose the best ones. Where are you going?"

"Choir practice. And then some of us are going to Regina and George's."

"So who cares if you're late? You see them all the time. I'm here only for another two weeks. There, that's the last of them. I give up—I can hardly breathe. Hold it steady now."

"I've got it."

"We'll have to give all these shelves a good dusting." Michael had reached the ground; he brushed off his sleeves and legs. "Maybe Neelam can do it."

"You want to send Neelam up a ladder?"

"No, no, she can do the lower shelves. We'll have to do the rest. Nothing to it." Michael clapped him on the shoulder. "My brother, the bachelor," he said. "Don't worry, we'll get this place in order before I go."

Two months after Toby and Jean received their degrees, Toby asked his father where his mother's gold was kept. He had taken up his post in the business with his father and uncle. Fernandez Printing was a hive of rooms on the ground floor of a small building, its outer walls blackened with dust and street fumes. Toby didn't speak until they had gone inside. A boy of fourteen or fifteen leaned near the doorstep, waiting to bring them tea.

"I'm asking Jean to marry me." The words had more force than he'd intended, and it occurred to him that he should be asking his father's permission instead of announcing his intentions. Surely it would have happened in such a way if his mother had been alive to consult. They would have conducted themselves as families do. But he had spoken; there was no point in trying to go back over it.

"Yes," his father said. "It's been some time, hasn't it?"

"Well, now I'm settled here . . ."

His father nodded. They had reached the office he shared with Toby's uncle, and he paused in the doorway. The rings were kept in a suitcase, he told Toby, with all his mother's jewelry. It had a lock, and he had added a padlock as well. "Tonight I can give you the key."

Toby struggled to say something that would end this exchange properly. "It's good of you, Dad. Thank you."

"You can give Regina the key once you've found a ring. There are other things in the suitcase. Bangles, whatnot. Let her take what she wants and keep the rest for Louise." He cleared this throat. "I wonder where your uncle is?"

"I don't know," Toby said.

A week later, he told his father Jean had said yes. Toby's father looked down with a smile that was at once shy and elated, as though his joy was too powerful to risk a direct gaze. He kissed Toby fiercely on the cheek and hugged him for longer than Toby knew how to be in such an embrace.

"Son . . . listen, son! There are some nice necklaces in the suitcase. Tell her to choose one from me."

A few days later, before Jean had returned, Regina and George came to dinner. That weekend Regina was throwing one of her big bashes in honor of Colleen, who had settled in the States and was visiting Santa Clara.

Regina had come with a list. She needed to borrow various platters. "And tumblers for wine. Just reach up there, Toby." She flapped around the kitchen like a large bright bird while Toby packed plates and glasses in paper. Neelam seemed even smaller than usual. She stood in a corner, watchful, unmoving, waiting for the bird to find its way out the window again.

"Will Jean be back in time for the party?"

"I don't think so. I rang up Ruby and I think she comes a few days after. Anyway, I said we'll do something with Jean later. A smaller group, maybe."

Toby did not know how to hide his disappointment, or even why it was so acute. Regina was right; it was likely he would see Jean. But not in the way he had begun to imagine, with all the old gang around them and everyone their old selves again, a reprieve from all that had happened to leave them as they were now. He reached in his pocket for his cigarettes, despite what he knew Michael would say about smoking in the kitchen.

"It will be good to see Colleen." He spoke with more energy than he felt. "It's too long since she's come."

"So strange she never married."

"I'm sure she knows what she's doing."

"The two of you. Hopeless." Regina poked her brother's shoulder. "You'd be married in a snap if you bothered to ask anyone."

"I've asked before."

Regina's face softened, but she spoke briskly. "All that is in the past. Children have been born and raised and turned out of the house since the last time you asked anyone."

Toby made a point of exhaling near the open window. He could see the smoke curling away against the dark sky.

"Actually, there's a girl coming to the party. Nice girl, very sweet. Neil's cousin, I think. She's been living in the Gulf, but she's just been posted here."

"Enough. Go and pester Michael."

"He's got a wife." But she went, leaving Toby with Neelam. From the other room, where Michael's photo project was still spread over the table, Toby heard his sister's voice: "Oh, hell! What's all this?"

Once she had gone the kitchen was still. Toby tapped his cigarette against the window railing. Eventually Neelam emerged from her corner to resume preparations for dinner.

"I'll move all this later," Toby told her, motioning to the boxes. "Are they in your way?"

She tipped her head from side to side, neither yes nor no.

"Toby, come and see!" He could hear Regina laughing, could hear Michael's proud voice urging her to look at this or that. "There's a funny one here of you and Colleen!" He waited one minute more, thinking of Jean, thinking of nights when he and Colleen used to share cigarettes, thinking it was good, very good, that his friend had come home, even for a short time.

• • •

They were engaged six months when Jean spoke of postponing the marriage. "You do understand, don't you?" She caught Toby's hand between both of hers and held it tightly.

She had won a fellowship for her first year of graduate work. After that, the doctoral program was fully funded.

He had known, of course, that she had applied to study in the States. But it had all seemed so remote: the chance of a scholarship that would transport her to a world he had seen only in glossy brochures. Tall stone buildings and brightly colored leaves. He had not found it possible to think of Jean in those pictures.

"You do understand?"

They were outdoors, sitting on a bench near the sea. It was evening and the tide was so far out that he could not see the waterline. Birds stalked across flat dark rocks, and near the seawall village children chased one another in small ragged circles. He could smell their mothers' fires and the heavy stench of dried fish. He could not imagine what Jean would see or smell or hear, so far from home.

"Toby?"

He could hear how badly she wanted both to go and to reassure him. Still he would not look at her. A dim pink sun faded into the haze that hung above the horizon. One of the slum children wore a rough green woolen hat that tied around his chin, a long shirt that flapped around his knees, and no pants or shoes. He ran and ran as if he would never tire.

"I thought we'd be married next year. It's a long time to wait."

"It seems that way now, I know. But it won't be forever."

He thought of his life in the printing offices. He realized how small it seemed, a son sliding into his father's business, and that Jean had never said so. Nor would she say now that she must go. She would only pick up his hand and hold it tightly. He wondered whether her mother would protest, how her father would greet this news. But it did not occur to Toby to refuse her.

After so many years, the idea that Jean would soon be in Santa Clara affected Toby more than he liked to admit. At work he was able to absorb himself, but at home he soon remembered both the electricity and the humiliation of waiting. Michael's invitations to come along and have a jog—usually a point of irritation—now brought welcome distraction, and the brothers spent every evening at Sunset Park, pounding side by side around the red dirt track, not talking but breathing hard in a kind of unison.

The photos waited for them at home, a patchwork record of years that Toby didn't care to contemplate. The day before the party, Michael spent all afternoon tapping nails into the walls and by evening, the apartment was suddenly populated by faded brown versions of them all: their youngest sister, Louise, hauled up on Regina's hip; Michael and his cousin Stephen swaggering with cricket bats; Toby as a small boy, barefoot on a beach he could not remember.

"Is it Juhu?" Michael peered closely, as though an examination of the grainy sand and sea would reveal some distinguishing mark.

"It may be," his father said. "You've worked very hard, Michael."

"Nothing, Dad, nothing at all! Happy to do it." But Toby could see his brother was pleased. They moved on to a packed shot of cousins, all crowded shoulder to shoulder. Toby noticed his mother appeared only in her wedding photo, their father standing carefully beside her. Hanging nearby were wedding pictures of Michael with Sabine and Regina with George.

"What's happened to all the pictures of Mum?"

Michael shrugged. He never spoke much about their

mother; it was clear he could not see the point of dwelling on such things. "I've put some back in boxes."

Toby had lost his appetite for pictures and with a pang remembered Neelam. She was waiting in the kitchen, hunched on a low stool and chewing the tail of her sari. She looked up when Toby entered and pulled the tip of fabric from her mouth. It lay on her shoulder, wet and wrinkled, distracting him.

"You can bring the food," he told her. She pushed herself up from the stool with difficulty and walked as though ready to drop.

"We shouldn't have been so late tonight. Tomorrow you must sleep. Don't get up to make Dad's tea."

He had hoped for evidence of relief or gratitude, but Neelam offered neither. The skin around her eyes was slack and swollen, the eyes small and numb inside their pockets of flesh. Toby turned away from her with the uncomfortable feeling that he could not make himself understood in his own home, and called the others to the table.

Twenty months after she left for America, Jean phoned to tell Toby of her engagement. "His name is Ranjit," she said.

It was shortly after dawn. Toby had stumbled out of bed to answer the phone; he had not had his cup of tea yet. He stood at the table where the phone was kept, rubbing his forehead.

It had happened so quickly, she told him. She hadn't expected it.

"What time is it?" he asked suddenly. "There, where you are. What time is it?"

For the first time she hesitated. "It's early evening. Eight o'clock, thereabouts. I wanted to call when I was sure you'd be there. I don't know when you leave for work."

"There's static on the line," he told her. "It's not a very good connection." Perhaps she would hang up and call back. They would start again.

"I can hear you. Can you hear me?"

"I can hear you."

"So I'm—we'll be married in the spring."

"You're marrying him?" He began to grasp what he was being told. "How can you—I don't—"

"It's only just happened. I mean, he's only just asked . . ."

A ring, she mentioned. A picnic. A rainstorm. A mother, his mother. Toby could not remember the name.

"What was his name? Tell me the name again," he said stupidly.

Ranjit. Ranjit's mother. Ranjit's mother who was sick and could not travel. So they would marry there, Jean said, and they'd visit Bombay soon after. He was Hindu, but they'd hold a prayer service in St. Anthony's.

She would be staying in America, he suddenly understood.

"You were coming back. You were going to get your degree and come back."

"I know, but . . ." She had been homesick, she had made friends with a boy in her program whose family had moved to the States from Delhi. Ranjit's mother had cooked for her. It had all tumbled ahead so quickly.

He shook his head. A hand in his hair. He shook his head again. "But what about us?"

"I didn't expect this." She rushed on, nervous. "But I'll be here so long, we couldn't really think that would last, right? I mean, I've changed. And you too, you've changed."

"I haven't changed."

"Of course you have—"

"I haven't. I haven't. I love you."

She paused, and for one desperate moment he thought that now something would be done about the whole sorry mess. Something would be put right.

"No, no, you don't. You really don't. You're just fond of me."

He had not known how to protest or what the point of such argument would be. She had sent his mother's ring home through a friend, Ranjit's friend. He could pick it up from her parents. "I see," he said and felt breathless, as if he had turned hollow and there was not air enough in the room to fill what had deflated. "But— " A moment later, because it no longer mattered what he said, he told her he had to go.

It sometimes seemed to Toby that his life turned out the way it had from a failure of imagination. He had lacked sufficient vision; he had not dreamt clearly enough for even those things he desired most to materialize. He sensed that other people, his friends, had envisioned their futures with a definition that bordered on will. They had seen themselves with husbands or wives, had seen houses, plum jobs, children. Nothing had turned out exactly as they imagined, of course. And many had gone. To England or Canada or the States, to the Gulf or Australia. Whole families slipped away to other parts of the globe, wives following husbands, brothers following sisters, elderly parents persuaded to live in suburbs with grandchildren, shopping malls, washing machines.

But whatever eventually happened to them, Toby knew his friends had begun with the idea that a particular life was waiting for each of them. They sat in somebody's garden, young and fearless and certain, talking politics and a bright new India, falling in love with one another and dreaming futures they could name. They seized them the way they grasped the necks of bottles, and they tipped their heads and drank. For a time, Toby waited to catch up, and then slowly came the idea that he never would. Something sharp in them was, in his own nature, blunt. He could feel it even as a young man, even when Jean was by his side, sitting among them in a garden lit with lanterns and listening as one quick voice replaced another.

"What do you think, Toby?" (It might have been anything—women's rights, the cut of a new suit.)

"I think I'd better have another." Appreciative laughter. He hadn't a strong singing voice or charm or looks, but he was easygoing and loyal—a sweet fellow, Colleen called him—a general favorite. He held his own.

Eventually there would come a call for music. Glasses refilled, a raucous chorus, chairs pulled in an untidy circle. Jean, who always sang flat, clapped her hands until she could resist no longer and then joined in, defiant and joyous, grinning when the guitarist told her to move, she was putting his instrument out of tune. Toby pulled his chair closer to hers. After they had gone through several rounds, a few people began to yawn. Some set off for home, dropping their hands on the shoulders of those still sitting, kissing cheeks. The songs grew quieter. Colleen sat on the ground, her back to Toby's chair, her legs stretched out before her. At dawn a small group would still be talking, fingertips smelling of cigarettes, empty glasses clustered near the legs of chairs. Jean had gone, but Toby could not tear himself away. Someone's sister, looking pale and tired, would lean forward to convince the boy she thought she would marry (in fact it would be another, asleep on the sofa inside) about the work she intended to do in a literacy program. How urgent she was, how hoarse-voiced, how lovely, pushing an unruly bit of hair behind her ear. It was all too important to sleep.

Toby always stayed to the end of such gatherings, nights that felt so much like this one, twenty-odd years later. Regina was badgering someone to join the tutoring program she ran at St. Anthony's for children in nearby slums. A couple of others were telling filthy jokes. Some of the women were clearing the food away, with George presiding over the sink, a dish towel that someone had tucked in the back of his pants hanging down like a tail. Five or six people were talking politics. Michael had left a few minutes before, hinting that it was late and Toby should do the same. But Toby wandered back toward Colleen, who was stretched out in a lounge chair looking rumpled and girlish, her shoes kicked off and her hair pulled back with a wide band, the kind she used to wear when they were young. She drew in her legs so he could sit at the foot of her chair.

"You're the life of the party, Tobes."

"Yes," he said firmly, raising his glass high and making her laugh. It occurred to him that the home he'd tried to envision all those years ago, the children he'd idly imagined, were phantoms. He could scatter them with another swallow. It was his memories that felt real, and this garden, his friends, the glass in his hand, the cigarette smoke. He drew it in slowly, filling his lungs, and offered the cigarette to Colleen, who took it. The sharpness in his chest might have been longing but not for anything that needed chasing after. He wanted another round of songs; he wanted Colleen to sit back down again.

"I'm just helping clear. You stay put, lazybones." She looked up and saw Neil's cousin, whose name Toby couldn't remember. "Here, come and sit. This fellow's perfectly happy on the floor." Toby grinned.

"Why not?" He patted the chair in extravagant welcome until the other girl had joined him.

Or not quite a girl anymore. She laughed and joked like a girl, she tapped his shoulder and flirted rather sweetly, she let her hand rest on his arm while she told the story of taking her little nephew on his first flight; she worked for an airline. But her hair was beginning to gray and the skin of her hands strained at the tendons. Her lipstick had faded so that her mouth seemed cracked with fine, dark lines. Even when she smiled, even in the dark, she did not quite seem youthful. None of them were young anymore. Their houses were real, their children off at parties, as old as he had been when he first thought of Jean. Toby rocked his chair back on two legs and the garden tilted. Black, with streaks of green where the torches spilled light against foliage. He watched swirls of cigarette smoke, lacy, slow-turning. Beneath it he smelled the lush scents of flowers. All the voices and laughter slid together and he smiled. "What's so funny, Toby?" The girl put an arm around his shoulder. "Toby's keeping secrets over here!"

"No, no," he protested thickly.

"Better give it up, man. She'll get it out of you before long."

"I have no secrets," he said. He thought a bit longer. "Well, maybe just one."

The girl at his side who was no longer a girl took his glass away. "That's it for you," she said gaily. Someone started singing and he joined in, words and notes so familiar that he did not need to think, and when they had gone through all their favorite songs, George and Regina and the girl, whose name was Violet, pulled him to his feet—"Come on now, up you go"—and made sure he reached home.

Toby was shaken from sleep early the next morning. "Son. Son, get up. Get up. Something's happened."

The light was still pale and watery outside his window. His mouth tasted of ash, his head felt like something he would have to pick up with his hands. "In a minute," he told his father.

"Now, son. Come on."

When he was finally roused, he followed his father to the storeroom. A pipe leading to the hot-water tank had sprung a leak. A large patch of plaster near the ceiling was soaked and water had gushed from a hole in the wall onto the highest shelf. Old cardboard boxes were sodden and dripping. Already a puddle covered much of the floor.

"What the hell!" Michael had awakened and stood in the doorway. "What is this?"

"It must be the pipes. Or the water heater may need replacing. Anyway, we must call that fellow, what's his name?"

Michael touched the toe of his slipper to the water. "First we should get Neelam. We need some towels. Thank God I took out the good photos, no? They'd be gone otherwise."

Toby stared at the wrecked cartons, thinking of the photos Michael had not wanted.

"Go and call, son. See if he can come."

Toby's head felt as if cement was hardening behind his eyes. "Right."

But Michael frowned. "Who's this guy you're calling?"

"Satip. The pipe man."

"Is he the one who put these pipes in? What's the point of calling him? We can swab this up with some towels. Or Neelam can do it."

Toby rubbed his face. "This is too much for Neelam, Michael."

"What's too much? Wiping the floor with towels? Never mind, you and I can manage."

"Of course we can manage, but we still need someone to check the pipes. We can't even turn on the water until we know what's happened."

"So his pipes cause a flood and you turn around and give him business?"

Toby stared at his brother. Michael's face was grizzled, his hair flattened from sleep. "What's the matter with you?"

"Son—"

"No, Dad. I can't call a plumber when there's a flood?" He shook his head. "What do you do in your house, Michael?"

"I don't let the place go to pieces. I don't stay out all hours with my friends like a bloody teenager."

"I'm forty-six years old. You think you have the right to come into my house and tell me what to do?"

"This is not your house. This is Dad's house!"

"That's enough," their father said firmly. "Michael, that's enough. Toby, go and call Satip. Go."

Toby turned in disgust and went.

He had not known what to say to his father when Jean announced her engagement. He had known for two days before he ventured to break the news. Even then he could not bring himself to mention Ranjit's name.

"Jean has decided to stay in the States."

They were at the dinner table.

His father paused. "Is it definite?"

"Yes."

"I see," he said finally. They ate for a time in silence. Toby imagined the way Jean's voice would have carried them through such meals, how happy his father would have been with grandchildren at the table.

"There are other girls," his father said.

"What?"

"Maybe a friend. Sometimes in these matters, it's better to think of a friend. Someone who will be a good companion. It's so many years . . ." He spoke slowly but evenly. "The other way can be difficult."

Toby did not know what to say.

"Not right away, of course. But maybe someday."

Toby shrugged.

"I'm sorry, son," his father said, as though he had been the one to fail them.

Some weeks later, Toby went to Colleen with his mother's ring. She fingered it while he talked.

Then she looked up at him, eyes wide and frightened beneath thick dark brows. "What are you saying?"

"We could have a good life," he told her. "I think we could be happy—"

"No."

They both were quiet. She continued to turn the ring over in the palm of her hand as though it were a pebble, and he felt lodge in him a final disappointment. He thought she must feel the same way, because eventually, when she relinquished the ring, she told him she did not think she would ever marry.

Michael seemed to abandon any plan of swabbing and disappeared to Regina's. Toby did not want to disturb Neelam, so he did what he could with rags and began to carry wet boxes to the garden. The sunlight was so bright that it seemed to buzz. The water had made pulp of his mother's books and letters, and Toby's arms ached with the strain. At first when he thought of Michael he wanted to thrash him, and then after a time he wanted simply to drop out of their arguments, to sit outside the circle of what they could not understand or explain. He found a photograph of his mother holding Regina and hung it on the line to dry.

He had brought down five loads when he heard a commotion at the construction site. Women were arguing. A few men's voices joined the clamor, but Toby did not bother to look until someone began to wail. From his gate he could see a familiar figure in a bright pink sari, standing with a pack of angry workers around her. She swayed on her feet, and her wail turned into a stream of abuse.

"Neelam!"

She paid no attention; he did not think she had heard him. She had not stopped talking. Her son would come soon and then they would see, she was not alone in the world, her Oorjit would protect her, they would all be sorry, yes, every one of them. She spat on the ground and nearly fell.

Toby crossed the street to the construction site. Neelam's sari and one side of her head were chalky with cement dust where she had lain. She had not troubled to brush herself off.

"You know this woman? Get her away from here," a

heavyset woman told him. A child advanced a few steps and she pulled him back against her waist. "You can see what state she's in."

A thin man in a lungi had picked up a handful of gravel. "Go on. Go!"

"My son will kill you!" Neelam screeched.

Toby could smell the sweet, rotted stench of feni as he stepped closer. The tail of Neelam's sari was dry but wrinkled from where she dipped it in liquor and sucked. Later he would find the bottle George had given him two months ago, all but empty. The whiskey, half gone; the vodka low. He would call Regina with this news and learn that Neelam's son had died the year before. "Some kind of accident in the Gulf. That's why I took her on—poor thing, she's got nothing. I had no idea she drinks. Oh, God, Tobes, what a scene!"

But Neelam had not screamed again, as Toby had feared.

"Neelam, it's time to go."

Her eyes were murky and bloodshot, narrowed in anger like a wild boar's, and then she seemed to see Toby for the first time. "Oorjit," she said to him. "My son is coming." She stumbled, as if rage alone had been holding her up, and he took her by the arm and led her home.

Two nights later Jean came to see them. She had aged since he'd seen her. Her hair was cut short and she did not color it. She had put on weight. But her face was unlined, her skin soft when he kissed her. She wore a long skirt and leather sandals.

Her sons were staying with Ranjit's family, she told him. They couldn't miss school. But she had wanted to come back for a few weeks.

"It's good to come home," Toby's father said firmly. He sat next to Toby on the sofa. The pipes were being replaced, so they had both gone to Regina's to bathe and had returned with damp hair, clean clothes. Toby worried that they seemed like a matched set, with only a short span of years separating them—that Jean might too easily see what Toby would become.

"Yes, Uncle, you're right." She smiled and Toby was struck by a new gentleness in her, both sad and tired.

"I'm sorry about Ranjit," Toby said, and she thanked him.

"These things are difficult." Toby's father cleared his throat. "Terrible. But then you go forward. And you have your sons, that is the important thing. All these difficulties—" he flicked a hand through the air, his wrist thin and fragile—"they come and come. But children are the reward." He did not look at Toby; he spoke as though Toby weren't in the room.

"Thank you, Uncle," Jean said. Toby saw her eyes fill with tears, though she tried to smile. "Actually, my parents are trying to convince me to come back to stay. But there's the house, the boys are in school . . . Dev wants to be a doctor. He wants to go to Cornell."

They spoke of her family, of the party she had missed. A few minutes later his father got up to kiss Jean. "Good night," he said tenderly, reminding Toby of what his father had lost when Jean didn't come back.

Jean stood, looking after him, and then she turned to Toby. "Your father looks good. Tired, maybe."

"It's been a crazy week." Toby told the story of the flood. He told it the way Regina might tell it at a party months later, as though it had all been funny, the brothers and the pool of water, the sleeping servant, Satip and the promised new pump. He did not mention Neelam. He did not mention the packet of letters his father slipped from the waterlogged boxes of his mother's belongings, though they must have been illegible. He did not mention Michael, who had come from Regina's at sunset to suggest a jog.

"I've taken up running," Toby told her.

"Good for you."

When she had finished her drink, Toby walked Jean to the gate.

"Oh, God, all this construction! It doesn't seem real." She looked across to the site where her family's house had stood eight months before. The workers had retreated into makeshift shelters around the property, and Toby thought of Neelam, asleep in her room. Michael had objected to keeping her on, but Toby had insisted. Where else could she go? And anyway, he was fond of her. She would stay until the priests at St. Anthony's had found a clinic to accept her.

"I still can't believe the house is gone." Jean stared at the flat building. "I know Dad had to do it, but don't you hate this? Don't you hate looking at it?"

Toby didn't mind terribly, but he knew it wasn't the moment to say so. For the first time he realized he had not thought to follow Jean. She had gone and he had stayed; he had chosen India. It had never before occurred to him to think in such terms. He had barely noticed the choices he had made or that they were choices at all; one thing seemed to lead to the next and he had fallen into a life that had not seemed to require much vision. But perhaps he had seen what he needed.

"I miss the garden," Jean said. "I miss all the gardens. And all the trees . . . Do you remember the day Stephen told us there was a cobra in the brush pile? You went dead pale. Mummy thought you would faint."

That was something Toby didn't remember. "Are you sure that was me?"

But he let Jean tell him the story and then he kissed her good-bye and promised to see her again, once more at least, before she had to go.

We Think of You Every Day

At first letters from Simon came two or three times a week. The morning postman, who was stout, preferred not to climb the steps to put his deliveries directly into the hands of the waiting Almeidas. Instead he called up from the gate each day until someone from the house came down to meet him. Though Essie had complained about such laziness (and at Christmas made a point of giving a more generous tip to the afternoon postman), going down to collect the mail had become a fixture in her daily routine. She stopped whatever she was doing—folding the washing or scrubbing the carrots—and wiped her hands on her skirt, and shook her head at Lila, the kitchen girl, who had long since stopped offering to fetch the mail herself. If the baby was awake, he went bouncing down on his mother's hip to meet the postman too, and when Essie came up again with a heavier step, the baby's arms around her neck and a thatch of mail in one hand, she could be heard grumbling about fat men who could do with a bit of stair climbing instead of expecting heaven and earth to come to them. Lila suspected that Essie guarded this task so jealously—and towed Jude along—because she was determined that the postman should see firsthand the inconvenience he caused. Essie even put off her marketing until he had come.

When she had brought the mail upstairs, the baby, who was three, was released to run in circles around the chairs and table, and before anything else—before resuming her work with the laundry or vegetables, before setting out to market at last—Essie sifted through her letters. Lila had learned never to interrupt her. Letters for her husband, Francis, were kept aside, unless they were business matters that Essie intended to discuss with him, or from mutual acquaintances who surely intended Essie to have their news as well, or represented any kind of mystery, which she could not resist. Bills, invitations, notes from cousins, aunts, her brother in Coimbatore—she flicked through them without stopping, pausing only when she found something from her elder son, Simon. Usually this was addressed to Essie and Francis, and she took it at once into her own custody. Occasionally Simon sent notes to his older sister, Marian, who was twelve, but Essie did not believe in secrets between mother and daughter and kept these as well.

She did not have time to open these letters right away. In another hour the tiffin-wallah would arrive to pick up Francis's meal; two hours later, at midday, Marian would come home from school to eat. Essie folded her son's letters carefully into the crocheted bag with drawstring handles where she kept her prayer cards and rosary. She tucked the bag beneath her pillow or in a corner of her cupboard, someplace where a small treasure might be stowed, until a lull in the afternoon when she had leisure to read and answer it.

Only when the mail had been sorted did her day resume: wet bedsheets, heavy as canvas, flung over the lines to dry; her stained blade against the carrot; the baby's sticky fingers leaving marks on the chair; and the trip to the market, where the best fish would have already gone.

• • •

That was during Simon's first term at St. Stanislaus School for Boys in Mysore, where he began to board when he was eleven. The school was an offshoot of St. Stanislaus Seminary, intended to educate boys who would go on to the priesthood, and it was a point of family pride that Simon had been selected. "Actually, he's won a scholarship," Essie did not mind telling the mothers of less-fortunate sons. Her husband's sister, who lived across the street, had a son nearly Simon's age who seemed chiefly interested in bugs. Little Michael Fernandez, born only a week before Simon, with nice fat legs that Essie had envied all the long, worrying months when Simon seemed unable to put on weight, had grown into a sluggish boy. She could put all that behind her now; she could walk to church imagining the way her pride would multiply, like the fish and the loaves, on the day when Simon took Holy Orders. She could shake her head with a modest smile when other mothers congratulated her. "God has been very good to us."

In fact, Simon's marks were well above average but not outstanding. His admission was largely Essie's achievement, the result of a long and vigorous campaign. Within Santa Clara, seven parishes flourished in a grid of streets named for saints and martyrs, and Essie had thrown herself into the workings of St. Jerome. She taught Communion classes, served on the Catholic Charismatic Renewal Council, and also on committees for church improvement and charitable outreach. She had cajoled her husband to pull whatever strings he could to secure support for Simon from his university contacts, and she had begged recommendations from the priests. One day she took Simon to town, his hair combed back sharply, his face scrubbed clean of any expression but acquiescence, to meet Bishop Percival Fonseca, who agreed to write a letter on the boy's behalf. She herself had kept up a tireless correspondence with the priests of St. Stanislaus, some of whom she had befriended when family matters took her to Mysore. For three years she had shaved what she could from the household budget to spend on Simon's tutoring, after-school sessions in Latin and religious history to prepare him for the rigors of the pre-seminary program. The news of his acceptance had rung through her with the power of a great cathedral bell toll, solemn and magnificent. She sat, trembling, felled by it. Simon would be a priest, respected, secure. His future was assured.

In the afternoons, when Marian had gone back to school and the baby slept, when the kitchen might be quiet for an hour, Essie read his latest letter. When she was finished, instead of closing her eyes herself, she sat in the front room to answer him. For as long as she could spare, she wrote, her shoulders rounded, her head bent, her pen moving ravenously across the page. Six, eight, ten sheets might be swallowed up at a sitting. She stopped only when she was interrupted by the arrival of the afternoon post. This postman knew to come right up the stairs to the landing. Sometimes she kept him waiting while a last urgent sentence spun from her pen, trailing up the margin if she had run out of space. "Much love," she murmured, "Mummy." One minute, one minute only, she assured the postman while she hurriedly addressed the envelope. She snatched a stamp from the little table where she kept her notepaper, a bird's nest of clutter that one day soon she meant to clear, and finally let the letter go.

In the evenings, after supper was finished and the baby put down, Essie made a point of sharing Simon's letters. Sometimes she passed them to Francis or Marian, so they could see for themselves the spiky handwriting, rising up like the points of a fence from sharp hand-ruled lines. These were mostly composed in supervised sessions, in times set aside for the boys to write home, and the Simon of these letters did not sound to Marian like the brother she missed. There was nothing about cricket or football or checkers, nothing about the way they used to signal each other through the open door between their rooms after they'd been put to bed. This Simon reported that Father Ivo was coaching him in Latin. His schoolwork was difficult, but he was trying to keep up. He wrote about the dormitories, the way the boys were taught to keep their beds and cupboards, the medicine he had been made to swallow when he was feverish. Marian caught a glimpse of the brother she knew when he sent a message to Lila that he missed her chapatis, but in most of these letters, he seemed farther away even than Mysore: a twenty-four-hour trip by train, with a gulf of several months before his first visit home.

Francis did not like to make a show of clinging to his son's letters, as Essie did. But he put on his reading glasses and inspected those specimens that came his way. "He needs help with Latin?"

"He's had a late start. Other boys in his class have been at St. Stanislaus's for two, three years already. Simon will have to work harder than the others at first."

Francis did not like the idea of his son at a disadvantage. "I'll write to the head and explain the matter."

Essie clicked her tongue. "Don't make trouble, Frank! The school is aware—already they're helping him. And I've written to all his teachers."

On other nights, she scanned the letters and read only bits aloud. "Most of the other boys seem friendly enough." She bit her lip. "Of course, most of them already know each other. Simon is new to them; it may take some time before he feels comfortable. Poor fellow, he's feeling homesick." She tried to smile at her daughter. "Write him a note, my girl. He says he misses you."

Marian had trouble knowing how to respond to this. She knew, of course, that her brother missed her; she knew it without being told. She and Simon were only a year apart; they had never been separated for more than a few days. But she never imagined that the words themselves—which seemed to belong to aunts and grandparents—would pass between them. When Simon used to tease her too badly, Marian grew very quiet until he left off. When their mother was ill—all the strange, sharp days after the twins were born and one did not live—Simon and Marian spent hours in a dusty corner of the veranda discussing the names of imaginary horses, the places they would go if their father bought a car, the ways they would spend a lakh. Simon, she knew, would buy a drum set, a motorcycle, a house with its own cricket pitch. "Good-bye," he said briefly when it came time for him to leave, though Marian could feel him trembling when she hugged him.

But her mother insisted on more-direct exchanges. "Encourage him a little, darling. These first months are always difficult. Tell him he'll soon make friends."

Mum thinks you'll make friends soon, Marian wrote. But it embarrassed her to make such bold reference to his distress, as though she had caught him in a private sorrow and hadn't the decency to look away.

Francis occasionally scratched a note of his own, a single stern page with news of the university or local politics. But it was Essie who kept in constant contact, Essie who wrote to Father Ivo for news of Simon's health and demeanor, Essie who reminded Father Ignatius that Simon must drink only goats' milk. "A little cows' milk in cooking is not always harmful," she explained, "but too much upsets his system."

She had always liked the hours after eleven, when the house seemed to belong only to her. Francis kept to a strict sleeping schedule, and the baby seldom woke before morning. For a brief time nothing was required of her, and she was free to follow the course of her own thoughts without interruption. But Simon's letters introduced an element of disturbance, and she spent her nights writing to him until her fingers cramped. *We think of you every day, my son. When you're feeling lonely, trust in God's strength; He is always with you.* She tried to ignore Simon's pleas to come home; she knew she must not encourage such lines of thinking. But alone with his letters, she could not help herself. *God knows your pain, my son. He has given you this opportunity. Think of this time as a sacrifice for your future happiness, and offer up all your hardships to the Lord. He will hear you.*

When she had finished, Essie folded her son's latest letter to keep in the back of her wardrobe with other papers she had saved, some since her own childhood. She had covered small boxes with pretty paper to hold Simon's letters and already, after only half a term, the first was nearly full. She imagined boxes stacked from floor to ceiling by the time he had finished his tenure at St. Stanny's: a tower of his faith and hers.

When Simon had been at school two months, his letters took on a new shrillness. It seemed to Essie that she could hear her son's voice, a thin, high spire rising from the pages he had written. He begged to come home.

Essie read these letters in silence, lips pressed tightly together to prevent the voice in Simon's letters from finding breath in her own person. It was for Simon's own good, she decided, that she must shield Francis and Marian from such raw appeals. Marian was too attached to Simon to view this period of adjustment in its proper context. And Francis, she knew, would not have the stomach for it; he did his utmost to avoid tension of any kind.

"He's working hard," she told them brightly. "Exams are coming, so of course he's feeling anxious. He's given up sweets for Lent."

In fact, Simon had not responded to his mother's queries about his preparations for Easter, or even to Marian's halting questions about the cricket team. But Essie persisted, writing every day with some new prayer or inspiration. During Lent her letters increased. Meditations on Christ's agony, the fear that surely must have sickened Him, the temptations He endured while fasting in the desert, were set against a record of her own self-denial. She had foregone all meat and poultry and sometimes experienced dizzy spells, when the earth stopped revolving but her blood still whirled with echoed motion. At such times her pen against paper seemed to anchor her, and she wrote to Simon as if he were already the priest she dreamt he would become. It was for his sake, she told him, for the sake of his future, that she endured the pain of their separation. But the truth was that she felt a new and glorious intimacy with this son. Before he left home he had begun to seem remote to her—already on his way to being a man she would not understand. Now only the deepest expressions of her faith could sustain him. Words flooded through her, a stream of such ceaseless power that she believed her discourse with her son had been in some way sanctified.

One night, she went to sit with Marian. It was long past the hour when Marian should have been sleeping, but she stirred when Essie sat on the edge of her bed. "Awake, my girl?" She stroked her daughter's hair. "You know my brother John went away to boarding school when he was even younger than Simon. Such stories he used to tell us!" It would be that way for Simon too, she promised Marian. He would make friends to last a lifetime. He would be invited all over the country by other boys' families, lavish trips to Delhi or Madras—places he could never go on what their father earned. As she spoke she began to see the world her son would inhabit: the kind, learned priests, the laughing young boys, the pillow fights and tuck-box feasts.

When Marian fell back to sleep, Essie remained beside her. Already her girl was twelve. In another twelve years, Essie might be sifting through proposals. She lay down next to her daughter and tried instead to think of the stories she had told about Simon, stories certain to come true.

In April the days swelled with heat. The sky stretched overhead, tight as a blister, and the baby's fever spiked. Essie thought he had heatstroke until his face erupted in a rash. The next day it had spread over his body; he pulled at his clothes and cried when anyone tried to pick him up.

Essie dashed off a quick note to Simon. *I may not be able to write for the next few days. Your brother has a bad case of measles—his temperature is running very high. Keep him in your prayers.*

On Good Friday, when Jude's fever had dropped nearly to normal, Essie decided she could get away long enough to attend the Passion. She had sent Marian to an early service, so the baby would not be left with only Lila. "I'll sit on the right side, near the aisle." She took up the crocheted bag that held her rosary and looped it around her wrist. "If anything happens, let Lila stay with the baby and you run and find me, you understand?"

When she had gone, Marian sat in the dusky light of her mother's bedroom and watched her brother sleep. All the shades were drawn; he had grown sensitive to light. The rash on his face was beginning to fade, but patches of his skin appeared darker, stained—the color of water from rusty pipes. She wondered about the twin who had died, whether that baby, her sister, would have had the measles too. She and Simon had gotten measles at the same time.

She read her book for a few minutes, but in the dim light her eyes began to ache. It was a relief to hear the bell at the gate jangling; she ran downstairs, where the afternoon postman was reaching into his sack.

"Coming down to meet me!" He smiled. "Handsome boys are already writing?"

Marian shook her head no—of course, no—and he laughed at her vehemence.

"Soon, soon," he said, in the same tone her grandfather used when he was pretending to search his pockets for a five-rupee note he intended to give her: half a joke, half a promise. Marian took the mail and said nothing, though he tapped her chin with the back of his finger and laughed again before going.

A letter had come from Simon, addressed to her mother. It did not occur to Marian not to read it. "It's a family letter," Essie said lightly whenever anything was addressed to Marian. "Of course it's meant for us all."

After the brightness of the afternoon sun, the bedroom was dark and close. Jude had fallen into a deeper sleep, still and sweaty. Marian listened to the woolly sound of his breathing as she read. The letter was short, not much longer than the telegrams their grandfather sent on birthdays. Simon mentioned none of the progress her mother had described, none of the boys who had become his friends. He could not keep up in Latin. He could not sleep at night. An older boy woke him up again; he did not know what to do. Please, could he come home?

Marian put the letter down in confusion. She understood at once that her mother had deliberately hidden Simon's misery, but the revelation jolted her—a sudden stop on a carnival ride, leaving her swinging in midair. She had been with Simon at Juhu the day she rode a Ferris wheel; she had clutched Simon's hand until the nausea passed and she could look down to where their mother smiled and waved below. She looked different, small, from such a height. They had spotted camels, a juggler, a family of five boys, all dressed alike. The sound of voices drifted up to where she and Simon hung suspended in the sky. Then the car had lurched, tipping forward, and they trundled back down to earth, everything its proper size again.

In the bedroom, faced with Simon's letter, Marian suddenly saw her mother from an alarming new angle. She had heard Essie lie before, of course: small white lies, the sort of lies routinely forgiven in confessionals. False appointments to avoid unwanted meetings, overblown courtesies, a quick twist away from one topic or another when she wished to deflect Francis's attention. But the idea that her mother was keeping such a secret as this bewildered Marian so much that her own course of action was not quite clear. Even Simon's unhappiness was distorting. Dimly she imagined cruel older boys shaking her brother awake to tease him, and she felt convulsed with a pity too powerful to express.

Jude put a fist to his eye, frowning in his sleep. He would soon wake, her mother would soon be home. Marian realized she must speak to her father, but she could not admit to having seen the letter—her mother would be furious. She stuffed it back in its envelope and then into her pocket. Later she would put it at the bottom of the rubbish pile, where it would not be found.

"What's this I hear? Simon wants to come home?"

Essie looked up in shock. "What's this nonsense?" she asked sharply. "What makes you say such a thing?"

For several days Francis had not acted on the news that his

son was unhappy at boarding school. His initial dismay had curdled; he could not think of Simon without reflecting with irritation that Essie had landed them in this mess and now he had been dragged right to the center of it.

They had just finished dinner. Marian had excused herself to study and Jude had fallen asleep, still weak though the worst of the fever had passed. Francis saw with some satisfaction that his wife had gone absolutely still, clearly taken aback.

He shook his head sagely. "You're not the only one who can read and write. People other than you receive letters."

"But what has he said to you?" She stared at him, her face drawn and tight. Francis did not answer right away, enjoying the rare knowledge that his wife was anxious to hear what he had to say.

"He doesn't like the school—that is the point." He could hear for himself how negligible such a complaint would sound to his wife and struggled to recall some sharper detail, something to reveal his unexpected acquaintance with Simon's predicament. "And there's this trouble with Latin."

Essie shook her head briskly and began to spoon the last of the raita into a glass, as if the matter had already been settled. "Don't be ridiculous, Frank. He's only been there one term. He needs time to adjust."

"There's no need for all this adjusting difficulty if we bring him home. I've been thinking he's better off here."

"Oh, you've been thinking! Suddenly you've been thinking!"

This was less a question than an opportunity to broadcast her derision. She pushed plates into one another, an angry clattering, and Francis raised his voice over the din.

"He's a young boy still. Time enough later to send him to school." He thought of Simon the day they took him to the station. They had handed him over to the teacher who would oversee the journey to the school and said good-bye on the platform. Francis found it painful to remember how small his son looked in the uniform jacket, like a child in a man's coat. Essie had cut it far too large in the shoulders, hoping it would last two years at least. "The point is, we can wait a year or two." He tried to speak with decision, as though to his subordinates at the university. He was a man of authority, of judgment, he often wished to remind his wife. All day long students and their parents flocked to his office, seeking his opinion.

"Listen to him! One of the best schools in the country—and the child has won a scholarship! All that is lost if we bring him home now. What happens in a year or two, Frank? Suddenly you can pay for his fees?"

Francis flicked his hand through the air, brushing away the familiar issue of his own earnings. She had begun to speak loudly, as though to an audience in other rooms, and Francis wondered if Marian could hear them. "Leave it for now," he said. "We can discuss it another time."

But Essie would not be stopped. She had begun to talk past Francis, as if he had already left her presence. "Suddenly he comes pushing his nose in. Where is he when I need his help? And I should say nothing, is that it?"

She did not give him time to answer; her stream of grievances rolled on. Francis did not indulge her with even the appearance of listening but poured himself a glass of water and drank deeply. He had the feeling, as often happened when it came to the management of the children, that he was standing by the side of the tracks with one hand feebly in the air as a train barreled past. Usually he did not permit this state of affairs to worry him. He enjoyed various offices he performed—counting out money for new shoes each year, examining papers with good marks before kissing one or another on the forehead. He enjoyed the pleasant sensation, as he cycled home each evening from the station, that his household was in full swing. A meal would presently be served, his children gathered around the table. He was not inclined to view his wife with any particular satisfaction; such hopes had not survived the raw silences of their first months together. But they had produced a house full of noise and purpose.

And it was not as if the children themselves were rushing away, helter-skelter, to some distant station. To Francis, despite the evidence of churning change, they remained constant. They filled his house, they cycled through illnesses, they replaced toys with books. He knew Essie lamented the loss of baby fat, the outgrown garments; she had cried over the christening dress all three had worn as infants, now packed away in camphor. But Francis preferred to take a longer view. They would always be his children. Better, perhaps, to wait until they were older, when Essie's iron hold on them had weakened, before he staked his claim.

"My son could go to one of the top schools in the country or he could go down the road and waste his best chance, but I should keep quiet . . ."

Essie's grievances billowed between them, black as smoke until it was difficult to breathe. Francis thought of the cool relief of the street, his wife's voice dissipating to nothing, the promise of a hand of cards at his club. It occurred to him that in a few years he could take Simon with him.

She stacked the dishes—usually a task she left to the girl, but one she had now taken on with alarming fierceness. Francis expected something to shatter. "Lila, come and take these!" Suddenly she turned on Francis once more. "He's a young boy—naturally he's homesick. How many boys go to boarding school? You think it's different for any of them? You think it's easy for me to send my son away? But I am thinking of his future."

The suggestion that he was soft was Francis's undoing. "Enough," he said, a grumbling surrender, and got up from the table, leaving Essie to bang the pots and pans and carry on muttering long after he had gone.

A week after Simon came home for the summer break, he told his father he did not want to go back to school.

"Still unhappy? Why?"

Simon did not answer. He seemed well enough—not too thin, though Essie had made a fuss. A bit more quiet, perhaps, and shy at first with his sister, but Francis supposed they had reached an awkward age. Simon's marks were good enough and would surely improve.

"What's the matter? It's this Latin course? We can hire a tutor."

Simon's eyes swam with tears, which embarrassed them both. His twelfth birthday was only a few months off, and it seemed to his father that he had grown taller after only five months away. But his face was still a young boy's, soft and hopeful. "Come, what is it?"

"I want to stay home." Simon rubbed his eyes with his fists. He promised to study every day, to be at the top of his class in his neighborhood school. He would work in the house and the garden, he would help take care of Jude. He would not ask to play cricket if Mummy said no. His voice rose, pleading, as he tried to bargain, and then his eyes filled again so that he could not speak. He did not cry out loud when Francis told him the fees had been paid, the scholarship granted, he must go back. But his tears came more swiftly, running down his cheeks and along the sides of his nose, trembling on his upper lip.

"Take." Francis gave him a handkerchief. "You may grow fond of school," he said while the boy blew his nose—and though Francis believed it, he knew he did not sound as if anything could be true but the sight of his son crying. He turned away, as though to give the boy a moment's privacy, when in fact he could not bear to look at him.

But Simon stared at him, a taut and ravaged look, and Francis felt a surge of anger. Essie should have let well enough alone; he did not see the point of all this commotion. The child would have been fine in the local school, which had sufficed for Francis and his brother and most of their friends. But she was always pushing one thing or another, and he knew his house would be turned upside down if he brought it up again. Besides, they had made a beginning. They had scrimped to find money for the fees, the uniform, the tuck-box and trunks. Francis himself had applied to colleagues for their backing. What would they say if he pulled the boy from school so soon? It wasn't only a matter of his own reputation, but of Simon's as well. The boy would be considered too soft, too weak. *And look at him,* Francis thought with sudden pride. He had grown nearly to his father's shoulder. His arms and legs were strong. Francis imagined other days his son would come home from school, clear-eyed and brave, a boy fit for anything. Francis would tell him then that he needn't go on to seminary, he could study whatever he chose. Not to worry, he imagined saying. I will see to your education. But what was the point of such conversation now? It would only prevent the boy from settling down. He wanted to tell his son not to worry, not to be ashamed; such changes were always disruptive. You are stronger than you know, he wanted to say.

"Try one more year. You've been through the worst of it already."

Simon was no longer crying, but his breaths came in jerks. The answer his father had already given him seemed to harden on his face, a thin and brittle mask, holding the muscles tightly in place. Already the boy had mastered himself.

"You'll be fine," Francis told him.

• • •

The year Simon turned fifteen, Jude Almeida, seven years old, felt his first loose tooth. Several boys he knew had lost teeth already—even his cousin Mark, who was four months younger than Jude. Mark lived across the street and came over at once to bare his teeth for Jude. He poked his tongue into the blank space. "See?"

"Where did it go?" Jude had a horror of swallowing his tooth, of feeling its thorny passage down his throat and into his belly. He could not even take the tablets his mother gave him with water; they had to be crushed with fruit.

Mark opened his fist. The tooth was small and not as square as Jude had expected. "I was pushing it with my tongue and suddenly I felt it go. I spit it out on my plate." Jude imagined a clean plate and the glassy clatter of the tooth upon it. Mark held his open hand up higher. "You see? Just there? That's blood at the tip," he said with satisfaction.

Jude would not allow himself to ask if it had hurt. "What will you do with it?"

Mark closed his fist, as though the question posed a threat. "Mumma kept Ian's first tooth in a little box and now she's choosing one for me." His tongue found its way to the gap again, pressing there for a moment before he told Jude that he thought he could feel the new tooth growing in already.

It was Palm Sunday. Both boys were dressed in good shirts and shorts for Mass, but Aunty Grace came out on her veranda to call for Mark—had he washed his face properly, and no, he couldn't take his tooth to church. Mark started back across St. Hilary Road while Aunty Grace held the door open. She smiled at Jude. "Lucky boy—your brother is coming home! When does he get in?"

Jude did not know the exact time. But Simon's train would arrive in the evening, and Simon might reach Santa Clara before dinner. He had not seen his brother since the Christmas holiday.

Inside his own house, Jude found his mother moving between her bedroom and the long mirror in the hallway where Marian stood braiding her hair. His mother wore a deep blue underskirt that rustled as she walked, and one hand was behind her back, clutching her sari blouse shut. "Just do me up, darling." Jude watched as Marian let go of her own braid (it sprang partly loose) and began to fasten hooks and eyes.

The rest of the family would eat after Mass, but Jude had not yet received his First Communion. He ate a cold chapati rolled up with jam and a banana, then slowly began to peel another banana. His mother had tucked one corner of her sari into the waistband of her skirt and quickly pleated the rest of the fabric. "Marian! You're ready? We must go!"

Jude's father was sitting on the balcony, reading the newspaper. He consulted his pocket watch. "There's forty minutes still," he said, with no sign of making a movement.

"What's wrong with you, Frank! All the good seats will be gone!"

"We'll go now and keep seats," Marian said. "Dad can bring Jude in a few minutes."

"Is it too much to ask that the family go together?" Jude's mother said in a grumbling voice, but she looped the crocheted bag with her rosary and prayer cards around her wrist and swept away with Marian.

Jude's father looked up briefly. "We'll go in twenty minutes," he said, and returned to his paper.

In the room Jude shared with Simon (when Simon was home, twice a year), both beds had been freshly made. When Simon was at school, his bed was usually covered with clothes to be washed or mended or with old linens intended for the ragman. But now all that had been cleared away, the cotton cover pulled tight over the pillow, Simon's bed waiting for him. Jude sat at its foot, took a large bite of his banana and felt it catch, just for a moment, on his loose front tooth. He had forgotten about it until the sudden tug reminded him; now he tested it with his thumb. Still stiff—like the old hinge downstairs that needed oil, his mother said—but it moved a bit. He wondered if he had grown since Simon's last visit, if Simon would notice.

When he had finished the banana, he threw the peel in the kitchen pail and wandered through his mother's bedroom, which smelled faintly of rose water and more strongly of camphor. Another of her saris lay thrown across her bed, a spill of watery silk that Jude would have liked to roll in. He did not dare; that was the sort of thing she always discovered later.

Opposite the bed were two large wardrobes where clothes were kept away from damp and insects. Jude backed against one to measure himself, his hand rolling off the top of his head and finding a slightly different spot each time; it was impossible to know if he'd grown one inch or three or not really at all. He would ask Simon. Then he remembered what Mark had told him about Aunty Grace's boxes and wondered if his mother had kept one of Simon's teeth all this time, or even one of Marian's. Perhaps she already had a place put aside for his own.

The wardrobe doors latched in the center, and Jude opened them wide, like shutters. The scent of camphor intensified, a strong, musty smell that Jude associated with the scratchy woolen sweaters he wore in the cool season. On one side was a dense thicket of skirts and saris, on the other a rack of shelves for clothes and papers. His mother's slippers were tumbled on the wardrobe floor (though Jude was made to keep his shoes neatly in pairs and not to scuff them). Stacks of folded clothes slid into one another—such a jumble of blouses and slippery scarves that at first Jude did not see the box his mother kept behind them. It looked far too large for teeth, but Jude pulled it out anyway.

Inside he found letters. At first he was disappointed; her closet was full of papers, most soft and yellowed with age. But the writing looked familiar, and as Jude read he realized the letters were from Simon. He had never read letters from his brother—except for birthday cards once a year, which were given to Jude after his mother had opened them. Simon rarely wrote to the family, not even in the cards, which Jude knew his mother bought ahead of time and packed in Simon's trunk. At best he scrawled a few cramped words beneath the printed message. But here were pages and pages of letters, more words than he could imagine his brother saying. It did not seem strange or wrong to want to read them.

His father called to him; it was nearly time to go. Jude took a handful of the letters—not enough to be missed—and put the box back into the closet, making sure to cover it again with clothes. He hid the letters beneath his pillow, then worried that his mother might find them there if she turned down the bed when it was time to sleep. He slid them beneath the mattress and ran, quick, quick, before his father called again.

Simon's train arrived at Churchgate over an hour late. A teacher and two older seminary students had been engaged to accompany all the St. Stanny's students from Mysore to Bombay, and Essie and Francis had gone to meet Simon at the station. Jude waited in the garden, wiggling his tooth or climbing the gate to keep a sharp lookout for taxis. Occasionally his impatience sparked to runs to the corner of the road, to see if they were coming. Finally Marian called him upstairs; it would soon be dark.

He had read a few of Simon's letters while the household napped after Mass, and he'd found them encouraging. They were written four years ago, but Simon had missed home so keenly that he had begged to return. Jude imagined that this new Simon, the Simon of the letters, would be so happy to see them all that perhaps he would give up his school, his friends, even his football team, and stay in Santa Clara. Jude and Simon would share a room all year. Simon would teach Jude to bounce a ball against his feet, thighs, and head without ever letting it touch the ground.

It was nearly time for dinner when the taxi finally pulled up at the gate. Jude went running down to meet them, Marian following right behind, and though Simon smiled at them both and hugged Marian briefly, he seemed more tired than happy. With that, all their rushing came to a halt and they fell back from him, strangely reticent, as if the journey and all the months away still set Simon apart. He stood near the taxi door while the driver and Francis struggled with the trunks.

"Such a long trip," Essie fussed. "More than twenty-four hours, and then this delay! Come, son, come and eat something and then you can sleep early."

"I'm fine," Simon said in his rough, low voice. Jude wanted to pull on his brother's hand, to explain about his tooth the way he would have explained to the Simon of the letters. But that Simon, a Simon he had never met, already seemed closer to Jude than the brother who stood before him: fifteen years old and as tall as his mother, dark hair on his upper lip, not smiling now but watchful. Even Marian felt shy of him and took Jude's hand as they went inside.

At dinner, Essie kept up a constant chatter, throwing questions this way and that as if conversation were a ball that must stay airborne. Jude tried to show Simon his loose tooth, but she clicked her tongue. "Not at the table, darling!" She laughed, looking around at all of them but especially at Simon, as if Jude had told a joke and she must encourage them to enjoy it.

Later, when she had bathed Jude and dressed him for sleep, she sent him to say good night to his father and sister. Jude slowly made his way to the front veranda, where his father was smoking, and then step by step to the dining table, where Marian studied each night for exams. By the time he came back, his mother was sitting at the foot of his bed, telling Simon all the visits she had planned for them the following day. "So many people are waiting to see you!" When she noticed Jude, she got up and clapped her hands twice. "Into bed, Master Jude."

"I want to show Simon my tooth."

She pretended to frown but waited in the doorway to watch. "Go on, then."

Jude had cleaned his teeth with extra vigor (in hopes of advancing his case), and he thought it was possible that he had made a real difference. He stood before Simon, his mouth open and his top lip curled back, rocking the tooth back and forth between thumb and forefinger. It was not as wobbly as Mark's tooth had been, but it was certainly moving.

He could not tell what his brother was thinking. Simon reclined against his pillow, a book of guitar chords in his hand. His hair was longer than Jude had ever seen it, falling past the tops of his ears.

Jude leaned closer and spoke around his fingers. "Schee?" he lisped.

His mother laughed. "It's not ready yet, son. There, that's enough for one night. Time to sleep. Simon?"

"What?"

"Yes, Mum," she prompted, and waited until he had mumbled the words back to her. "You should sleep soon too, son. All the traveling, you must be exhausted."

"In a few minutes."

"Ten minutes only. I'll come back to turn off the light. Jude, kiss your brother and climb into bed." She lingered a moment longer and then moved away.

Jude stood at Simon's bedside, waited for his brother to kiss him good night. "You're too old for all that," Simon said gruffly.

Jude stood staunchly in place, still thinking of Simon's letters. "Next year I could go to school with you."

"Don't be stupid."

"But I could! I wouldn't be lonely." Already, though, Jude was counting the lonely months ahead. Simon would be in Santa Clara only until the beginning of July, when St. Stanny's resumed. He would not come back until Christmas. "Or you could stay home. Just tell Mummy you want to stay home."

Simon looked up suddenly and for a moment Jude felt his brother's breath, hot and close on his own face. He could see dark hairs on Simon's chin and upper lip, the nose that had never been broken but looked as if two pieces had been jointed together, the fierce dark eyebrows. Simon stared at him, his eyes narrowed.

"Let's see that tooth again," he said. Jude's mouth yawned open, and Simon prodded the tooth as much as it would go. "Mum doesn't know what she's talking about. That could come out anytime. We could pull it right now."

For a moment Jude wavered.

Simon shrugged. "Shouldn't hurt too much. It'll be over in two minutes. Then you can surprise everyone tomorrow."

Jude thought of the tooth in Mark's hand, how small it had looked. He nodded.

"Good." Simon moved with sudden energy, rummaging through the cupboard until he had unraveled a length of thread. Soon Jude was standing in a doorway with one end of the thread tied around the tooth and the other end tied to the doorknob. He stared at the open door with dread. "One quick jerk," Simon said. "Ready? Ready?" and without waiting for an answer he slammed the door shut.

The tooth did not come out on the first try. It was wrenched nearly free, but though Jude was howling, his face pale and streaming with tears, though Marian and Essie came running and even Francis hurried up from the veranda with a sudden stab of fear that his boys, who had seemed safe, were all along in danger, the tooth still clung to Jude's bloody gum and had to be yanked again.

"What is the matter with you!" Essie cried when she saw Simon's mutinous face. He looked at his little brother, the thread still dangling from Jude's wet mouth, and then he looked at her and whatever sorrow or tenderness the sight of Jude had awakened was gone. He stared at Essie, hard and unflinching, someone Essie had never imagined or met. She stopped shouting. Her mouth flew open, filled with what she might once have said to him, but no sound came. Simon waited until she ducked her head, defeated, before he turned to Jude.

"You'll be fine," he said, and left them.

Marian watched in astonishment. Normally her mother would have flown into a rage at such behavior, but Essie only caught Jude in her embrace, her arms crossed over his chest. "Hang on, son, just one pull more." She sounded shaken, even afraid; Jude began to cry again. "Go on, my girl, finish it." Marian picked up the string and tugged and before Jude could cry out again the tooth had clattered to the floor.

Marian picked it up and washed it. She took a rag from the kitchen and cleaned the thin bloody swirls on the floor. Simon had gone, perhaps to the veranda with Francis, and Essie was holding Jude in her lap. She helped him hold a clean cloth, doused in ice water, to the gap in his mouth. He could not speak when Marian showed him the tooth, but his eyes, still huge with pain and shock, moved to her face. "I'll keep it for you," she offered.

"Go back and study, my girl. We're fine here." Her mother rocked Jude against her chest. "There, son, all finished now. Older boys can be rough, that's all. You don't be frightened. Boys who go away to school are rough."

Marian stood on the far side of the door for a moment, out of her mother's sight but listening. She felt the current of some greater violence running through her family, but she could not put her finger on what any of it meant or even how it had begun. She wondered how much her mother knew; if even Simon, somehow at the center of it all, could have explained. Years later, when she thought back to the letter she'd destroyed and understood its full meaning, she pushed the idea that her mother must have known the truth as far from her mind as she possibly could. Occasionally, at odd moments, it sprang back to catch her: once when she found a rosary in her nightstand drawer; once when a deliveryman came to her door with a package; once when she was pregnant and a wave of nausea reminded her of the Ferris wheel. She remembered how small her mother had appeared that day at Juhu, waving foolishly from the ground, her tiny voice calling out not to be afraid.

Carrying

For weeks Rowena has intended to tell her husband about her appointment, but on the morning of her meeting, when the telephone rings, Rowena snatches it up before Mark or his mother, Grace, can answer.

"Who is it, darling? Who?" Grace asks before the caller has a chance to speak. Her voice is high and curious, with a touch of irritation; the phone is one of Grace's greatest pleasures and Rowena knows that by picking it up she has crossed one of the lines her mother-in-law will never admit to. Rowena and Mark are visiting Grace in Santa Clara, a suburb just north of Mumbai where they both grew up before moving to the States.

"Is this Rowena speaking? Rowena, Sonali here." Sonali's voice is so strong and resonant that Rowena imagines Mark can hear every word through the receiver. She turns away from the breakfast table, where Mark holds their daughter, Lizzie, in his lap. Outside, palm fronds hang in the sky, dusty and still. Rowena remembers what it was like to smoke out of windows before she quit, imagines her voice drifting out over the garden.

"Yes. Hi, hi—" She does not want to say Sonali's name in Mark's presence. "How are you?"

Grace has not let the matter drop. "Of course it may be for you, I don't know who you've given the number to . . ."

Rowena says as little as possible while Sonali briskly confirms their appointment.

"Can we make it a bit earlier, in an hour or so?" Sonali asks. "I have to go off to some terrible luncheon in Colabo, a committee to form a committee to do God knows what. But come beforehand, we can have a few minutes at least. You have the address?"

Grace is still waiting when Rowena puts down the receiver. "It was Aunty Beryl," she says quickly, "just telling me where to meet her for lunch." Rowena's aunt Beryl lives in nearby Pali Hill, in the house where Rowena was raised after her own mother died.

"But I've been wanting to speak to Beryl! I meant to phone her yesterday."

"I'm sorry, Mum. I would have put you on, but she was rushing out of the house."

Grace looks away, her lips moving briefly against each other in a gesture of such delicate agitation that Rowena is reminded of a cat. "It's strange she didn't ask to speak to me."

Mark looks at Rowena over Lizzie's head. "She's meeting you in town?" Lizzie is trying with both hands to grasp his cup of tea, but Mark catches her fingers and holds them fast. "That's hot," he warns her. "Wait 'til it cools." Lizzie puffs her cheeks and begins to blow. She is four years old, their only child. Rowena would like another. Mark says he's happy as they are—a temporary stance, Rowena believes. A kind of indolence from which she must rouse him.

"You should ride in with her," he says.

"She has to see someone first." Rowena busies herself with the kettle, pouring a cup of tea she will not have time to drink. She keeps her voice calm, her hands steady, though her stomach feels sour. She has told Mark and Grace that she will spend the day shopping in the city, a story that, she comforts herself, is at least partially true. She had not intended to invent a lunch, to involve Beryl. "Actually, she may not be able to get away in time to meet me. We'll see."

For the past several days, Rowena has worried that all her plans will go awry, that Mark will announce he'd like to join her. They used to go on such outings together: wandering in and out of shops, choosing bedspreads, letter paper, a small carved wooden screen that Mark fit into their canvas duffel for the trip back to the States.

But he just nods, one arm looped around Lizzie, the other holding the *Times of India*. His hair is still thick and curly but beginning to gray. He hasn't shaved in two days, reminding Rowena of days when he was a resident and buried his face in her neck the moment he came home. "You're taking the train in? Maybe she can give you a lift home."

"Oh, no, darling! Not the train. It's so hot and dirty! And pickpockets everywhere. Take a taxi. I can give you money if you need."

Grace has never liked the commuter train, which is so crowded during the morning and evening rushes that men near the open doorways have been known to fall off. When Rowena and Mark were first married, they used to laugh off her objections and take the train together, Rowena passing up the peace of the ladies' compartment to ride in a regular car with Mark.

"A cab might be simpler if you have bags." Mark returns to his newspaper. "Just pay the guy to stay with you all day."

Rowena has bathed and dressed early, but Mark hasn't yet washed. He is wearing an old T-shirt, bright red running shorts, and reading glasses. His slippers are tumbled near the door, where he left them early that morning. He spent nearly an hour walking with Lizzie at dawn, up and down the driveway and on the sandy bit of road outside the compound. They only arrived from the States a week ago, and Lizzie has not quite adjusted to her new nights and days.

Now she hangs over Mark's teacup, clamoring for a sip, and Grace holds out her arms to the child. "Come, baby, let Daddy have his tea. I'll give you your own cup, all for you." She fills a mug with milk and adds a thin stream of tea from the kettle.

"Now you stir," Lizzie tells her.

"That's right." Grace laughs. "Where's our spoon? See, now we're happy. Look at Mumma, doesn't she look nice? She's going to town."

Rowena has dressed as though for work at home, in a pharmaceutical firm where she has cut back to three days a week since they brought Lizzie home. She adjusts the strap of her shoulder bag, Lizzie's adoption files zipped carefully inside, out of sight.

Lizzie considers her mother. "I want to go too," she says stoutly. She is a happy child, fat and healthy, with curly black hair all over her head that looks like Mark's. When people notice a resemblance, Rowena says nothing to dissuade them.

"No, no, baby. You stay with Grandma." Grace hugs her, realizing her mistake, and Rowena moves quickly to kiss the child—a smacking kiss to make Lizzie laugh. She and Mark prefer not to make a production of leaving.

"You can play with your cousins," she says in a bright voice. Mark's sister and her family live in the same building, in a flat upstairs; there is a new baby, three weeks old, whom Lizzie adores.

"And later on you have a special visitor coming," Grace adds. "We can make a cake for her." In the holiday season visitors dropped by nearly every evening, and tonight Sister Agnes is expected. After another week she will return to Mysore, where she has worked for years at Holy Family Orphanage. It was Sister Agnes who took Rowena through the wards, the first time Rowena saw Lizzie.

Grace glances at Rowena. "Tell Beryl to come too, if you see her," she offers stiffly.

"I'll be back before dinner," Rowena promises before turning to Mark. "You'll be okay? You may need to lie down with her later." Grace's apartment is still a foreign landscape to Lizzie; when she's tired, the strong-tasting milk or the angry red light of the hot water heater can reduce her to tears. In bright sunlit hours Lizzie is content to be without her mother, but before and after sleep, she has been clinging to Rowena.

Mark yawns widely, the paper rustling between them. "We'll be fine."

Grace smooths Lizzie's bangs from her forehead. "I'll nap with her. Happy to, darling."

"I'm not napping," Lizzie announces.

"After the cake, darling. Not for a long while. Rowena, you have your wallet? Keep it at the bottom of your bag," Grace warns.

"I'd be better off if she left the wallet. Don't go crazy," Mark calls after her—a joke that seems as if it ought to belong to another sort of couple, nothing Rowena imagined she and Mark would become. But she doesn't say anything, just hurries away before Lizzie notices she has gone.

For the first few years, Mark and Rowena both laughed at the postscripts in his mother's letters. He used to read them aloud to her in bed at night, Rowena's head tucked against Mark's chest, his arm reaching around her shoulder to hold the thin blue aerogrammes Grace sent every week. Spring swelled into summer. In the small, dark bedroom of their first apartment, an electric fan trained on the bed and the sheets of the letter trembling in its breeze, Rowena pressed against Mark and listened to rambling accounts of the extra bit of fish his mother bought at the market or the cousin who came to visit and stayed only twenty minutes or how much she gave to the lady collecting for little slum children. Always at the absolute bottom of the last page, Grace sent blessings, hugs, kisses. A month after the wedding, the postscripts began. *I am praying for good news soon.*

Twelve years later, Rowena could still call it all to mind: the futon, soft and warm as bread dough; the fan blades rattling in their cage; the old bureau they shared, its surface littered with matchbooks from bars, Rowena's hair clips and jewelry, Mark's watch, a few crumpled receipts. In those days Mark wore a faded Harvard T-shirt to bed, the letters cracked and flaking, and Rowena used to drag a finger along his ribs in a slow, serpentine motion while he read aloud. She knew the days when he had used her soap, could feel as well as hear his voice, rumbling beneath her cheek. Sometimes she tried to match her breathing to his, deep and even, in perfect accord.

In the taxi, her nerves are loose and jangly as pocket change; she cannot collect herself. Traffic is heavy and she worries that she'll be late. The window is smeared with grime, and she rolls it down to a blast of fumes and hot air. The taxi heaves forward, past a rattling red bus. A brisk commerce has struck up beneath the new flyover, where vendors have set up stalls despite municipal notices. The taxi driver grumbles and they lurch into another lane. Rowena slides hard to one side of the vinyl bench seat, empty except for her small frame. For a moment, her relief at having concealed the meeting from Mark is replaced by the feeling that she is completely alone. What began as an omission has taken new unsettling form, become a secret.

Rowena has kept secrets before, secrets that only her body knew. "There are tests we can run, but the truth is, we may never know why this happened," the doctor told her after the first miscarriage. She had shown Rowena a picture from the week before, when the baby was still developing normally. "This is what I expected to see," she said gently, and then she pointed to the picture she had just taken. Rowena nodded. When she had to speak—to schedule a procedure, to refuse assistance from the nurse—it was in quick dry bursts, like dust beaten from cushions. She drove herself home and did not call Mark for several hours.

There were clinics and specialists, tests. Grace's postscripts advocated prayer or special diets; she wrote at length to urge a course of homeopathic medicine that had worked for someone's niece. At first each month's disappointment felt short-lived, a misstep, luck stumbling before they moved forward into their real life. But eventually it seemed to her that all along, their hopes were being funneled slowly, painfully, away. After the third miscarriage, Rowena woke in the middle of the night in an empty bed. She heard Mark's voice and slipped downstairs to find him hunched on a kitchen stool in the dark, his back to where she stood in the doorway. He was speaking softly into the phone, warning his mother not to mention anything upsetting. Rowena went back to bed before he discovered her. When he finally came up, she pretended to be asleep.

A few years later they adopted Lizzie, and the family that had once seemed lost to Rowena came rushing back, possible once more. She was not prepared for Mark's reluctance when she mentioned a second child. Rowena remained on adoption list servers, kept in contact with families in various stages of waiting, considered herself in a waiting stage. She only needed more time to convince Mark. Then a few days before her thirty-eighth birthday, she faced the mirror, running her fingers through her hair to find the silver strands beneath. Soon she would be forty. Her children would only know her as an older woman, a woman who had to dye her hair. That was the day she wrote to Sonali.

• • •

Sonali is a wealthy, stylish woman in her mid-fifties. Her two grown sons are in university, but the house is kept lively with three foster children, girls no one has wanted. One, a toddler, is underfoot during their meeting. "Kripa loves to be where the action is," says Sonali fondly. The child breaks Rowena's heart—bald-headed, skin patched together as though by a ragman. Her lips are more like scars, shiny and misshapen. Her arms and legs seem to be flaking away and even her eyes are affected, the eyelids scarred and heavy, the pupils strangely fixed. She stands between Sonali's knees, barefoot, in a pink cotton dress that hangs nearly to her ankles, and picks up one after another of the ornaments on the coffee table. "She loves to organize things—right, my precious? And she loves to help me find my spectacles. Kripa! Where are my spectacles, Kripa?"

The child gropes along the table.

"Can she see?" asks Rowena.

"A little yet. The sight is gone in one eye. Ooh! *There* are my specs. *Thank* you, Kripa. Now take that box and play with it, yes?" Kripa laughs and tries to grab the glasses from Sonali's face. "We'd better get this monkey out of here, or we'll get nothing accomplished." She calls for one of her servants to take Kripa to the kitchen. "Give her some coconut. She'll be feeling hungry soon."

"Poor little thing. Was she burned?" Rowena asks when the child has been led away.

"Born like that. The family kept her for a month or so, waiting to see if it would go away. I suppose the mother was petrified, a village girl. Just as well. Baby would have died without special care." She looks toward the doorway through which the girl has gone and smiles as tenderly as if Kripa were still there. "No one thought she would live past a year, and now she's fifteen months. Doctor says who knows, now she may be out of danger. She's a happy little thing, with all she endures. You know, we have to bathe her twice a day to clear away the skin, even in her ears. It scales away constantly."

"Is she in pain?"

"She is uncomfortable if we don't tend to her. There are medicated lotions we must use, and we're careful with her diet. Her feet become irritated when she walks too much, but she's always wanting to run around."

Rowena imagines the child's cracked skin peeling away like the outer layers of onion. All that was dry and discolored would fall away, and Kripa would emerge unscarred, smiling with fresh new lips. "And she'll improve?"

"They say not. This is for all her life."

Rowena tries to absorb this and cannot. It seems impossible that a child should be locked in her own skin, that no treatment, no medicine, can help her.

"But we've fallen in love with her," Sonali says warmly. "Such a funny little creature, you can't think. So adventurous, so determined. More stubborn than either of my boys. And they adore her, they send e-mails that I read to her at bedtime." She crosses her leg. "Now. You haven't come here to speak about Kripa."

Rowena shifts in her seat, knits her hands in resolve. "We want to adopt another. We think it's time. And we both come from big families. That's something we've always wanted." Her voice is firm and even; there is enough truth in what she is saying. She and Mark had both hoped for many children—until he changed his mind.

"Good news, good for you!" Sonali checks her watch. "I have twenty minutes before I dash. So let's be quick. You're what? Thirty-eight?"

"Thirty-nine in October."

"Then we must hurry. It will probably be a girl again. You can request a boy, but that may cause a delay and everything becomes more difficult once you're past forty."

"No, no, a girl is fine. A girl is wonderful."

Sonali nods briskly. "Right, then. How long are you here?"

"Three more weeks. I thought I could begin with the paperwork on this end."

"Good. Your fingerprints and all will be on file from the last time, but you'll have to turn in your application right away so it can be processed before your birthday. You have your U.S. application ready? You and Mark have signed everything?"

"There wasn't time before we left," Rowena says smoothly. "I've prepared nearly everything, but we haven't turned in the final paperwork." In fact she only needed Mark's signature. She had even written the statements from the parents.

"Fill out the financial records at least, and send those in. You go home in three weeks and work on the rest—submit them as quickly as you can. Now it won't be as easy as with Lizzie. The government position has changed. They're pushing for children to be placed with Indian families."

"But Mark and I both—"

"You're nonresident Indians, you have different status. And you know there's a bias toward Hindus."

Rowena feels a familiar twinge: always the chance that it will not happen after all. "But it's not impossible?"

"Not impossible." Sonali takes Rowena's hand, a sudden swift motion that threatens Rowena's composure. "You must be realistic, that's all. The child may be a few months older or have some minor condition. Or she may just have darker skin, who knows? Let's go one step at a time; we'll see what happens once the papers are in. I'll do everything I can for you. How is Lizzie doing?" she asks abruptly.

Rowena recovers herself, smiles. "She's fine. Perfect. The apple of her father's eye. He's so in love with her he can hardly imagine another."

"They always think that." Sonali shakes her head. "Until they meet the next one. Then suddenly they can't imagine their lives without. Nikhil is crazy about Kripa."

"Will you adopt her, then?"

Sonali shrugs. "I am fifty-five, Nikhil is sixty. We have to think about the boys, since they may well land up with her care. And we don't know yet what that means. She's been good for the boys. They look on her as a little sister, very protective, very loving. But adoption is a big step. *You* know." She laughs. "For now, the little one rules the household. Absolute dictator, I'm telling you. We may not have a choice in the matter!"

Just before it is time to go, Kripa comes rushing back into the room, clapping hands that resemble paws. Rowena thanks Sonali; she kisses Kripa on her forehead—the bald scalp like paper beneath her lips; she walks out into the dazzle of midday sun. She moves quickly through her shopping and eats near a children's store Sonali recommended, where she buys a mirror-work outfit for Lizzie and a small embroidered top with matching pants, size six months. She has begun to see her next child, asleep in the crib they will bring down from the attic, or sitting in Lizzie's lap for a picture, both in their Indian outfits. When she puts up her hand to hail a taxi, her bangles fall toward her elbow and make a noise that reminds her of her mother, who died when Rowena was seven.

Rowena sits in the taxi, clinging to a leather strap as they jounce over ruts in the road. She hardly notices the city neighborhoods outside her window except as another portion of her journey accomplished. The road is clogged, even in midafternoon, and bicycles edge in and out of crowds. A motor scooter carrying a family of five draws close, and though such sights are commonplace Rowena is struck by them. They fit together like nesting bowls, the smaller boy tucked against the older, the older boy leaning into the father. The mother sits in the back, a baby tight to her chest. They move at roughly the same speed as the taxi, surging briefly ahead and then dropping behind, until eventually they turn off somewhere near Worli. Rowena feels oddly bereft as they curve away from her. One corner of the woman's dupatta has slipped free from beneath her and it flutters behind them, a rippling wave that Rowena watches until the taxi pulls forward and the motor scooter has moved out of sight. She does not notice the cyclist on their other side until the cab jerks and she sees a shape all in white come hurtling over the hood. It hits the window like a bale of cotton, a dull, soft thud that jars the whole car so that Rowena is still shaking when it is all over and the man and the taxi are still.

The bicycle carcass lies a few meters back from the scene of the accident, its front wheel bent and twisted from the impact. Almost at once, with no time to have been summoned, three policemen in khaki shorts appear; presumably they were on duty nearby. One of them instructs Rowena to stand out of the way and motions her to a spot near the bicycle to wait. The taxi driver is explaining loudly that the fellow came out of nowhere, though no one seems to be taking his statement. A crowd of passersby has formed, and the police move slowly around its perimeter, calm as shepherds, occasionally consulting with one another. Traffic has not been diverted, but cars, buses, and brightly painted trucks slide past in the narrow channel of road left to them.

Rowena cannot see the cyclist, who is blocked from view by the crowd. But she caught a glimpse of him lying in the road before she was ordered away—a heavyset man in late middle age wearing a white kurta and white drawstring pyjama pants. His small white hat had tumbled from his head and his eyes were closed. She cannot be sure, but she does not think he was moving. Already people had crouched near his body; she could not see any blood nor guess at the extent of his injuries.

"Is he breathing?" she calls to one of the police. Her voice flutters like a weak pulse; she tries again in Hindi. "Can you tell me if he's breathing?"

The policeman saunters closer. He is shorter than Rowena, with a full lower lip beneath his mustache and plump, pockmarked cheeks. "He will go to hospital."

"Let me see him."

He shakes his head, a lazy movement, as though nothing of urgency has happened. "He is hurt here." He waves a hand near his own hip. "You cannot see. You are needing a taxi?"

Rowena feels as if she may vomit. "I am waiting to see what happens to him."

The policeman glances at her, the Western clothing and the shopping bags she has put down in the road. "You are from where?"

"Santa Clara."

"You are living there?"

For a moment it seems simplest to lie to him. But she tells him no, not now. "I grew up there." She takes off her sunglasses, shields her eyes with her hand. "My husband is Indian also. He is a doctor. I can go with this man to the hospital."

He inclines his head, appears to accept this remark, and drifts back to one of the other officers. They confer, both glancing toward Rowena at intervals. She has put her sunglasses back on against the glare. The sky is stony with heat; she is rocked by the motion of passing cars. She can hear nothing over the noise of the crowd and the din of motors and horn blasts. After a minute the other policeman approaches. He is tall, with dark, incurious eyes and a sunken chin. "You can pay this man half," he tells her.

"What man?" Rowena wants to laugh when he jerks his head in the direction of the taxi driver. "He's hit someone, how can you be thinking of the fare?" But she has no intention of antagonizing anyone; she walks over and tries to hand a few bills to the driver. He tosses his hand, refusing the money, refusing even to look at her; he clearly expects nothing but trouble from all this. The policeman does not press the point. He moves past Rowena and into the moving stream of traffic, his whistle to his lips. Before she has had time to argue, he flags down a passing taxi. It's already occupied, Rowena can see. A middle-aged woman in a sari sits in the back. The policeman gives the driver brief instructions and turns to Rowena.

"Challo," he says. Go on.

"No, no, I want to stay!"

He picks up her shopping bags and places them in the vehicle, leaving the back door open.

"Okay. Challo."

The people inside stare at her, waiting also. Some of the men who are in the crowd tending to the cyclist have turned to watch, and the younger police officer comes forward, looking concerned. Rowena begins to imagine that she is the piece of accident that must be cleared first, before any other progress can be made. She looks uncertainly at the taxi. A fresh garland and a figure of Ganesh dangle from the rear-view mirror. Then she reaches into her purse and writes her name and Grace's phone number on the back of a receipt. She holds it out to both policemen, insistent, until with a quick glance at his superior, the younger one takes it.

"That is where I'm staying. I want to know what hospital he goes to, yes? I want to know what has happened."

He turns it over and inspects both sides. She does not get into the car until he folds the slip of paper and tucks it in his chest pocket: the only agreement she's likely to get. The older policeman ushers her in and closes the door behind her like a hotel attendant. She is going to Santa Clara, he tells the driver. They move slowly away. The other passenger pulls a worn red leather handbag onto her lap and pushes back Rowena's shopping bags when they tip against her. "So sorry."

Rowena gathers them closer, distracted, still craning to see the injured man as they move past, though the crowd has closed around him completely and he is swallowed up from sight.

Rowena directs the driver to Beryl's house. She is not prepared to face Grace or even Lizzie; her hands are still shaking when she loosens her grip on her bags. And Mark has become a region of difficulty, the person to whom she must either continue to lie or confess the truth. The idea of seeing him exhausts her.

The taxi snorts as it pulls away, leaving Rowena at the gate with her shopping bags. Even in the cool season the sun is strong enough to drive people indoors; the street is all but empty. Dogs sleep, flung on their sides. The fruit seller has set up his cart at the corner, but he sits on his low stool, dozing. At the far end of the street, a parish house and a tea shop intended to attract university students conspire to stay busy all day long. Rowena can see a crosshatch of figures moving back and forth at the juncture. But she feels far from such activity. After all the chaos of the accident, she is suddenly doused in the afternoon quiet. She would like to sink onto a bed, to sleep.

She does not bother to ring the bell but slips her hand between the bars of the gate to lift the latch, the way she used to as a girl. The grass is cropped close, and a stone bench blazes white in the afternoon light. Rowena squints. The house is built around an inner courtyard, and she follows a path to the kitchen entrance. The sounds of insects merge into a single felted buzz, and the heat holds everything in place: a broad, shining blade of grass, distinct from any other; clay flowerpots standing just so on ledges of the stone wall; a beetle. Beyond the garden is the old cashew tree where

Rowena and her brothers and cousins used to play as children.

When her mother died, her father was still in the army, posted in a cantonment town. Rowena and her brothers were sent to live with Aunty Beryl and Uncle Oliver. She can remember sitting out on the balcony with her cousins and brothers, all of them bathed and dressed for bed, her hair combed back so that the wet ends pricked her neck and shoulders. In the spring they leaned over the railing and picked guavas. In the stifling weeks before the monsoon, they slept outside. The nights seemed larger than the days, as though a caul of sun and dust had slipped away to reveal what lay behind the featureless Bombay haze. The sky no longer pressed down but spun outward, and Rowena, lying on her back, stared up at the stars until some seemed to drift away and others to slowly settle closer to earth. The boys knew the names of the constellations and pointed them out to one another—straight lines and sharp angles meant to describe the flank of a bull or the curve of a thigh. But Rowena could never see the pictures they saw. She looked up and up until she felt dizzy, and then she reached for somebody's hand to anchor her. There were always people nearby, her older brothers or Aunty Beryl's sons, and no one objected when she held onto them. She was seven and her mother was dead.

Inside, the household is quiet. Even the kitchen work is conducted in a kind of stupor. The servants are stone-faced, two day girls from the fishing village in T-shirts, skirts, and rubber slippers, and Bhavani, a wiry woman in her fifties who already seems old to Rowena. One girl sifts rice, and another straddles a low wooden bench, shredding coconut against a long curved blade. Aunty Beryl has bought an electric grinder for twenty thousand rupees, and Bhavani tends it with an abstracted air, as though hardly aware of the crush of spices that pulses within. Her head floats with the sound of its whirring. The two younger ones say nothing to Rowena when she passes, but Bhavani, who has lived with the family for years, smiles when she sees her and pretends to scold.

"Where is Baby? Why have you come without Baby?" Baby is the name she uses for a daughter of any age, for Rowena as well as Lizzie. When Rowena came to see them the first day of her visit, Bhavani seized Rowena's hand, grinning at the sight of her. "Baby has come!"

The house belongs to its women in the afternoon. The men are off somewhere—in clubs or at cluttered desks in the city. But in the back bedroom, coolest at this hour, Rowena finds the women draped across a narrow double bed: Aunty Beryl; Uncle Oliver's niece Cuchu, who is living there while her parents are posted in Delhi; and Cuchu's grandmother, Aunty Vinnie, who is no relation to Oliver but is frequently there with Cuchu. Fifteen-year-old Cuchu sleeps facedown on the coverlet, her legs crossed and white socks (looking dirty and gray) at her ankles; she is wearing the bright green uniform of St. Gregory's School, and a matching green headband has been tossed on her pillow. The two women are curves and spills of cotton. Their bodies seem supple in repose, and the colors of their salwar kameez are softened in the dim light. Rowena feels tall and angular, standing over them in her narrow black slacks.

"See who's come!" Aunty Vinnie says in a hushed voice.

"Here, beta, sit." Aunty Beryl pats a cushion next to her. "Such a lovely surprise! What have you been doing?"

Rowena leaves her bags in a corner and joins them. It is a wood-framed bed, slightly smaller than a double, but with room enough for all of them if they lie with some reference to each other's lines and curves. She thinks of the king-size bed she and Mark share in the States, the limbs flung mindlessly out in sleep.

"I've been to town, shopping," she begins, uncertain how much to reveal. She must pass along Grace's invitation, she realizes. She must explain away the lunch.

"You're looking tired." Aunty Beryl brushes the hair from Rowena's forehead. "You're not used to this heat anymore."

Rowena remembers the times when she was pregnant, the sudden waves of fatigue, the drag on her limbs. The weight of what she has said to Sonali, what she has not said to Mark, has begun to feel like something she is carrying. She wants to pour out the whole story until it is just another soft shape on the bed. She imagines the women will shift their limbs to make room, that they will have no trouble accommodating her secret. Outside the heat has glazed everything to sharp edges, but surely here, in the dusky light, nothing is so hard or fast as it appears.

"She's still feeling all this travel. I don't know how you're running around town already—such a lot of hustle-bustle. I can hardly pick myself up to go." Aunty Vinnie is twelve years older than Aunty Beryl; her hair has grayed to a cloudy color, and her skin is slack and creased. Aunty Beryl's hair is carefully styled, a short cut that shows off her earrings.

"You went alone, beta?"

Aunty Beryl's voice is so gentle that Rowena finds, to her shame, she is in tears. It is her chance to mention Sonali, but instead she tells them about the accident.

Aunty Beryl shakes her head over the unorthodox behavior of the police. "And they didn't tell you what hospital he'll go to?"

Rowena shakes her head no.

"They may not have known. If you haven't heard anything tomorrow, I'll make some calls."

Cuchu groans and lifts her sleepy head, wondering what the commotion is.

"Nothing, nothing." Aunty Vinnie pats Rowena's hand.

"Rowena has had a shock. But not to worry. I'm sure the fellow isn't dead."

"What fellow?" Cuchu props her chin on her elbows.

Aunty Beryl puts a restraining hand on Cuchu's shoulder. "Come, we'll talk of something happier. How is Biddy's little one?"

Mark's sister has had her fourth child, a girl. For a moment, Rowena imagines she can feel the clutch of the baby's fist closing around her finger. She had pulled gently, for the pleasure of feeling a pull back. The newborn's fingers were delicate as the ridges of a shell, the knuckles watery hollows. Had Lizzie grasped a finger so early? Rowena has no memory or even photos of Lizzie at that age; she first saw Lizzie at three months, the earliest she could be released from the orphanage.

"She's very sweet. Lizzie adores her."

"She's not too thin? These babies now are seeming so thin, and then they grow up like sticks." Aunt Vinnie looks longingly at Cuchu. "You can eat a little more, darling. A few more bites at every meal will make all the difference." Cuchu groans and pushes her head under a pillow. "At least she has Grace to help her. I went home to my mother to have all of mine. That used to be the way of it, no? We all went home. And such care they took! Bathing us, massaging us. My mother had a girl come just to rub the baby's head with oil, to shape it properly. After the birth, you know, the heads were always looking too pointed. But they used to rub"—she lifts Cuchu's pillow aside to demonstrate the technique—"See, a firm touch, just so. They did this every day for such and such a time, and eventually baby's head was rounded."

"Not now, Grandma!"

"Nice round-shaped heads everybody had," says Aunty Vinnie.

"This baby has a good enough head, I think," Aunty Beryl says with decision, and Rowena smiles.

Cuchu rolls out from under her pillow. "Actually, I am very good with babies. I don't know why. But they just seem to gravitate to me." She nudges Aunty Beryl's leg with her foot. "I tell you, it's a remarkable thing."

"Maybe they sense you'll share your books with them, hmm?" Aunty Beryl pinches her.

Cuchu still prefers comics and children's books to the novels her class is reading. She has fallen behind in school. Aunty Beryl and Uncle Oliver are trying to push her toward more advanced reading.

"No, I think I'm just naturally good with them. When I grow up, I'll have lots of babies."

"You'd better learn to look after yourself first." Aunty Beryl laughs at her.

Rowena leans back. Her neck aches, and she wonders if she has strained it in the accident.

"Close your eyes, beta. Rest." Aunty Beryl draws Rowena's head to her shoulder and while the women speak softly, Rowena falls asleep.

When she wakes, the light is dim. It is not cold, but the breeze from the fan makes her shiver, and she rubs her arms. She can hear noises from the kitchen—voices and the clatter of pans—lively sounds. She gets up stiffly and looks out the window. The sun is low, a bulb of hot color behind palm trees. The ruckus of bird calls has quieted from a matted clamor to a single cry here and there, throbbing in a wide sky.

She splashes water on her face and walks along the courtyard. She passes the bedroom where Cuchu and Aunty Vinnie are staying, and she hears water running into a bucket. It is the time of day for baths. In another twenty minutes or so the women will emerge, fresh and clean, reborn into the evening. She hears voices in the front room, her uncle and perhaps one of her cousins, but she doesn't feel ready to join them. She goes instead to find Aunty Beryl, who is sitting on a bench in the courtyard with her legs spread wide, leaning forward as she brushes one of her several dogs.

"Had a good sleep?"

Rowena nods. She watches her aunt pull the brush through the dog's coat. "I'm running late—I must get back. But Grace wants you to drop by later if you're free. I should have told you earlier."

"Yes, she called an hour ago. I didn't want to wake you." Aunty Beryl smacks the dog lightly with the brush handle. "Off you go!" Long white hairs have drifted to the tile floor, and she bends over to sweep them up with her hands. "I need a whisk broom. What's all this about lunch?"

"I told them I might meet you." She looks out into the garden, down to the cashew tree. "I wanted a morning without Mark."

Aunty Beryl rises. She kisses Rowena on each cheek, the way she used to when Rowena was a child. "I told Grace I had to rush back from the city. But you know better, beta. Don't fall into bad habits. Next time just tell him what you want, hmm? Now say a quick hello to your uncle before you go."

"You missed quite a show." Mark raises his eyebrows. Rowena has put her bags in the bedroom they are using, where suitcases yawn open like books with cracked bindings.

"She wouldn't go down? Hang on, I just want to splash some water on my face before Sister Agnes comes."

"She's here already. She's taken Lizzie upstairs."

Rowena has turned on the tap, is leaning over the sink, but stops. "Upstairs? Why?"

"Biddy brought the baby down to say hello, and when she tried to go Lizzie had an absolute meltdown. She wanted the baby to sleep in her bed."

"Oh, God."

"She was just wailing. None of us could do a thing with her. And then she started crying for you."

It was Sister Agnes who managed to calm the child, Sister Agnes who took the newborn in her lap and held her up for Lizzie to see. "You can give baby a kiss," she offered in her slow, lilting voice, but Lizzie only stared. "Come," Sister Agnes said, and Lizzie reached out to touch the baby. "Gently, that's right. See how she's wrapped up tightly? That helps her feel safe, even when she sleeps by herself."

Sister Agnes handed the baby back to Biddy and drew Lizzie to her. "You see how she takes to you? She must know you're her friend. Now"—she glanced at Biddy—"If Aunty says so, we can go up together and say good night."

"They've gone up ten minutes ago," Mark tells Rowena. "Go on, wash your face. I'll pour you a beer. How was your day?"

When Rowena emerges, Sister Agnes is sitting on the sofa with Lizzie close beside her. Lizzie's face is streaked with dried tears, tragic in its small way, thinks Rowena. She pauses in the doorway. Lizzie is showing Sister Agnes a picture she has drawn.

"You see? This is Mumma and Dadda and me. This is Grandma, this is you . . ." Rowena cannot see the paper but imagines the tall, jagged lines her daughter has used to draw Sister Agnes. The glasses would be rings around the dots of eyes. The strip of blue sky, the sun like a round yellow cheese. The red slashes of mouths. "This is Aunty Beryl and Uncle Ollo. This is our house."

"A green house, just like this one!" says Sister Agnes. Rowena is amused; their house in the States is yellow.

"Yes, this is our house," Lizzie says easily. "And see, here is my sister and my other sister and here is our baby."

"So many sisters!"

"Her name is . . ." Lizzie thinks for a moment. "Diya!"

"I see! And what is this?"

"This is our coconut tree."

"You know, when you were a tiny baby, too tiny to remember, you lived with me. And even then you liked trees."

"What did I do?"

"You liked to see the leaves. Whenever you cried, we took you outside and held you up beneath the trees, right in the center of the branches, so you could look up at all the green." Sister looked up from Lizzie's dark bent head, saw Rowena, and smiled. Such a sweet smile, girlish despite the soft wrinkles, eyes shining behind her thick glasses.

"And then I stopped crying?"

"Yes, of course! Then you were happy."

"What else?" asks Lizzie.

Rowena moves quickly away, before Lizzie looks up and sees her. She can hear Grace's voice and Mark's, knows she must rejoin the others quickly. But she slips down the back stairs to the garden. To the west, over the Arabian Sea, the horizon is stained orange and lavender. The east is pale but darkening. At the back of the property, the neat flower beds give way to a fecund tangle of plants. A few old fruit trees have survived. One cashew tree has a long, low limb that reminds her of the tree in Aunty Beryl's yard. Rowena and the boys used to straddle it in a row, laughing and bumping shoulders and knees. They twisted and squirmed like a seven-headed caterpillar.

She is wearing slippers. The leather soles are thin and smooth, so she leaves them on the ground before she begins to climb. Beneath her feet the clay is rough and sandy-warm. She worries about her good black trousers scratching against the trunk as she pulls herself up. When she was a girl, one of the boys used to give her a boost, lacing his fingers into a stirrup, heaving her up.

Rowena sits on the branch, swings her legs through empty air. She misses her brothers, who are scattered all over the globe. One lives in Bangalore and will come to see her next week, but she wants something more: she wants the lot of them, and her cousins too, all together again on a single branch. When she tips her head back she sees leaves and more leaves, in layers that sift what is left of the light. The leaves are broad and thick and seem black in the twilight; the white chinks of sky shift like the patterns of a kaleidoscope. She thinks of Sister Agnes carrying Lizzie as a newborn, standing with her beneath a tree, and thinks this is what her daughter saw before she was her daughter: black leaves, white sky, tricks of light. She thinks of Sister Agnes walking other babies into the garden to gaze up through the branches, whether one of them might have been hers.

"Rowena!" Mark is calling. "Rowena! Where are you?"

She considers not answering. But she slides down from the branch, pushes her feet into her slippers. "Here."

He appears, brows pulled tight as shoelaces. "What's the matter with you? What are you doing out here?"

She shakes her head. She does not know how to begin. She has carried her secret too long. She knows how it will appear when it comes into the world now: distorted, grotesque in its scabrous layers. She had intended nothing so ugly.

"Someone from the police is on the phone for you—something about a guy who's broken his legs? What the hell happened?"

When she starts to cry, it is not for the man in the white kurta but for what cannot be helped, for Kripa, for the brothers and sisters Lizzie will not have, for Mark and herself. She does not know how they have stumbled into such betrayals: Mark changing his mind after all they have endured and Rowena forging ahead without him.

"What is it?" Mark has taken hold of her arms and shakes

her gently. "What's happened?" Finally he puts his arms around her. "Calm down," he says.

She rests her forehead on his shoulder, breathing in a faint trace of sea salt. Grace must have dried this shirt on the line. In another minute or two, Rowena knows, she will have to make a beginning. They will have to go upstairs; perhaps the policeman will still be on the line. She will have to show Mark the application. But for now, she is trying to calm herself—she is thinking past all that to tomorrow evening. If Lizzie has had a good nap, Rowena will bring her out to this tree. They can look up at the leaves together. Rowena can tell her daughter about playing on such branches as a child, and then, if Lizzie likes, she can repeat what Sister Agnes has told them. *When you were a tiny baby . . .* Soon, after only a few tellings, it will sound as if Rowena had been there.

This Is Your Home Also

Once the train had gone and the stirring of paper and rubbish in its wake had subsided, Santa Clara Station was quiet. Naresh watched the lights of the train curling away toward Juhu. "That's where I go," his father said. Naresh felt his throat tighten, but he was eight, old enough to be of use, old enough to leave home. He did not cry. Outside the station, autoricks were parked three deep, their drivers asleep on the benches inside. Naresh followed his father as they twisted farther and farther into the neighborhood. Dogs with thin hindquarters sifted in and out of the darkness, and they all seemed the same dog—watchful, silent. "You help wherever you can," his father told him. "Do what they say quietly. Listen to your grandfather. If they let you stay, they will give you things now and then, clothes and shoes. You can eat with your grandfather—he will have enough food."

Naresh nodded. His father was a groundsman at a Juhu hotel; Naresh could not possibly stay with him. But Ashok had been with the Almeida family for three years, and it was decided that Naresh might have a chance in that household.

He would be fed there, at least, and his family saved the cost of his food.

"You'll live well there."

One street tumbled into the next, and suddenly at a quiet turning was the street where Naresh would stay. He stared up at the Almeida house and tried to imagine its occupants while his father bent to wake a sleeping figure at the entrance to the compound. Naresh hung back. He had not seen his grandfather in over a year, the last time Ashok had made the three days' journey back to their village.

But his grandfather fumbled to his feet, weeping with a joy so great that it seemed to throb in his bones and muscles. Ashok's hands trembled as they held Naresh's face, in just the way his mother's hands had trembled when she said goodbye, and Naresh felt a wave of recognition. He would not be alone.

By daybreak Naresh's father had gone. Naresh squatted next to his grandfather and tried not to look at the place in the road from which he had seen his father disappear. The house was large and square and blank-faced. Ashok tossed a hand in its direction. The family was all but gone, he explained in a low voice, the grown children scattered.

"Gone where?" Naresh whispered. The whole world seemed hushed.

"Gone here, gone there. People with money can go anywhere."

Why would rich people need to leave their families? Naresh wondered. But he was less curious than convinced of their remoteness. "Who is here?"

The old parents only, Ashok told him. Memsahib and badasahib. And one son, Jude-sahib, who didn't go. "That is better," he added. "So few people here, who will mind if you've come?"

Naresh was sleepless, aching; he rubbed his eyes and listened to his grandfather's voice without hearing the words. A woman lit a fire in the construction lot across the street, and it seemed to hold the morning's only color. Everything behind it—the mounds of dirt and gravel, the figures just beginning to move about, the ruined garden—was blue and smoky. Naresh rocked on his heels and felt a small stone bite into his foot.

"They are nice enough people," his grandfather was saying. His voice took on a tinge of complaint. "Like any others, always wanting this or that. What is good enough?"

Naresh said nothing. He did not want his grandfather to see he was afraid.

"And I am older now, growing tired . . . but you can help me, anh?" He rested his hand on the top of Naresh's head and the boy felt its surprising weight. "I'm happy you've come, baba." Ashok smiled at him fondly, and Naresh felt a rush of affection for him.

The sun broke through the haze, and all around him St. Hilary Road began to take shape. What had seemed like crude ideas of trees—flat branches against a flat white sky—blazed to life and depth. Leaves shifted in layers, light filled the spaces between. Crows called from one place, then another and another, new points on an emerging axis.

"On this side is a school." His grandfather pointed. "Someone tore down the house opposite, and soon there will be a new flat building. On the other side is a house with no watchman." He grunted in disapproval.

Naresh stood, stretching his cramped legs, and surveyed the compound. Tied to the veranda post were two sleeping dogs; Ashok's small shelter of palms and burlap stood at the back of the garden; and in a corner lay a scuffed white ball. A football, the kind Naresh had seen but never kicked before.

"Whose is that?" He pointed, his voice rising in excitement.

But his grandfather put a restraining hand on his shoulder.

"That is memsahib's," he said. "We give all the balls to her." Perhaps he saw the boy's disappointment, because he smiled kindly. "You can give her this one yourself. She'll like that, baba. She will let you stay."

"He cannot stay." Memsahib straightened the folds of her sari. Her braid was long and wiry, her face set. She was much older than Naresh's mother, and the dark flesh of her belly was soft and puckered. "What is this? I'm not running a hotel, I'm not running a school for boys."

"But the father has gone to Juhu," Ashok explained. "There is no one to take him away."

"That is not for me to worry about! What business do you have, bringing a boy here without asking leave?"

Ashok rolled his head as a man with drooping shoulders came out to the veranda. He squatted to greet the dogs, who were tied to the porch and whined for attention.

"Jude-sahib, see baba here!" Ashok appealed to him.

Memsahib sniffed. "Don't go looking to him for soft treatment! I am talking to you!"

Naresh understood some English, but not enough to follow the drifts and swerves of their conversation. He watched Jude-sahib, whose round face and mustache reminded him of his father's, and waited to see what memsahib would make of him. When she turned to face Naresh, he felt as if she could see all there was to know about him. He clutched the ball he had found in the garden close to his chest.

Finally she sighed. "For a few days, no more, he can stay and work. But see, I haven't hired two for one post. In two days, maybe three, he is going. You tell your son in Juhu. Here—" She turned suddenly to Naresh. "You can give that to me."

Naresh surrendered the ball, wondering what she would

do with it. In his village the boys played cricket with sticks, football with green coconuts. He imagined the feeling of kicking this ball, its straight, soaring path. Coconuts always bumped off to the side.

But memsahib neither kicked the ball nor threw it. She only returned to the house, carrying it like a parcel.

Ashok put a hand on Naresh's shoulder, as if to steer him away, but Jude-sahib called down to the boy, "What is your name?"

Naresh backed into his grandfather's legs.

"Come, tell me!"

"Naresh."

"Naresh," Jude-sahib repeated. Then in Hindi: "My father is sleeping. He is old and tired. You must be careful not to bother him, understand? Even when he is awake. Otherwise you'll get a shout."

Naresh nodded.

"Mmm." Jude-sahib glanced briefly at Ashok, then returned his attention to the boy. "Will you like being a guardsman?"

Naresh did not know what to say. He smiled shyly and cocked his head, turning a toe in the dirt.

"It's an important job, you know."

He hesitated. Then suddenly: "I am working, my father is working, my grandfather is working," he said in a high, piping voice. "All working." He stood up straighter.

"Let's see how you like it, yes? If you take to it, I may give you jobs of your own."

The boy beamed. He would not disappoint Jude-sahib, whose soft eyes and grave manner held him spellbound.

"Go on, then. But mind the dogs. They'll snap until they know you."

• • •

For the first few weeks, homesick and ashamed to confess it, Naresh stayed close to his grandfather. Ashok sat in a chair near the gate, beneath a stand of bamboo trees that creaked in the wind. When anyone needed to be let in or out, he began the long business of straightening his limbs and hobbling forward. Naresh soon got into the habit of jumping up himself.

"This is how you help, is it? Two doing half a job," memsahib said when a week had gone by. "Where is this boy's father, Ashok? What have I told you? He is going, this one. Or I'm keeping him and you are going." But then she gave Naresh her bags from the market to carry, the heavy burlap sack of potatoes or the thin plastic bag that cut into the flesh of her wrist. *"Po-ta-to,"* she said in English. Then in Hindi: "You know the word? Say it with me. *Po-ta-to.*"

"Potato," said Naresh.

"Take it up to the kitchen. *Up. Up. Kitchen.*"

"Keetchen," said Naresh. He climbed the back stairs, which led to the kitchen, and gave the bag to Patty, the servant. It was the one room of the house where he was permitted, and sometimes he stayed to watch her as she made the masala. The sound of the grinding stone reminded him of his mother. When Patty chopped onions, he could feel his eyes filling, and it was a relief to cry.

But in the dim, whitish mornings, when Jude-sahib went to town in his car, Naresh opened and shut the gate for him. The smell of petrol lingered in the still air for a few moments—a sharp, busy smell, the smell of important doings—and as Jude-sahib drove away he sounded the horn especially for Naresh. He befriended the dogs, who strained on their leads to greet him when he passed. Even badasahib seemed to grow accustomed to Naresh's presence. He was a thin old man with the fierce eyes and scratching walk of a rooster. He spent his days at the gymkhana, and although he didn't nod or smile when he encountered the boy at the gate, he pulled Naresh aside from time to time.

"You there! Naresh, is it?" He fumbled in his pocket. "Take, take quickly." He pressed a few bills and a slip of paper with writing into Naresh's hand. "Give this to the man. One bottle only. And bring it to me here, in the garden, you understand? Not upstairs."

As the weeks passed, Naresh brought back two bottles, a third, a fourth . . . too timid to refuse the old man even though he knew what would happen. Whenever badasahib stayed too late at the gymkhana, Naresh was sent to follow him home—a quiet arrangement between Ashok and Jude-sahib.

"Go quietly," Ashok told him. "Otherwise he will see you and be angry. And if he falls, you come running here and tell Jude-sahib, yes?"

Jude-sahib did not smile or speak, only watched Naresh with a seriousness that filled the boy with pride.

"Jude-sahib only. Never memsahib. You understand?" Ashok pressed.

Naresh tipped his head back and forth, yes.

So on certain nights, at a word from Ashok or a sharp glance from Jude-sahib, Naresh left the Almeida compound. The dark streets reminded him of the night his father had brought him from the station, and the boy was pleased to think he had learned his way around the neighborhood. Even late at night, men and women hurried this way and that, intent on errands of their own. They made little noise—small disturbances of slippers against pavement or one trouser leg against another—and then, each with a brief, opaque glance, they were gone. Naresh wondered to where. He felt connected to them, all on the same brownish streets, beneath the same patch of sky.

Outside the gymkhana gate, he crouched beneath a clump of bougainvillea and waited. Often he waited a long time and his thoughts floated back home. What would his mother think of him, entrusted with such a job? What would she say when he gave her his earnings? When badasahib emerged, the boy trailed behind him. On some nights, curling beneath the scents of gardens, Naresh could smell the whiskey on the old man's breath. It leaked from his skin in a hot, sour cloud, and on those occasions badasahib walked so slowly that Naresh found it difficult to keep any distance between them.

Yet with all of this, Naresh's favorite task was collecting the balls that fell into the garden. The discovery of the football, he soon realized, was a regular occurrence. Every day balls flew over from the Hindu school next door, where a new games court left the Almeida house exposed to regular abuse. There had been incidents of broken windows, roof tiles brought down, and gutter pipes damaged. The wall of the house was pockmarked, and the garden had a gap-toothed look where flowers had been crushed.

Memsahib wrote letters and registered municipal complaints. She scolded the miscreants from the outdoor stair landing, which faced the games court and which she began to treat as a kind of pulpit. She even appealed to the parish priests, arguing that since the neighborhood had long been home to East Indian Catholics—Indians converted by the Portuguese centuries before—they must use their influence with the head of the Hindu school.

Some days later, two priests came to the house with a Hindu schoolmaster and three young boys, fresh and sweet in spotless uniforms. Naresh came up the back stairs and listened to their meeting from the kitchen. With priests in the next room, Patty was too harried for their usual chat, but she told Naresh to sit quietly in a corner and she would give him what she could when the priests had gone. She was Catholic like the Almeidas, from a village in the south, and when she spoke of priests her eyes grew large, as if the word itself were holy.

Naresh was Hindu, and he found the schoolboys far more

interesting. He squatted in his corner and tried to make out what was happening in the front room. His English had improved a great deal since coming to the household; memsahib continued to drill him with words she considered useful. "You might as well learn something, until your father comes," she told him. *Father. Learn.*

Scandal, expense, he heard now. Memsahib described the damage to her property in elaborate detail, her voice rising as she recalled each grievance. The schoolmaster passed his hand over his carefully oiled hair and met each charge with regret or satiny protest. The priests said little, although one had a dry cough and peppered the discussion with throat clearing.

Then Naresh heard the clear, high voices of the boys. "Don't be angry with us, Aunty."

Memsahib made a dubious clucking noise.

"We will do our utmost to *catch* the balls, Aunty!" another proposed.

Naresh, moved by this response and overcome with curiosity, slipped to the doorway just in time to see the smallest boy present memsahib with a thick packet. "These are letters we have written telling Aunty we are sorry."

"Most sorry, madam," the schoolmaster added. "Most regretful. Only see how hard they have worked at these letters! In their English class, they've written them. In English, for you." To the boys, in a tone of great respect, "Aunty studied in England when she was a student. In Oxford. If you study hard, maybe you can win a scholarship to England too."

"That is neither here nor there," memsahib said, shaking her head. But her voice had a new conciliatory softness and she grasped the letters tightly. "It is a serious thing, you know, the upkeep of property."

"Highly serious," offered the healthy priest.

"What could be more serious?" The schoolmaster nodded,

beaming. With that, the matter seemed settled. The boys were given a biscuit apiece, the men slices of plum cake, and the council soon departed with suitable expressions of thanks and best wishes, and frequent coughs from the afflicted priest.

The packet of letters from the Hindu boys became memsahib's triumph. For the next several days, she took to reading them aloud in the spare hour after tea. She sat at the front room table with the letters spread before her and read one after another with relish, repeating certain phrases as if to impress an audience with their significance. In fact, there was no one but Naresh to witness these sessions. At dusk, when the crows began wheeling through the yellow skies, he found it pleasant to sit on the balcony and listen to her reading. At that distance he could not quite understand her, but he let the English words float past him, faint and blurred and musical. His grandfather rested at that time of day. Jude-sahib was still in town, badasahib still hiding at his gymkhana. There was no one to interrupt the flow of apologies.

But this reprieve did not last long. Three weeks later, a ball crashed through the front-room window, upsetting a bowl of rice memsahib had left to soak on the sill. From that day forward, memsahib sent Naresh running whenever she heard a smack and a shout. "It's mine to keep. It's come on my property," she shouted when the boys hooted in protest. *Property,* she taught Naresh. *Hoodlum.* Naresh repeated the words back to her, strange sounds that had nothing to do with the feel of the ball in his hands as he began the slow climb up the stairs. *Lesson,* she called down to him from the landing. *Respect.* The smaller balls fit neatly in his hands; the big ones were heavy as jackfruit. *Enough,* she taught him. He offered them up to her, one by one, and watched as she held each scuffed hostage aloft for the Hindu boys to see. Then she tucked them all away inside the house—*Con-fis-cate*—where Naresh was not permitted to follow. By the time Naresh had collected three dozen balls for memsahib, she had stopped asking when his father would come from Juhu to take him away.

On a hazy day in January, five months after Naresh had come to the Almeidas, he lingered near the garden wall and listened to the progress of a game overhead. He could hear a ringing whenever the ball bounced off the rim, a jarring sound in the sleepy afternoon. It was after four o'clock. Classes had ended, the teachers had gone, the throng of autoricks and buses and bicycles and carts had all but cleared from the road. Only a few boys still hung about the grounds, dusty-legged, shirts pulled loose from their shorts.

At that time of day, the Almeidas napped through the afternoon heat. They closed their doors and windows against the din of the games court and ran all the overhead fans to drown out the boys' shouting. Ashok sat beneath the shade of the bamboo trees, staring through the gate to the light-glazed road until his head drooped and he dozed.

But Naresh enjoyed the sound of the game too much to sleep. When he backed away from the wall he could catch a glimpse of the ball, falling into a thicket of brown hands, popping free, and falling again. Suddenly a wild throw sent the ball well beyond the fingertips of the tallest Hindu boys. It smacked against the side of the house, bounced sharply, and disappeared behind a pile of earth.

"Oho!"

"Into the hornets' nest!"

Naresh ran to retrieve the lost ball, pretending that he was a part of their game. He knew what the ball's fate would be. But he longed for the chance to return one ball, if only to see whether he could clear the second-story wall.

"Were you aiming for the chimney?"

"It's gone into the back! Go and see. We'll wait."

"Why should I get it? I was throwing to you!"

By the time Naresh found the ball, nine or ten heads had lined up against the school wall, staring down at him from one side. Memsahib stared down from the other. She had just emerged from her afternoon nap, looking tired and cross. Her braid was a long frayed rope down her back.

"What have they broken today?" she asked loudly in Hindi for the boys to hear.

"Nothing broken."

"Nothing this time, you mean!"

The boys struck up their usual clamor, trying to appease her. Some called to her in English: "Aunty, Aunty, excuse!"

"I give it back and ten minutes later the same thing again. I can hardly close my eyes to sleep!" She leaned over the railing and pointed. "See the marks you've made on my house? See that crack there? It's like living opposite a cannon gun!" She directed her gaze back to Naresh. "Bring that ball to me."

At once the boys surged forward, leaning over the wall and shouting.

"Is this the way to treat a neighbor?" she demanded. "Pelting my house, day in, day out? Is this the way to behave?"

"Don't take our ball, Aunty!"

"We're playing only!"

But one boy turned his attention to Naresh, who stood beneath the commotion with the ball in his hands.

"Kutta! Ganda kutta!"

The other boys soon took up his cry, calling Naresh a dog, a rat, a thief for hire. This had never happened before. Memsahib threw her arms in the air, shouting, objecting, threatening a campaign of letter writing. "See how you behave when your teachers aren't here? Stop it. Stop it!"

Naresh did not much mind the names. He did not know these boys; he tried to think instead of Jude-sahib, who tugged his ear playfully now and then. He thought of memsahib and the letters he felt they had shared; he thought of his mother, who could not write him letters. He thought of his grandfather, who could sleep in the afternoons with Naresh to watch the gate. "See the blessing God has sent me," Ashok had taken to saying.

"Cuha! Cor!" called the student.

"You need a good slap, all of you!" memsahib said shrilly.

Naresh gazed up at the schoolboy who had started the attack. He was perhaps a year or two older than Naresh and wore a white button-down shirt. He had shoes, Naresh knew without being able to see them.

Something passed between the two boys as they watched each other. It was not that the student had a house somewhere with a toilet or that he came to school in an autorick each morning. Naresh enjoyed his smoky evenings in the shelter at the back of the Almeida compound. He had a mat on the floor and two good pairs of slippers. He was not bothered by the boy's tie, by his shirt or his shoes. But there was something.

"Ganda kutta!"

It was not even the names the boy shouted. Naresh felt only a single part of the distance between them: that it was so easy for this boy to drop balls down and let them bounce away. Standing beneath the games court, testing the weight of the ball in one hand, Naresh was filled with a deep wistfulness. He wondered what it would be like to hold a ball out into the air and watch it plummet from his hands. It would fall so quickly, bounce so high! And then he imagined throwing the ball from his spot in the garden, a perfect arc, sailing up, up, just over the boy's fingertips, just out of reach.

Instead Naresh surrendered the ball to memsahib. She put her hand on his shoulder, quivering with anger as she faced the row of boys. "I will write to your teachers! Do you hear? I will write to your parents!"

"Tilcatta!" the boy called merrily to Naresh. Already someone had found another ball. The faces vanished from the top of the wall as the boys resumed their game.

"What's happening here? What is all this?"

Naresh turned, still hugging the ball to his chest. Badasahib had awakened. He had no hair left on the top of his head, but the tufts around his ears were stiff and wild.

"These boys are up to their tricks again, that's what!"

"Tcha! They are boys, only boys. High-spirited," said badasahib. He looked up to the games court, but all the schoolboys were clustered beneath the basketball hoop. He chuckled and said, "When I was a boy, I could throw a ball like a shot, from one corner of a field to another. Every day we used to go and practice—"

"When you were a boy! When you were a boy you were a hooligan just like these ones here! And they go on with this behavior, totally unchecked. See what they've done." She pointed to chalky marks on the wall and a dented gutter. "Francis, you must go and see the head. This was a quiet neighborhood until that school came in. Now I can hardly shut my eyes for five minutes' peace!"

Badasahib squinted in the direction of the damaged tree. "Why do you interfere in these things? Just leave them be. You only make matters worse."

"I? What have I done? I put up with their noise and their games and their I don't know what, all day long, and I'm the one interfering, is it? Interfering!" Naresh saw tears spring to memsahib's eyes. "I'm left to manage everything on my own. No one lifts a finger to help me . . ."

Naresh slid against the railing, letting one foot drop to the step below. He thought of his grandfather, sitting quietly near the gate, far below whatever happened on the landing. Could Ashok hear them? Did he wonder where Naresh had gone? For a moment the boy considered slipping away with the ball in his hand but memsahib suddenly turned to him, her eyes bird-sharp again.

"Let them do what they like, then. Let them pummel my house and abuse this boy. *I* won't bother to stop them!"

"What abuse? What's happened?"

Naresh glanced quickly to the foot of the stairs, wishing Ashok would appear.

"They've insulted him. Right to my face. Such things they've called him—" She glanced at Naresh and set her lips firmly. "But the point is that all this business has gone too far. That I should stand on my own landing and be pelted at, that this child—come here, son—should suffer only for trying to help me." (*Son,* thought Naresh. *Suffer.*) Her fingers bit into the flesh of his shoulders.

"He looks well enough."

"Oh, what's the use, Francis—you might as well stay shut up in your room all day. What do you care about anything that happens?"

"Enough!" badasahib growled.

"Oh, enough, enough!" scoffed memsahib. Her arm looped around the boy's chest, pulling him closer to her. Naresh felt hot and cramped against her bulk, but he dared not move.

"It's time for my tea," badasahib added in a loftier tone. "I'll be late."

"Late to the gym! What's wrong with you, Francis? What's more important?"

Badasahib glared. His hair stood up from his ears more violently than ever, it seemed to Naresh, and his face was small and hard. Memsahib was strong and stout, but badasahib had shrunken to bone, to hip joints and chin, the plate of his forehead and the knobs of his knees. Wrinkles bit into the pouches of his cheeks, and his eyes were yellow at the corners. Naresh shrank away from his gaze.

"Well," badasahib demanded. Then in Hindi, "Is anything the matter with you?"

Naresh felt his face grow hot. He sensed that he had gone from the guard to the guarded and that badasahib had caught him in his shame. "Nothing is wrong." His voice piped, higher than he liked. "This ball came over and I found it for memsahib."

Memsahib shook him. "Tell the truth, son. What did they say to you? I heard as well as you."

Truth, thought Naresh, relishing the sound. He did not see the point of any of this. Only the ball, still in his hands, seemed solid enough to speak of. "This is the ball, here."

She sniffed, letting go of Naresh with a little push.

"That's an end to it, then," said badasahib. Naresh stood uncertainly between them, and at that moment a ball sailed over the wall and crashed into a guava tree, bringing down a scattering of leaves. Memsahib crowed, "You see! You see!" and badasahib shuffled forward, the bottoms of his trousers flapping against his ankles.

"You there!" He straightened, lifting a bony arm to the games court. His fist was tight and small as a child's. "You boys, there! How can a tree grow when it is battered like this?" He glanced toward memsahib, then turned back to the wall, speaking more gently. "I know you are only young boys playing. But you must take better care!"

"Sorry, Uncle," one boy chirped, but he was jostled away and three others appeared, older and taller.

"They'll keep our ball!" one of them shouted. "Thieves! Throw it back!"

"He can't throw it back! Look at him, with his arm in the air like a scarecrow." His friends took up the cry, some in English, others in Hindi. "Scarecrow, old scarecrow!"

Badasahib stood at the railing. His lips moved as if of their own accord; Naresh heard small smacking noises but no words. The old man's fist swayed gently overhead, nearly still, until a car horn sounded and the boys turned to go. Only when they had disappeared did badasahib let his arm drop to his side, as if he suddenly felt the weight of it.

. . .

The next day, the schoolmaster came to the gate, pressing his hands together in appeal. Ashok jerked up, stiff-hipped, to open the gate, but memsahib ordered him to leave the schoolmaster standing in the road. "What good does sorry do?" she said loudly, for the teacher to hear.

Sorry, Naresh heard. *Good.* Ashok dropped a hand to his shoulder and led him away before the schoolmaster answered.

"Leave them be," advised Ashok. "They have their own troubles. We have ours."

But Naresh turned back to see memsahib accept a fresh packet of letters through the bars of the gate. When the schoolmaster turned to go, she marched straight back toward the house.

"Memsahib?" Naresh broke away from his grandfather's hold and ran after her. He had been waiting in the garden in case she needed help. She had so many balls now that surely the schoolmaster had come to claim them. He thought he could carry them down for her.

But memsahib stopped only for a moment. "I am disappointed in you," she told Naresh in a low voice. "Disappointed," she repeated in Hindi, and he put his hands behind his back, scratching a toe in the dirt. "You did not tell the truth." She did not return any of the lost balls.

In the evening, when Jude-sahib came home from the city and memsahib had spoken to him, he called Naresh aside. Naresh told him of the first ball and the second, then he stared at his slippers. When he looked up again, Jude-sahib was still watching him.

"Then they spoke badly to badasahib," Naresh said softly.

"To him only? Not to you?"

Naresh said nothing.

"You can tell me. You've done nothing wrong."

It had not occurred to Naresh that he could do something wrong. He did what the Almeidas asked him, whatever each of them asked him. The idea of right and wrong beyond that made him puzzled and uneasy; he did not know how to answer. He wished his grandfather would come, but Ashok was in his shelter in the back of the garden. Naresh was alone. Again he said nothing.

A few minutes later, Jude-sahib rode away on his motorcycle. When he returned, twenty minutes later, he beckoned to Naresh and from behind his back produced a small bouncing ball. It was new, not dingy—red rubber, flecked with yellow. Naresh had seen balls like this one piled into baskets in front of the small, squashed shops on the Linking Road. He stared at it in surprise.

"You are a good guardsman." Jude-sahib had crouched before him. He offered the ball, then pulled it out of reach as if they were playing a game together. Naresh did not know whether to take the ball or let Jude-sahib snatch it away, but as suddenly as the game began, it ended. Jude-sahib tucked the ball into Naresh's hands and smiled at him. "Acha, acha. It's yours." He had not released the ball yet. "This is your home also," he said. "Don't let anyone upset you." Naresh did not know if he meant the schoolboys or memsahib or bada-sahib with his shaking fist.

That night, long past the hour when he usually slept, he sat with his legs spread wide and bounced his new ball in the patch of dirt before him. He was trying to keep time to his grandfather's snores, which rose and broke so loudly that the boy had grown accustomed to pulling his mat outside their shelter to sleep.

"You see?" Ashok had told him triumphantly when Naresh showed him the ball. "You see how it happens. Now they are giving you things. You will stay." Naresh had smiled shyly, thinking first of his mother but then of his father, working. His grandfather, working. *You are a good guardsman.*

In the darkness, the yellow flecks of his ball seemed white and starlike. Again and again, Naresh bounced and caught it, bounced and caught it. He found the rhythm soothing.

But a sudden thud startled him. Birds rose up from the trees and Naresh's ball slipped through his fingers. What could the Hindu boys be doing at such an hour? The school was locked each evening. By dusk the street belonged once again to its residents. By midnight silence hung over the school building like a drop cloth.

After a moment the birds resettled in the trees where Naresh could not see them. All was calm again. He groped for his ball and recovered it just as another thud sounded. Then three dull thumps and the birds clouded up again like dust from a whisk broom. Through the entrance to the hut Naresh saw his grandfather stir briefly, tucking one foot beneath the other. Even in sleep Ashok kept one arm across his face to ward off mosquitoes, which gave him the look of someone hoping to shut out the world for a few minutes longer. Naresh decided not to wake him. But he put his ball beneath a corner of the old man's mat for safekeeping and walked softly through the garden to investigate.

The moon was thin-shaven. It did not give much light, but Naresh's eyes were well adjusted to darkness, and he moved quickly around the front of the house. The tops of the palms were dense brushes against the sky, and the wall was clotted with vines and bushes. Behind it the school rose, huge and still. Naresh stared in bewilderment, as if he expected something to appear in the grainy darkness of the games court. It was difficult to imagine anything animate, anything lit, anything as crowded as a school for Hindu boys; the world in daylight was a far-off place and hardly to be believed. In this landscape there were only the sounds the boy had heard, and even they began to seem hollow and foolish as he faced the empty building. It was a cat jumping, he thought, or a falling coconut. And then a ball smacked to the ground. There on the second-story landing, high above the garden wall, was a thin, dark figure.

Naresh knew him at once. He saw the shaking arms, the crooked legs. He saw how slowly the figure stooped and rose again, ball in hand. He knew that badasahib was aiming for the games court because it was what Naresh longed to do himself, and he knew that badasahib had not yet succeeded because his shoulders drooped with each missed shot. He knew that even though badasahib had not gone to the gymkhana, the air would taste of whiskey if he climbed the steps to the landing. So he stayed where he was, in the cool, gray garden, and watched the balls come down in twos and threes. One bounced sharply off the root of a tree. A flat one thudded to earth and did not move. A small one careened toward Jude-sahib's motorcycle, and Naresh kicked it aside. Four more balls, and then silence. Naresh waited for the barrage to resume, but a minute passed and then another. He crept to the foot of the stairs and saw that badasahib had gone, leaving a single ball behind. It rolled lazily to the railing, bumped, and trickled back across the landing. Naresh could see it lolling at the top of the stairs, white and moonish, and he felt the pull of it as something he could not resist.

His feet made no sound on the weathered wood steps, and he had nearly reached the landing when he heard badasahib's scratching progress across the floor. Naresh pressed himself against the wall of the house just as the old man reappeared. His breath was a streak of something iron-hard in the soft night air, and his hand was wrapped tightly around a glass. Ice knocked against it with faint brittle sounds, as if tiny unseen things were breaking. Badasahib finished his drink and reached for the ball.

The night was so still that Naresh heard the whine of a

mosquito darting near and away, near and away. The boy felt a swelling in his chest as he looked at badasahib, his trembling legs, his spidery arms, and he was consumed with a fierce and angry pity. *Let the ball fly over, let the ball fly over.* He felt he would be furious with everyone if the shot didn't make it, with memsahib and his sleeping grandfather and even badasahib himself—when suddenly badasahib lifted the ball high in one hand and heaved it toward the school. The boy started forward with a soft cry, and then it was over, a wobbly throw that hit the side of the building well below the games court wall. It rebounded, thump, into the Almeidas' garden.

There was no time to run and hide. Naresh and badasahib faced each other. The old man's eyes were dark and glinting, oily with drink, but Naresh was neither frightened nor angry. His limbs felt slack and heavy, and he wanted to sit. He wanted both of them to sit. It pained him to see badasahib's legs, stiff and crooked and frail. One clawlike hand gripped the railing and the old man swayed, braced upright more than standing. He stared at Naresh with an expression the boy could not entirely understand, a dull bewilderment. Then his shoulders sagged. His gaze dropped. He turned slowly and went back into the house.

When he had gone, Naresh put the empty glass on the step. He left the balls where they'd fallen, like coconuts shaken down in a storm. That night, he slept in the hut with his grandfather.

The next day he was sent back to his village. Memsahib believed he had thrown the balls. "What are you thinking about, coming into the house at night, taking what you like without asking anyone? What is the meaning of this?" Naresh did not deny it, even to his grandfather. Ashok was grave and stricken, but he did not protest when memsahib announced the boy must go. "I am not waiting for any father from Juhu, anh? Today he goes. You will take him." Badasahib kept to his bed.

"It was wrong to go inside the house," Jude-sahib told Naresh, looking worried.

Naresh did not answer.

"I'll speak to her. She'll change her mind."

Naresh shrugged.

"You are a good guardsman." He lifted the boy's chin with two fingers.

But Naresh didn't mind his punishment, or even the strange new feeling that only he knew what had really happened to him. Even badasahib did not know all of it. He thought perhaps that it would always be so, that the world he'd imagined as common and shared was different for every man, for badasahib and his grandfather and every one of the Hindu boys. The idea made him feel lonely and powerful, and so he hoarded the secret of badasahib at the top of the landing. It struck him as a different sort of thing to be guarded.

And he was relieved to be going home. He was tired and he missed his mother.

Naresh kept the ball that Jude-sahib had given him and took it to his village. He and the other children played with it in a scrub field. It was too big for cricket, but they tried to bowl on the uneven ground. They dribbled it with their bare feet in football matches. They played a game in which one child tossed the ball high into the air, and the others scattered as far as they could—until the ball was caught and they stopped dead, laughing, panting, rooted to their spots, looking all around them to see who had run the farthest.

It was a game he remembered long after the ball was lost and memsahib brought him back to the Almeida household. *School,* she taught him. *Training. Trade.* Jude-sahib had shaved off his mustache, and his face seemed naked and fleshy without it.

By then badasahib had collapsed. On the rare occasions

when Naresh encountered him, the old man stared at him blankly. Once he wandered into the garden wearing his pajamas and Naresh found him sleeping in the flower bed. He helped him to his feet and brushed the dirt from his clothes before taking him upstairs. Badasahib clutched his hand. "Simon?" he asked. "Simon? Is that you, Simon?" Naresh thought of his grandfather, a hand pressed to the place in his hip that pained him; he thought of his father walking blank-faced on the twisting streets. He took badasahib by the arm and nodded. *Yes, yes, Simon.* One of badasahib's family who had gone, Naresh realized, and who would not be coming back.

Acknowledgments

I've enjoyed the chance to work with extraordinary writers and teachers whose support and example are a constant help. Many thanks to Robert Cox, William Pritchard, Brad Leithauser, Mary Jo Salter, Jan Sanders, David Turner, Hollis Seamon, Louis Edwards, Michael White, Rob Nixon, Magda Bogin, Binnie Kirshenbaum, Maureen Howard, and especially Caryl Phillips. The writing course I took with Helen von Schmidt was invaluable, but I am even more fortunate to have known her joy of reading—and her fine taste in writing—my whole life.

Thanks to my colleagues in workshops and writing groups, many of whom have gone on to write books I admire. Dave King, above all, found the time to read several versions of these stories, and his enthusiasm has been nothing short of a gift. I am also indebted to the American School of Classical Studies in Corinth and its director, Guy Sanders, for giving me such a remarkable place to write each autumn (and such excellent company).

I'm very grateful to Carol Janeway, who has been a wonderful editor in every way, as well as to Lauren LeBlanc and the rest of the team at Knopf. Thanks to Amy Berkower for all her support, and to Genevieve Gagne-Hawes and Michael Mejias of Writers House. My thanks to W. David Foster and

Douglas Mason for their expertise, and to my coworkers in Newport and New Orleans.

My greatest thanks go to my family and friends for their encouragement—especially to my parents; my brother, Chris; and my sister, Radhika, my first and best reader. A world of thanks to Drew, whose patience and faith seem limitless, and to H., who gave me the ending to at least one story.

A NOTE ABOUT THE AUTHOR

Nalini Jones was born in Newport, Rhode Island, graduated from Amherst College, and received an M.F.A. from Columbia University. Her work has appeared in the *Ontario Review* and *Creative Nonfiction* online, among others. She is a Stanford Calderwood Fellow of the MacDowell Colony and has recently taught at the 92nd Street Y in New York and Fairfield University in Connecticut.

A NOTE ON THE TYPE

This book was set in a typeface called Cochin, named for Charles Nicolas Cochin the younger, an eighteenth-century French engraver. Unlike many of his contemporaries, Cochin was as much an engraver as a designer, and was deeply interested in the technique of the art. Mr. Henry Johnson first arranged for the cutting of the Cochin type in America, to be used in *Harper's Bazaar.*

The Cochin type is a commendable effort to reproduce the work of the French copperplate engravers of the eighteenth century. Cochin is a versatile face and looks well on any kind of paper. The italic is delightful.

COMPOSED BY *Creative Graphics, Allentown, Pennsylvania*

PRINTED AND BOUND BY *R. R. Donnelley & Sons, Harrisonburg, Virginia*

DESIGNED BY *Iris Weinstein*